POKÉMON™

BLACK AND WHITE

VOL. 8

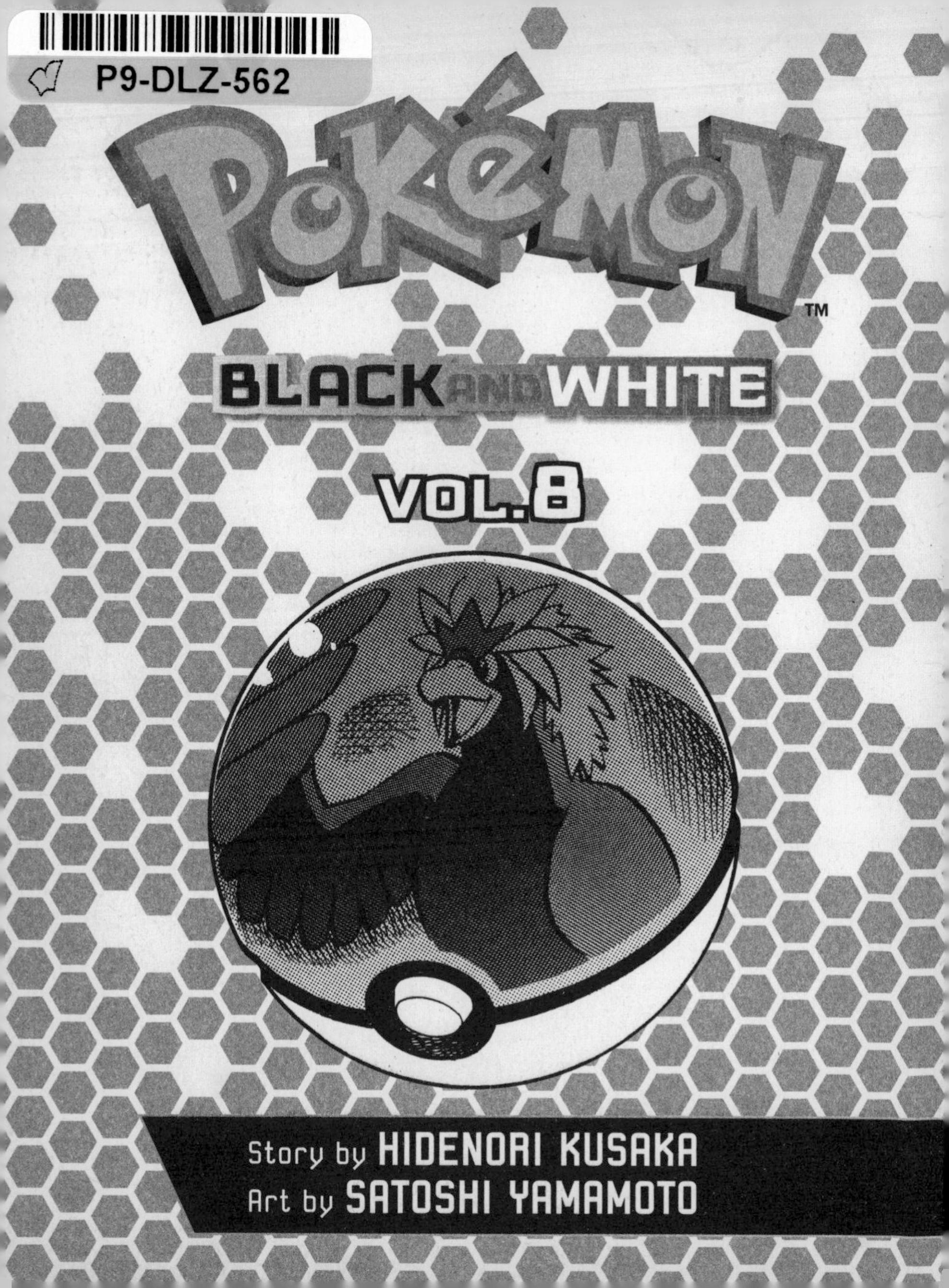

Story by HIDENORI KUSAKA
Art by SATOSHI YAMAMOTO

Pokémon Black and White
Volume 8
VIZ Kids Edition

Story by HIDENORI KUSAKA
Art by SATOSHI YAMAMOTO

© 2012 Pokémon.
© 1995–2012 Nintendo/Creatures Inc./GAME FREAK inc.
TM and ® and character names are trademarks of Nintendo.
© 1997 Hidenori KUSAKA and Satoshi YAMAMOTO/Shogakukan
All rights reserved.
Original Japanese edition "POCKET MONSTER SPECIAL"
published by SHOGAKUKAN Inc.

English Adaptation / Annette Roman
Translation / Tetsuichiro Miyaki
Touch-up & Lettering / Susan Daigle-Leach
Design / Fawn Lau
Editor / Annette Roman

The stories, characters and incidents mentioned in
this publication are entirely fictional.

No portion of this book may be reproduced or transmitted in any form or
by any means without written permission from the copyright holders.

Printed in the U.S.A.

Published by VIZ Media, LLC
P.O. Box 77010
San Francisco, CA 94107

10 9 8 7 6 5 4 3 2 1
First printing, July 2012

PARENTAL ADVISORY
POKÉMON ADVENTURES
is rated A and is suitable
for readers of all ages.
ratings.viz.com

www.vizkids.com

www.viz.com

POKÉMON™
BLACK AND WHITE
VOL. 8

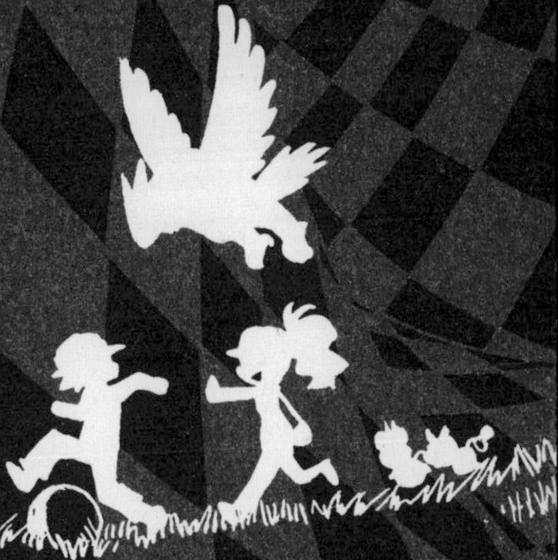

THE STORY THUS FAR!

Pokémon Trainer Black is exploring the mysterious Unova region with his brand-new Pokédex. Pokémon Trainer White runs a thriving talent agency for performing Pokémon. Now she has hired Black as her assistant. Meanwhile, Team Plasma is plotting to separate Pokémon from their beloved humans...!

BLACK'S dream is to win the Pokémon League!

WHITE'S dream is to make her Tepig Gigi a star!

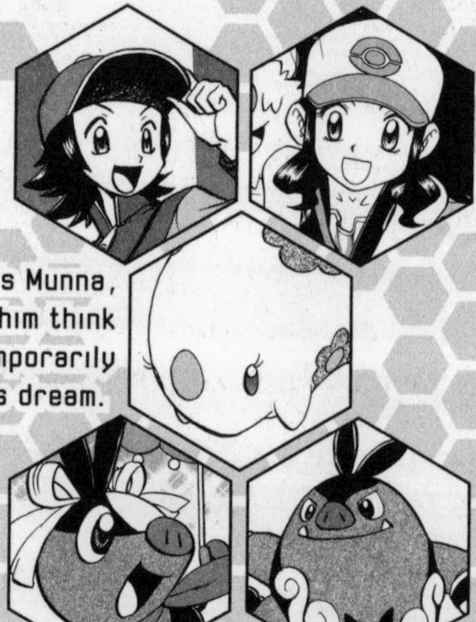

Black's Munna, MUSHA, helps him think clearly by temporarily "eating" his dream.

White's Tepig, GIGI, and Black's Pignite, NITE, get along like peanut butter and jelly!

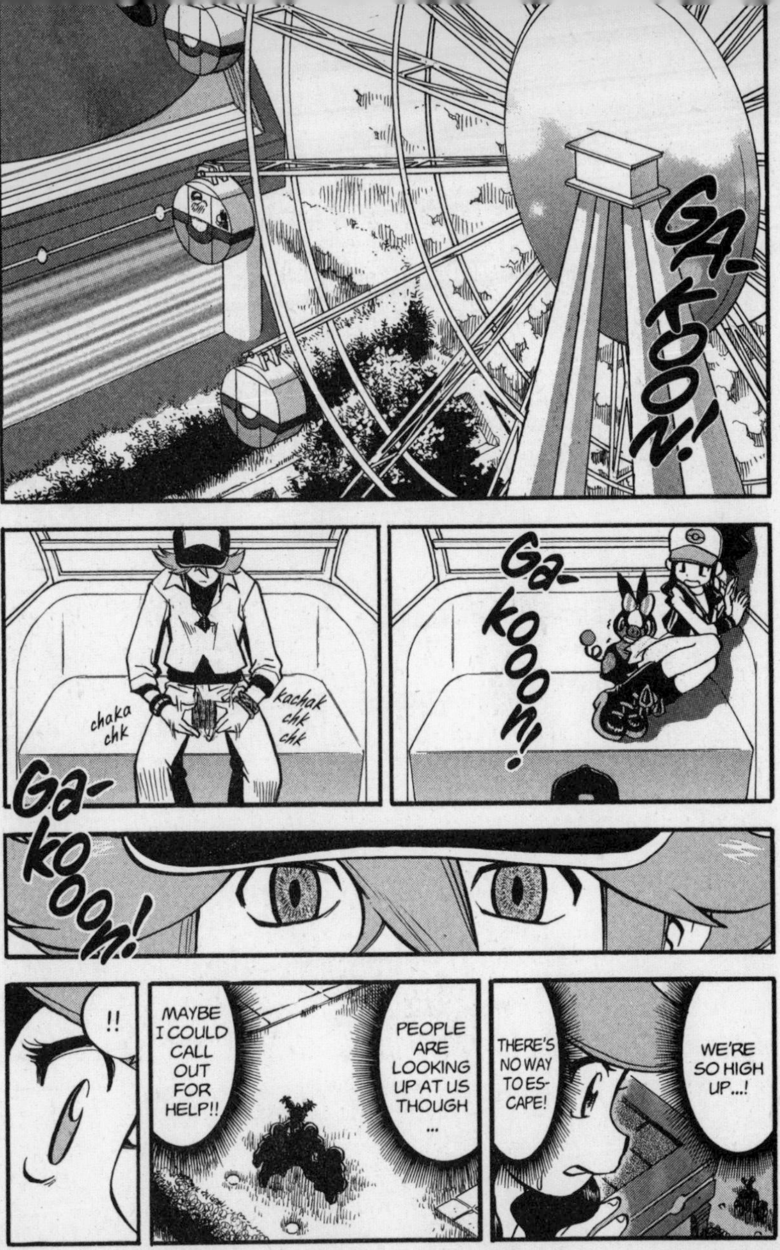
GA-KOOON!
Ga-kooon!
kachak chk chk
chaka chk
Ga-kooon!
WE'RE SO HIGH UP...!
THERE'S NO WAY TO ES-CAPE!
PEOPLE ARE LOOKING UP AT US THOUGH...
MAYBE I COULD CALL OUT FOR HELP!!
!!

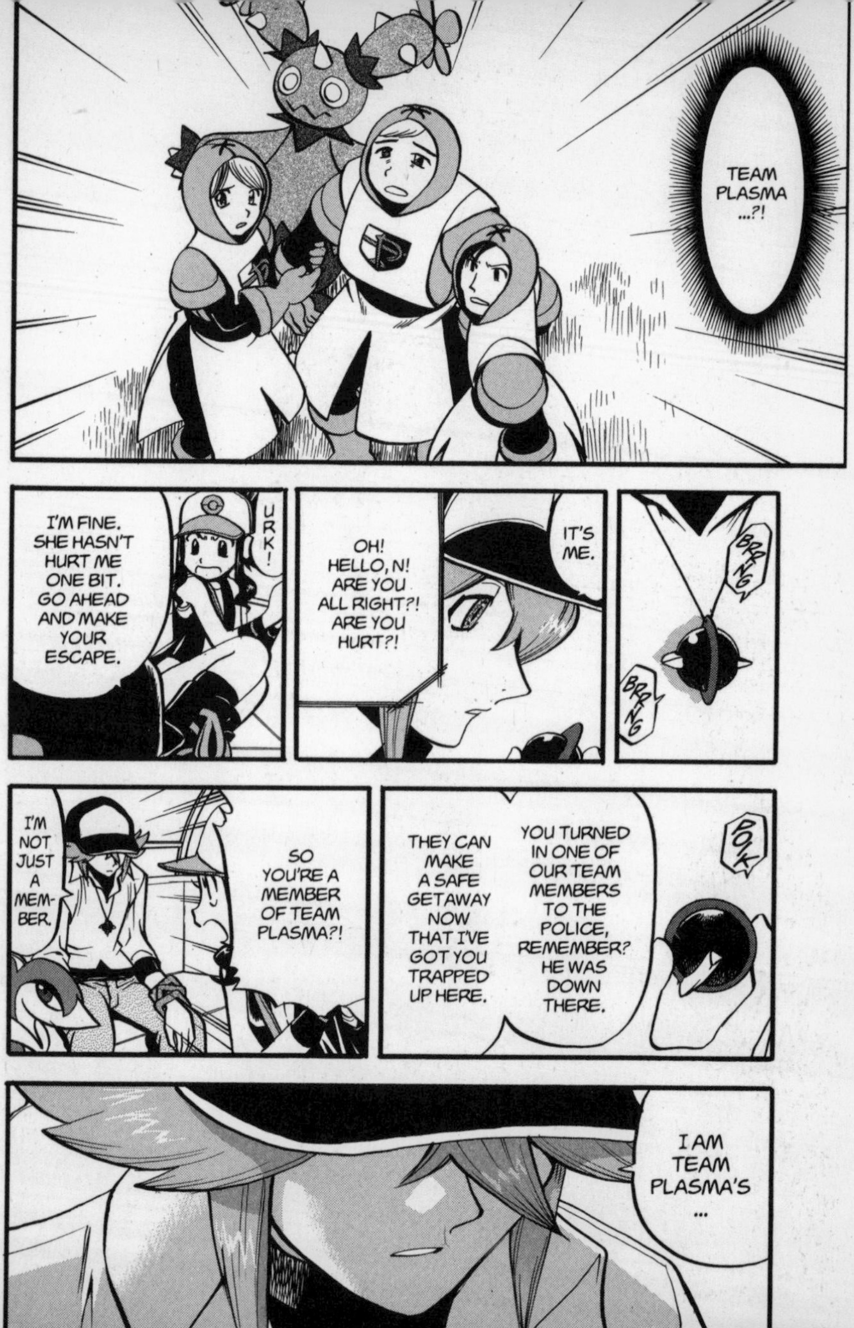
TEAM PLASMA ...?!
BRRING
BRRING
IT'S ME.
OH! HELLO, N! ARE YOU ALL RIGHT?! ARE YOU HURT?!
URK!
I'M FINE. SHE HASN'T HURT ME ONE BIT. GO AHEAD AND MAKE YOUR ESCAPE.
POK
YOU TURNED IN ONE OF OUR TEAM MEMBERS TO THE POLICE, REMEMBER? HE WAS DOWN THERE.
THEY CAN MAKE A SAFE GETAWAY NOW THAT I'VE GOT YOU TRAPPED UP HERE.
SO YOU'RE A MEMBER OF TEAM PLASMA?!
I'M NOT JUST A MEM-BER.
I AM TEAM PLASMA'S ...

Adventure (25)
Gigi's Choice

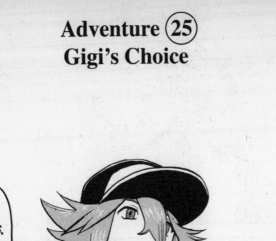

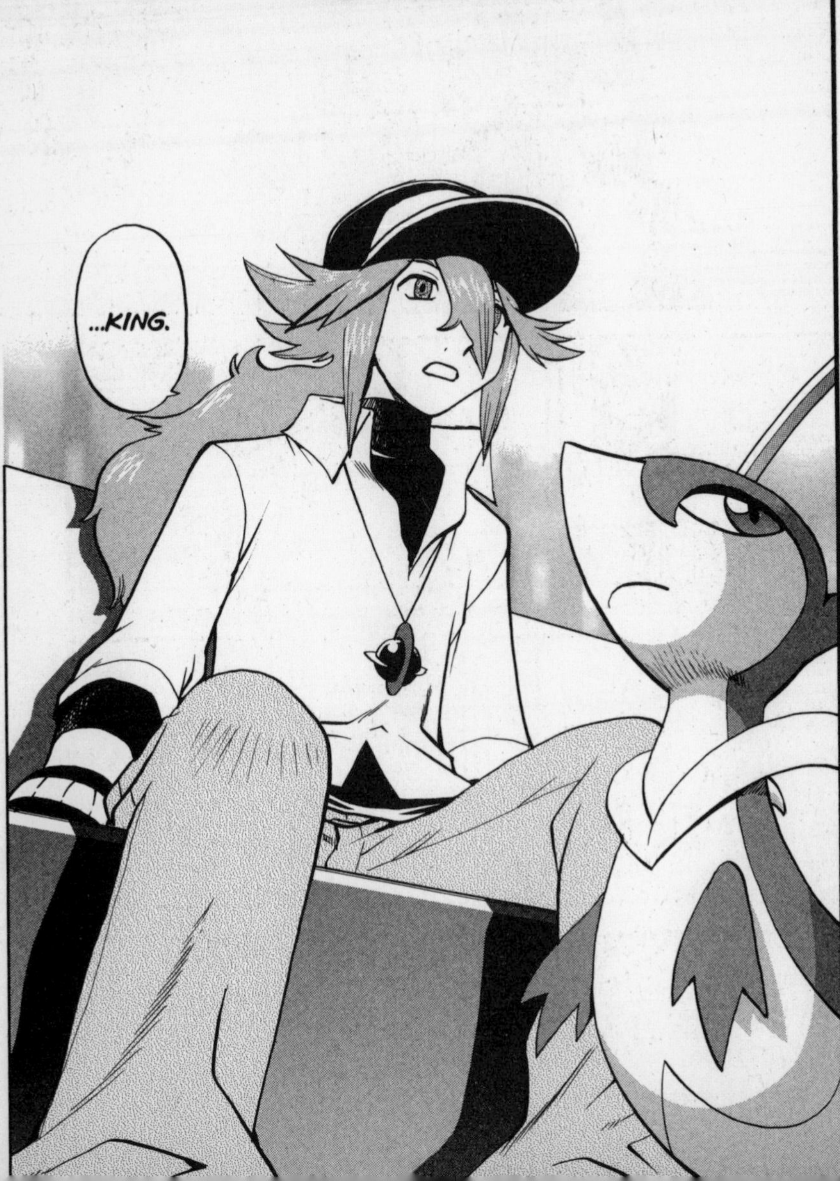
...KING.

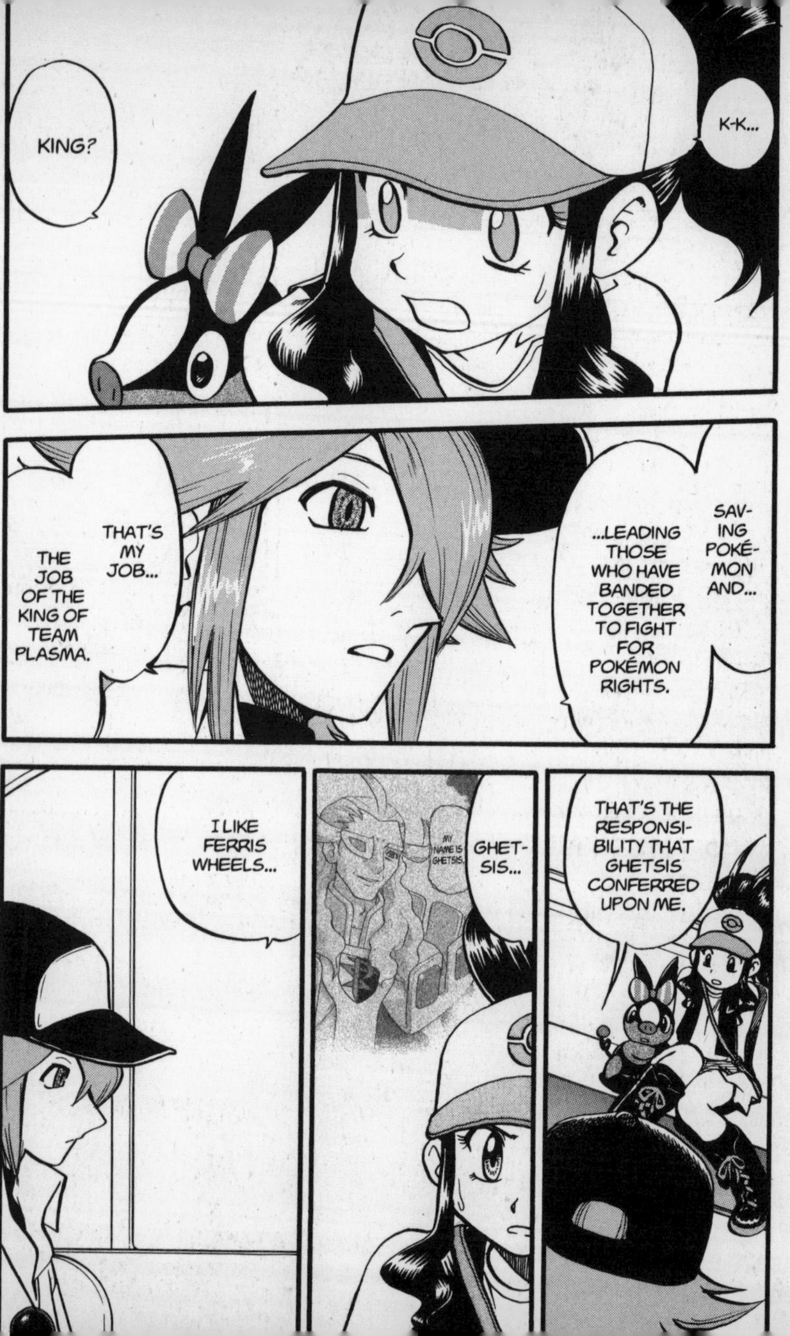
K-K...
KING?
SAVING POKÉMON AND...
...LEADING THOSE WHO HAVE BANDED TOGETHER TO FIGHT FOR POKÉMON RIGHTS.
THAT'S MY JOB...
THE JOB OF THE KING OF TEAM PLASMA.
THAT'S THE RESPONSIBILITY THAT GHETSIS CONFERRED UPON ME.
GHETSIS...
MY NAME IS GHETSIS.
I LIKE FERRIS WHEELS...

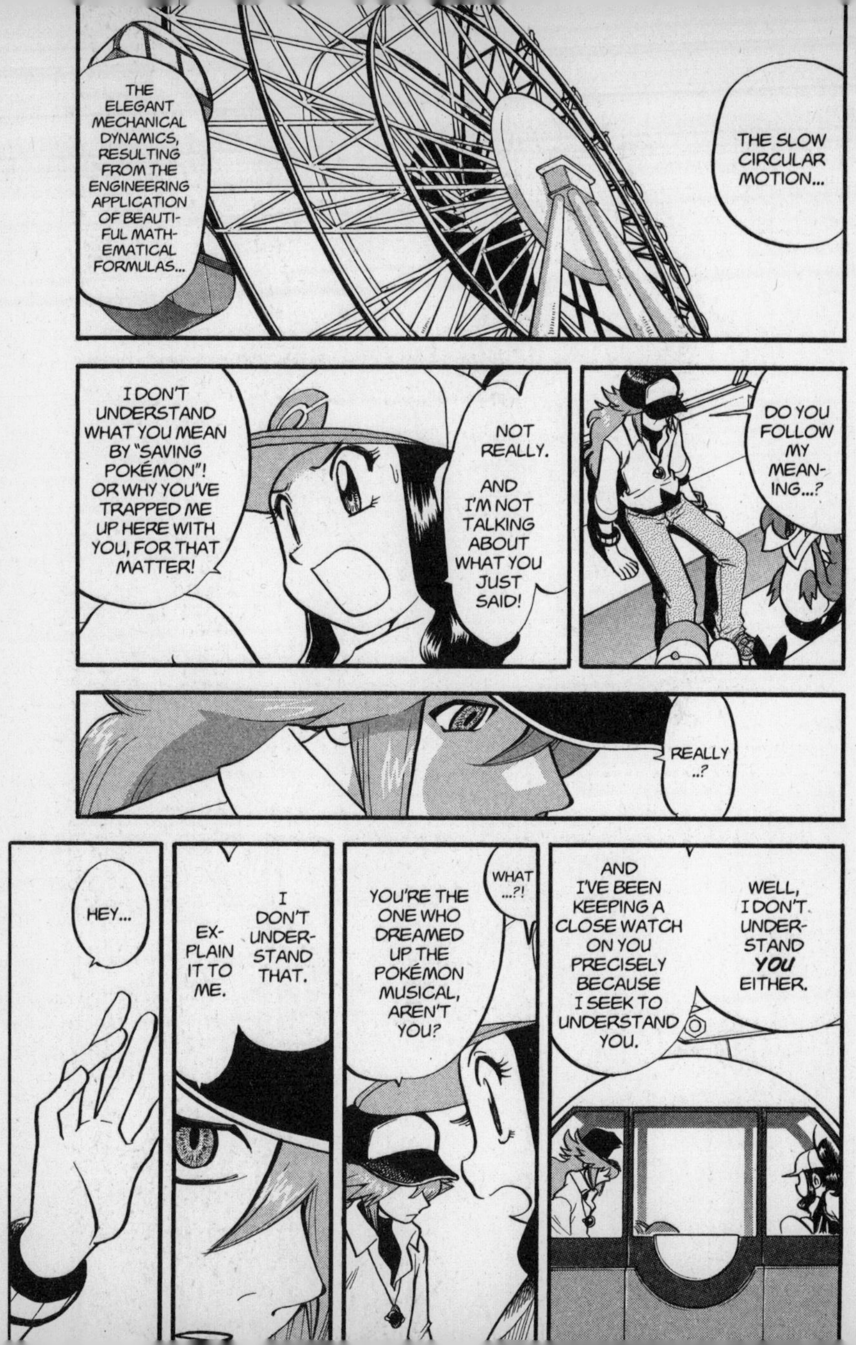
THE SLOW CIRCULAR MOTION...
THE ELEGANT MECHANICAL DYNAMICS, RESULTING FROM THE ENGINEERING APPLICATION OF BEAUTIFUL MATHEMATICAL FORMULAS...
DO YOU FOLLOW MY MEANING...?
NOT REALLY.
AND I'M NOT TALKING ABOUT WHAT YOU JUST SAID!
I DON'T UNDERSTAND WHAT YOU MEAN BY "SAVING POKÉMON"! OR WHY YOU'VE TRAPPED ME UP HERE WITH YOU, FOR THAT MATTER!
REALLY ...?
WELL, I DON'T UNDERSTAND ***YOU*** EITHER.
AND I'VE BEEN KEEPING A CLOSE WATCH ON YOU PRECISELY BECAUSE I SEEK TO UNDERSTAND YOU.
WHAT ...?!
YOU'RE THE ONE WHO DREAMED UP THE POKÉMON MUSICAL, AREN'T YOU?
I DON'T UNDERSTAND THAT.
EXPLAIN IT TO ME.
HEY...

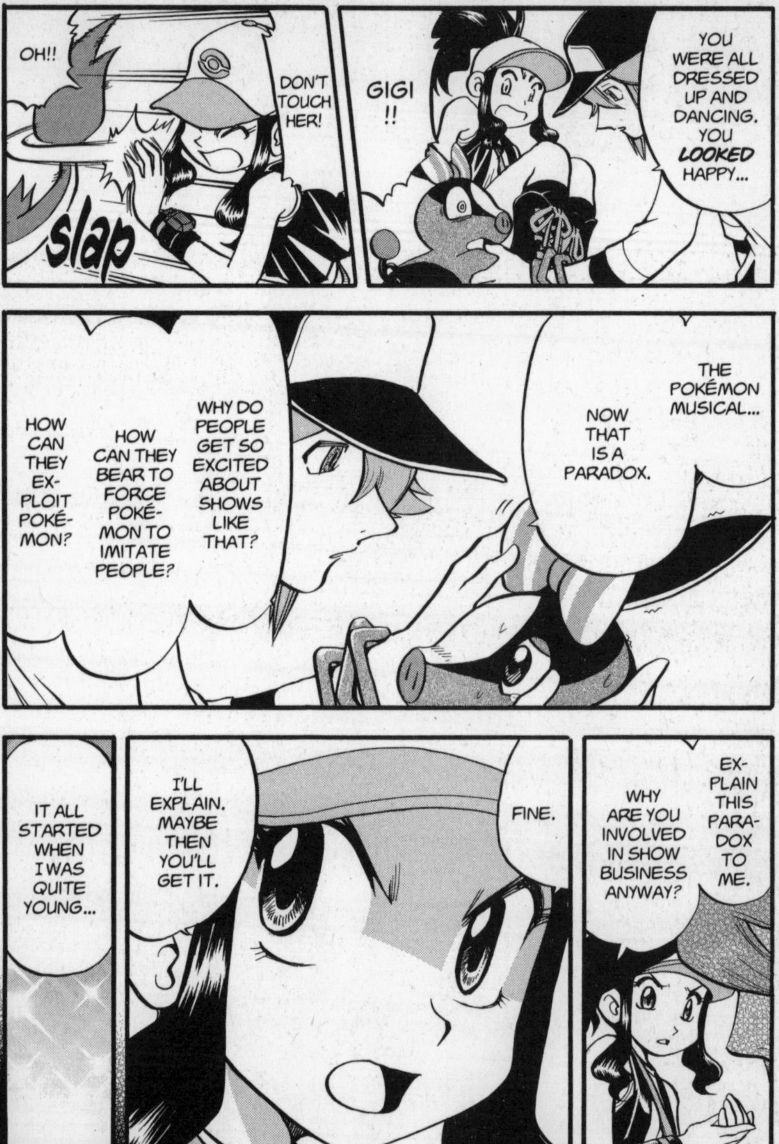
YOU WERE ALL DRESSED UP AND DANCING. YOU **LOOKED** HAPPY...
GIGI !!
DON'T TOUCH HER!
OH!!
slap
THE POKÉMON MUSICAL...
NOW THAT IS A PARADOX.
WHY DO PEOPLE GET SO EXCITED ABOUT SHOWS LIKE THAT?
HOW CAN THEY BEAR TO FORCE POKÉMON TO IMITATE PEOPLE?
HOW CAN THEY EXPLOIT POKÉMON?
EXPLAIN THIS PARADOX TO ME.
WHY ARE YOU INVOLVED IN SHOW BUSINESS ANYWAY?
FINE.
I'LL EXPLAIN. MAYBE THEN YOU'LL GET IT.
IT ALL STARTED WHEN I WAS QUITE YOUNG...

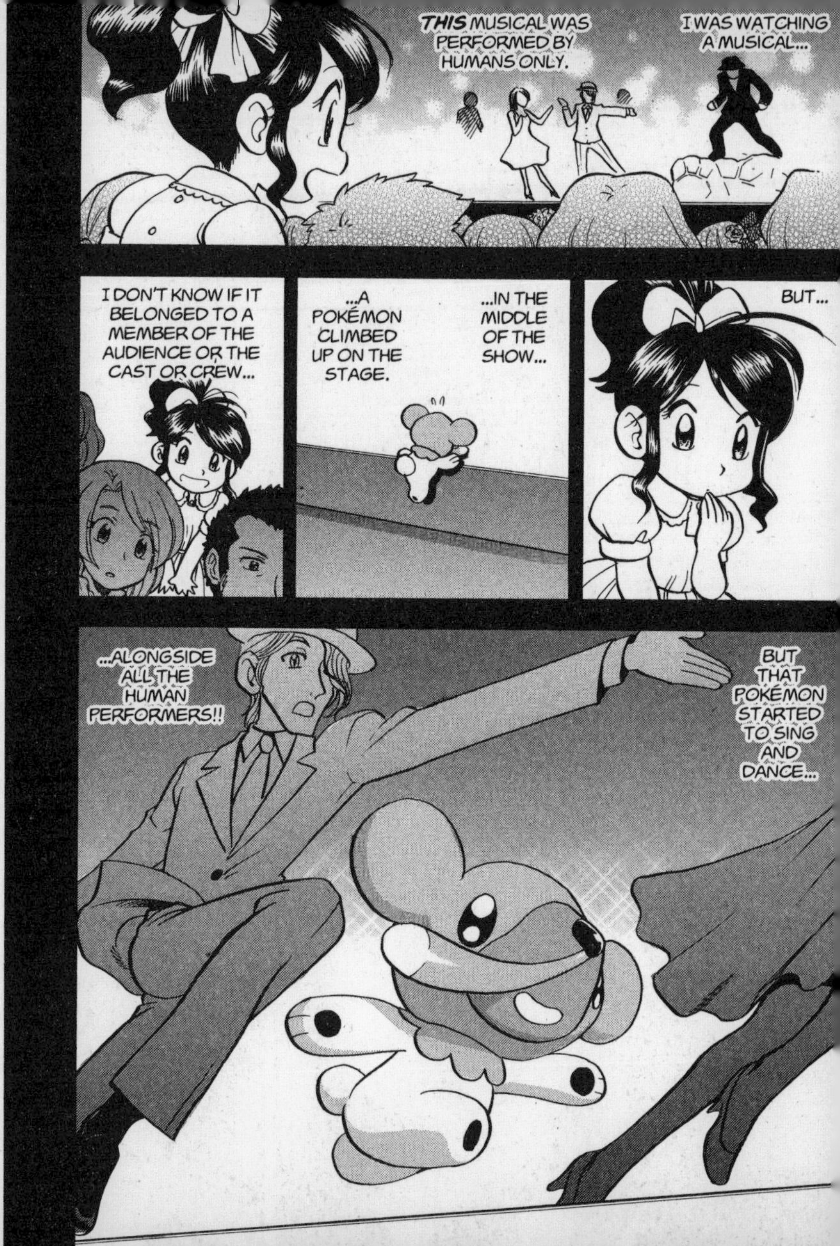
I WAS WATCHING A MUSICAL...
THIS MUSICAL WAS PERFORMED BY HUMANS ONLY.
BUT...
...IN THE MIDDLE OF THE SHOW...
...A POKÉMON CLIMBED UP ON THE STAGE.
I DON'T KNOW IF IT BELONGED TO A MEMBER OF THE AUDIENCE OR THE CAST OR CREW...
BUT THAT POKÉMON STARTED TO SING AND DANCE...
...ALONGSIDE ALL THE HUMAN PERFORMERS!!

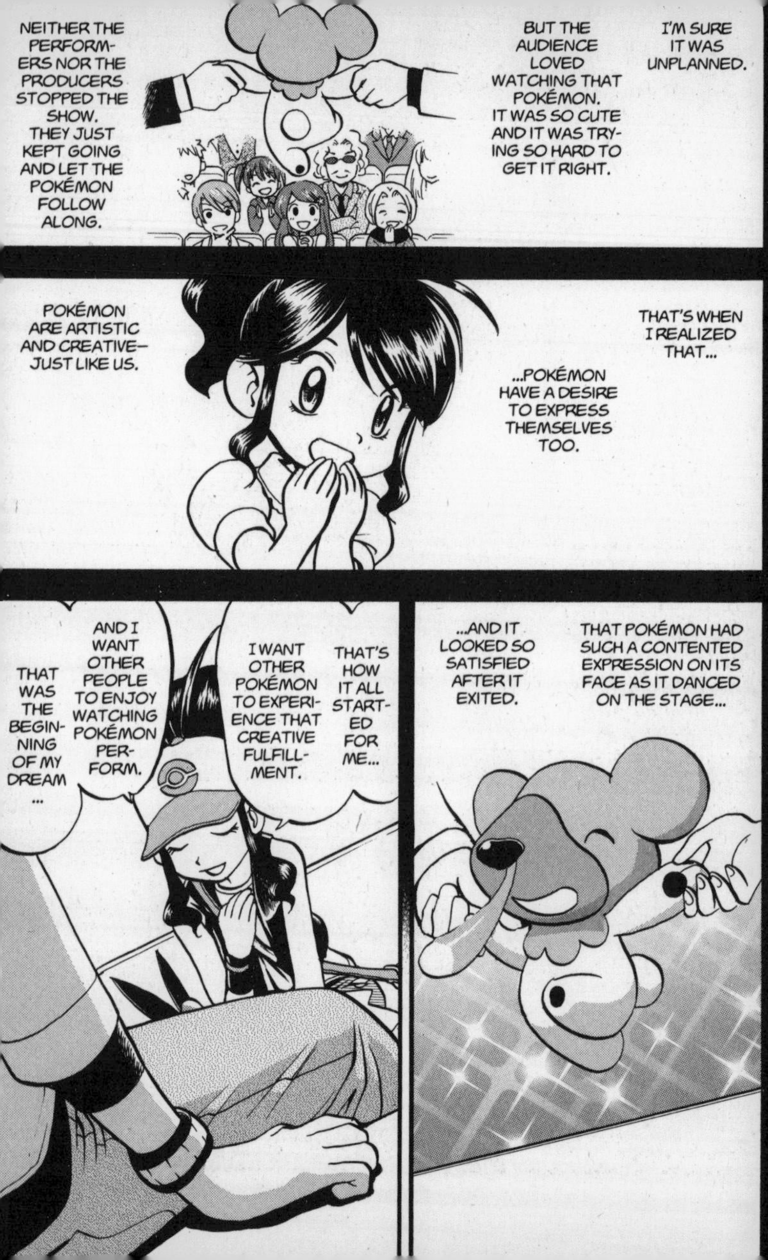
I'M SURE IT WAS UNPLANNED.
BUT THE AUDIENCE LOVED WATCHING THAT POKÉMON. IT WAS SO CUTE AND IT WAS TRYING SO HARD TO GET IT RIGHT.
NEITHER THE PERFORMERS NOR THE PRODUCERS STOPPED THE SHOW. THEY JUST KEPT GOING AND LET THE POKÉMON FOLLOW ALONG.
THAT'S WHEN I REALIZED THAT...
...POKÉMON HAVE A DESIRE TO EXPRESS THEMSELVES TOO.
POKÉMON ARE ARTISTIC AND CREATIVE—JUST LIKE US.
THAT POKÉMON HAD SUCH A CONTENTED EXPRESSION ON ITS FACE AS IT DANCED ON THE STAGE...
...AND IT LOOKED SO SATISFIED AFTER IT EXITED.
THAT'S HOW IT ALL STARTED FOR ME...
I WANT OTHER POKÉMON TO EXPERIENCE THAT CREATIVE FULFILLMENT.
AND I WANT OTHER PEOPLE TO ENJOY WATCHING POKÉMON PERFORM.
THAT WAS THE BEGINNING OF MY DREAM...

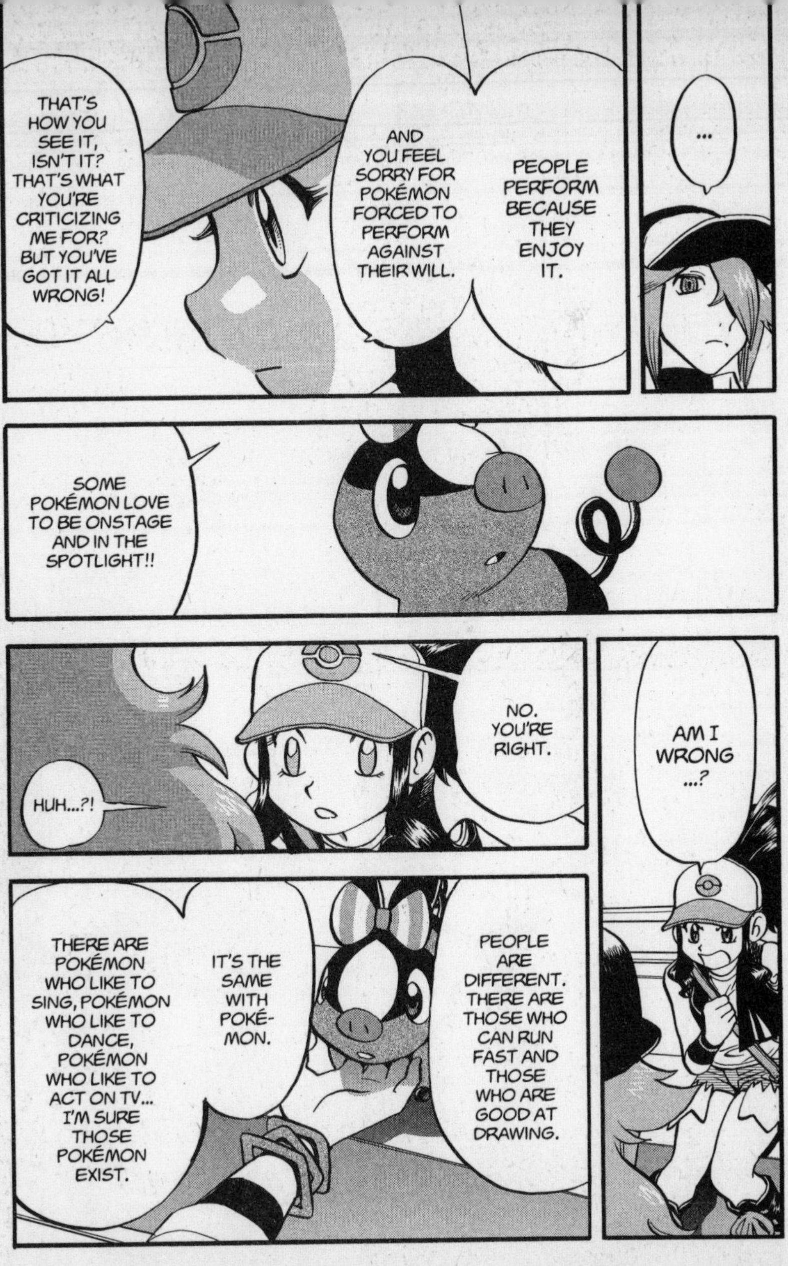
...
PEOPLE PERFORM BECAUSE THEY ENJOY IT.
AND YOU FEEL SORRY FOR POKÉMON FORCED TO PERFORM AGAINST THEIR WILL.
THAT'S HOW YOU SEE IT, ISN'T IT? THAT'S WHAT YOU'RE CRITICIZING ME FOR? BUT YOU'VE GOT IT ALL WRONG!
SOME POKÉMON LOVE TO BE ONSTAGE AND IN THE SPOTLIGHT!!
AM I WRONG ...?
NO. YOU'RE RIGHT.
HUH...?!
PEOPLE ARE DIFFERENT. THERE ARE THOSE WHO CAN RUN FAST AND THOSE WHO ARE GOOD AT DRAWING.
IT'S THE SAME WITH POKÉ-MON.
THERE ARE POKÉMON WHO LIKE TO SING, POKÉMON WHO LIKE TO DANCE, POKÉMON WHO LIKE TO ACT ON TV... I'M SURE THOSE POKÉMON EXIST.

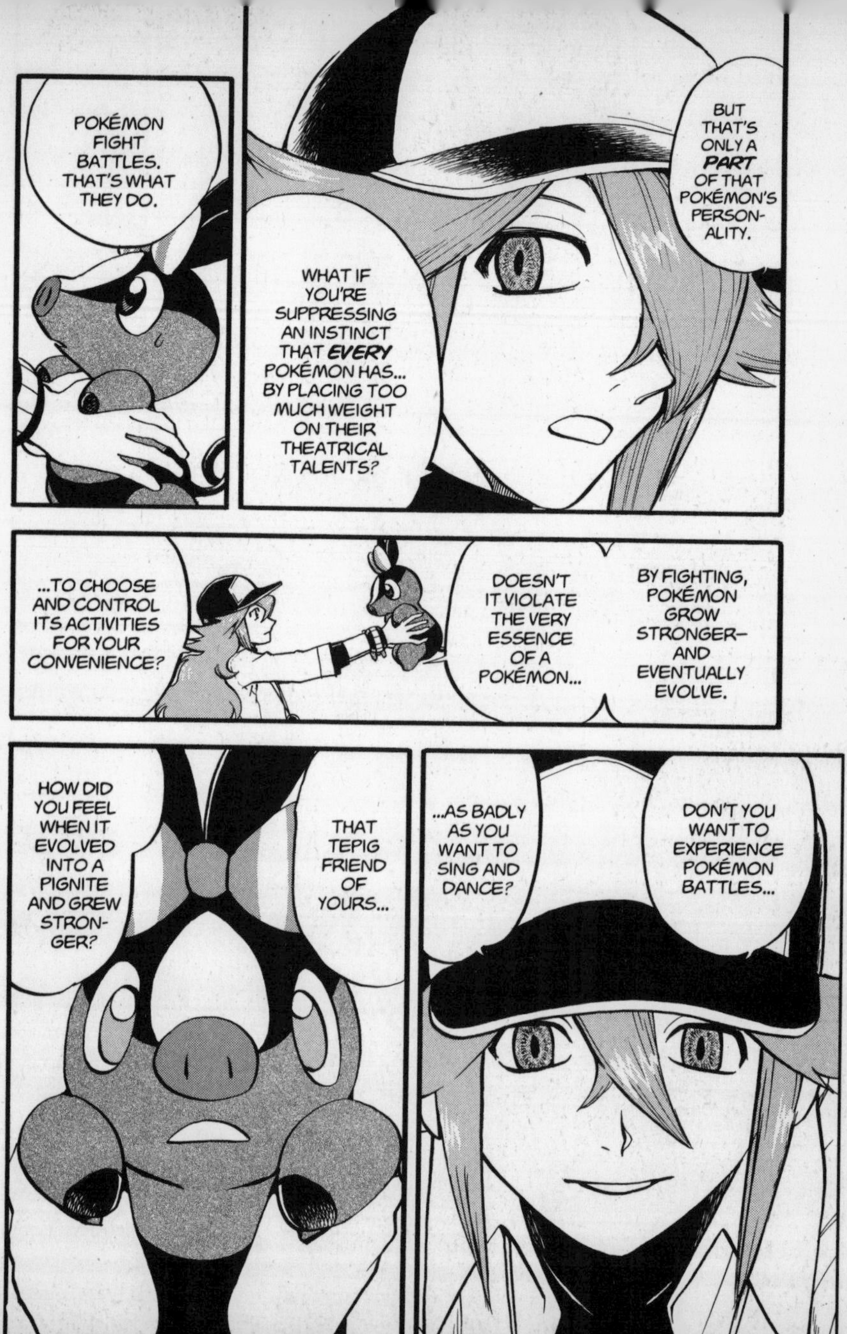
BUT THAT'S ONLY A **PART** OF THAT POKÉMON'S PERSONALITY.
WHAT IF YOU'RE SUPPRESSING AN INSTINCT THAT **EVERY** POKÉMON HAS... BY PLACING TOO MUCH WEIGHT ON THEIR THEATRICAL TALENTS?
POKÉMON FIGHT BATTLES. THAT'S WHAT THEY DO.
BY FIGHTING, POKÉMON GROW STRONGER— AND EVENTUALLY EVOLVE.
DOESN'T IT VIOLATE THE VERY ESSENCE OF A POKÉMON...
...TO CHOOSE AND CONTROL ITS ACTIVITIES FOR YOUR CONVENIENCE?
DON'T YOU WANT TO EXPERIENCE POKÉMON BATTLES...
...AS BADLY AS YOU WANT TO SING AND DANCE?
THAT TEPIG FRIEND OF YOURS...
HOW DID YOU FEEL WHEN IT EVOLVED INTO A PIGNITE AND GREW STRONGER?

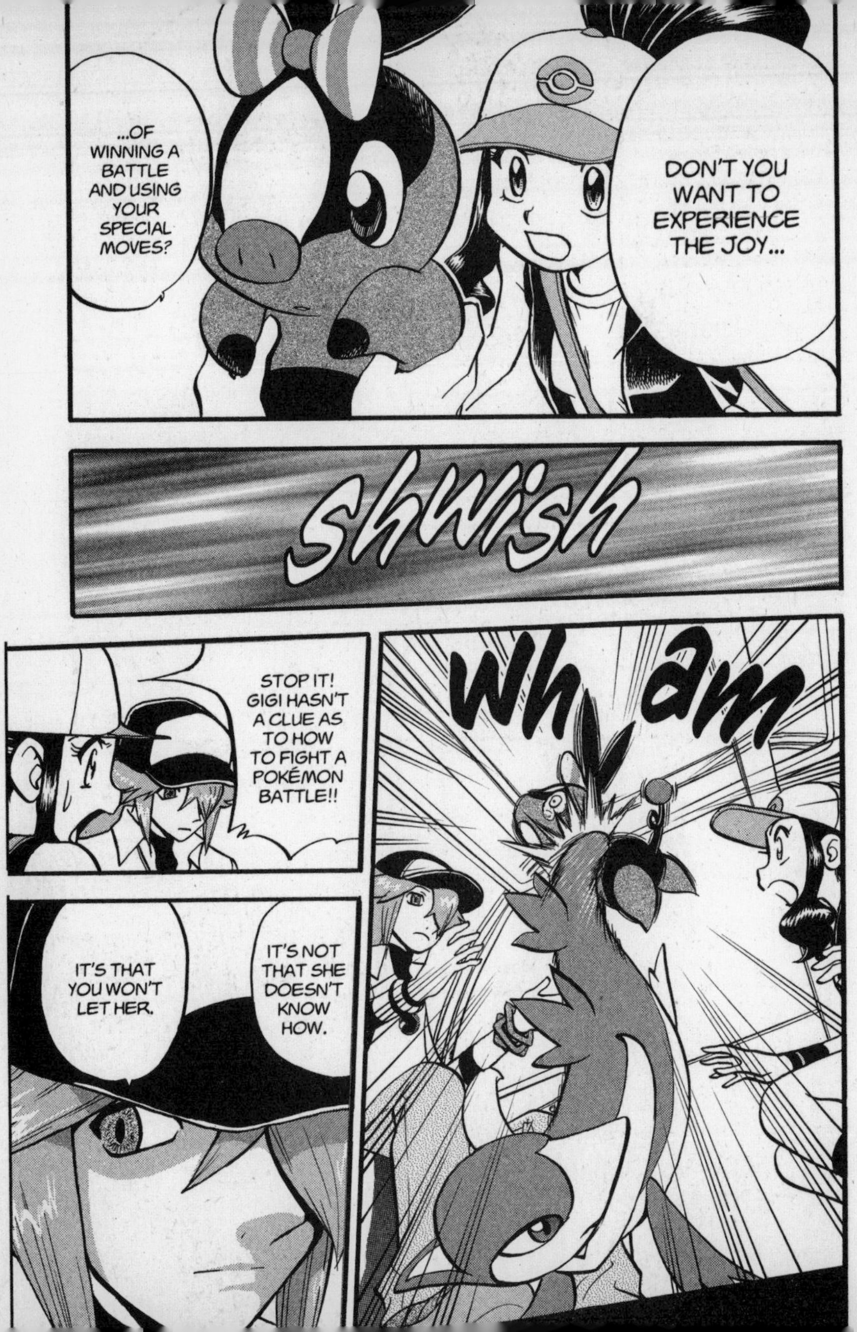
DON'T YOU WANT TO EXPERIENCE THE JOY...
...OF WINNING A BATTLE AND USING YOUR SPECIAL MOVES?
shwish
wham
STOP IT! GIGI HASN'T A CLUE AS TO HOW TO FIGHT A POKÉMON BATTLE!!
IT'S NOT THAT SHE DOESN'T KNOW HOW.
IT'S THAT YOU WON'T LET HER.

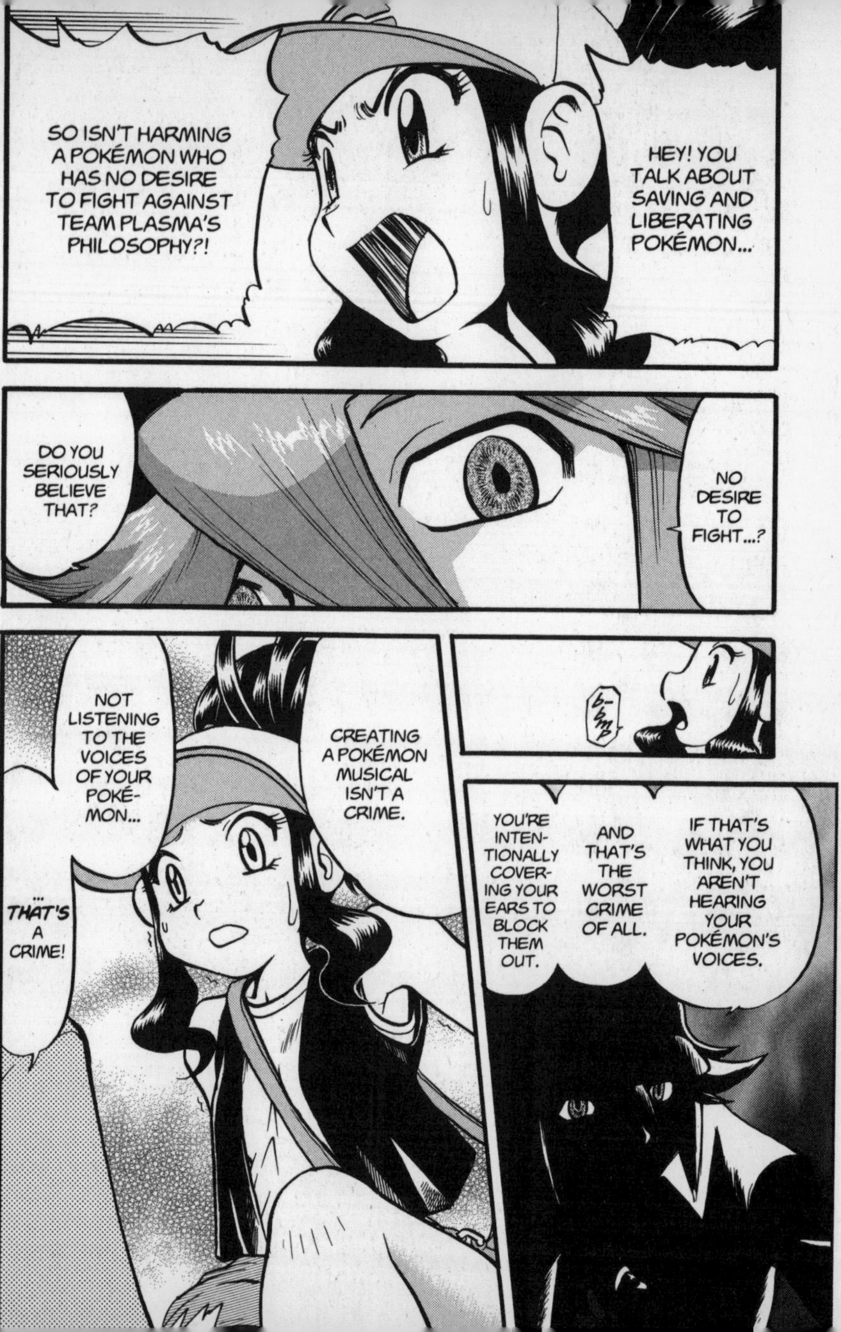
HEY! YOU TALK ABOUT SAVING AND LIBERATING POKÉMON...
SO ISN'T HARMING A POKÉMON WHO HAS NO DESIRE TO FIGHT AGAINST TEAM PLASMA'S PHILOSOPHY?!
NO DESIRE TO FIGHT...?
DO YOU SERIOUSLY BELIEVE THAT?
b-bmp
IF THAT'S WHAT YOU THINK, YOU AREN'T HEARING YOUR POKÉMON'S VOICES.
AND THAT'S THE WORST CRIME OF ALL.
YOU'RE INTENTIONALLY COVERING YOUR EARS TO BLOCK THEM OUT.
CREATING A POKÉMON MUSICAL ISN'T A CRIME.
NOT LISTENING TO THE VOICES OF YOUR POKÉMON...
...*THAT'S* A CRIME!

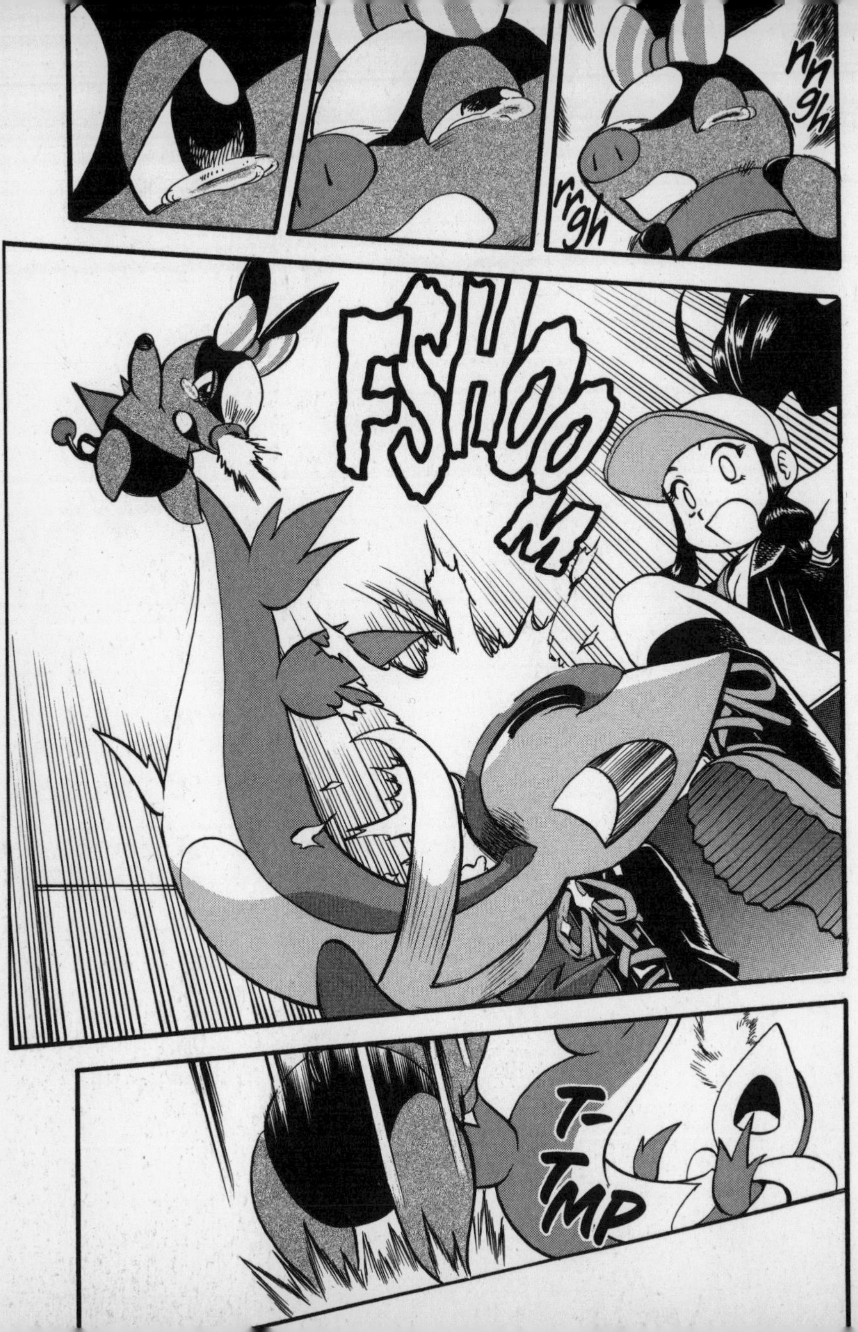

nngh
rrgh
FSHOOOM
T-TMP

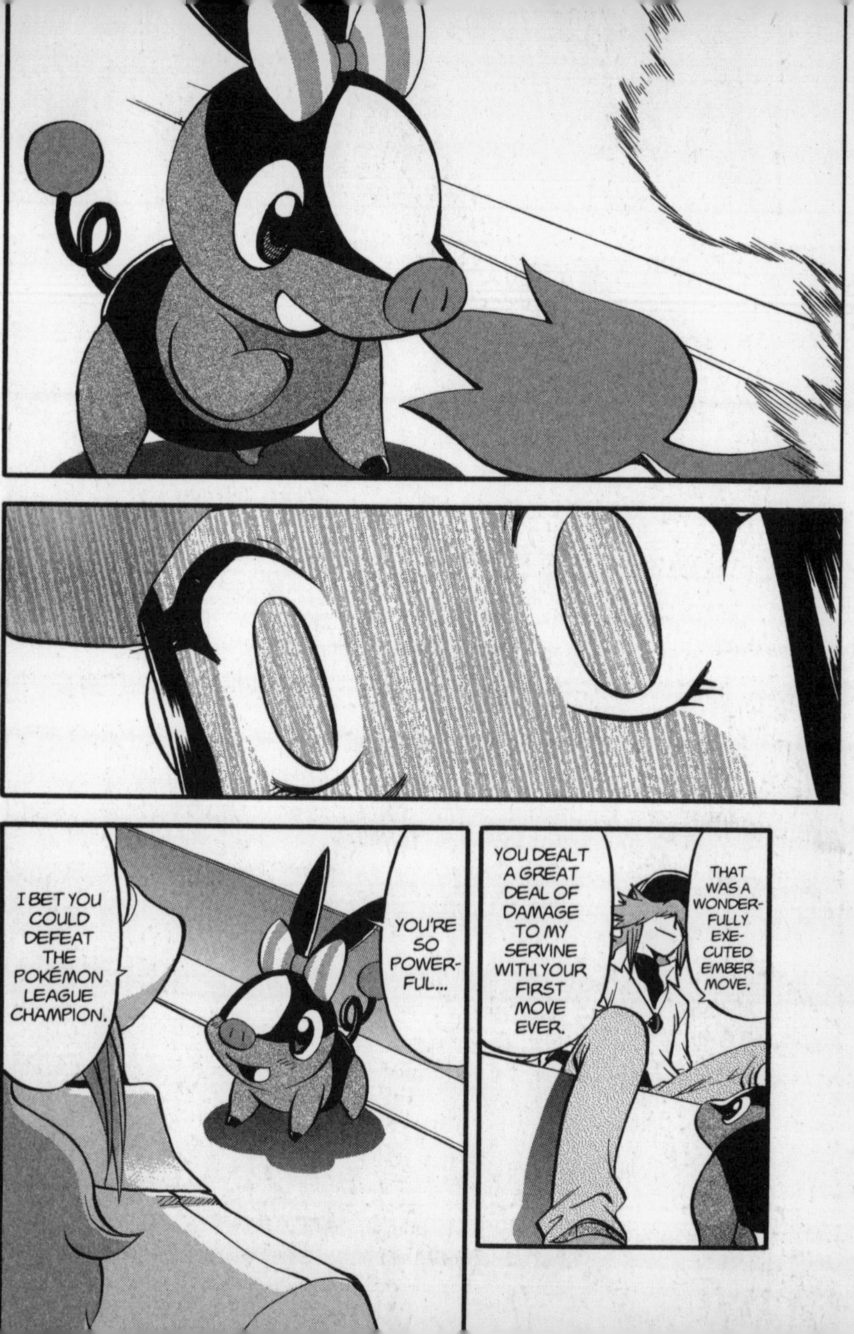
THAT WAS A WONDERFULLY EXECUTED EMBER MOVE.
YOU DEALT A GREAT DEAL OF DAMAGE TO MY SERVINE WITH YOUR FIRST MOVE EVER.
YOU'RE SO POWERFUL...
I BET YOU COULD DEFEAT THE POKÉMON LEAGUE CHAMPION.

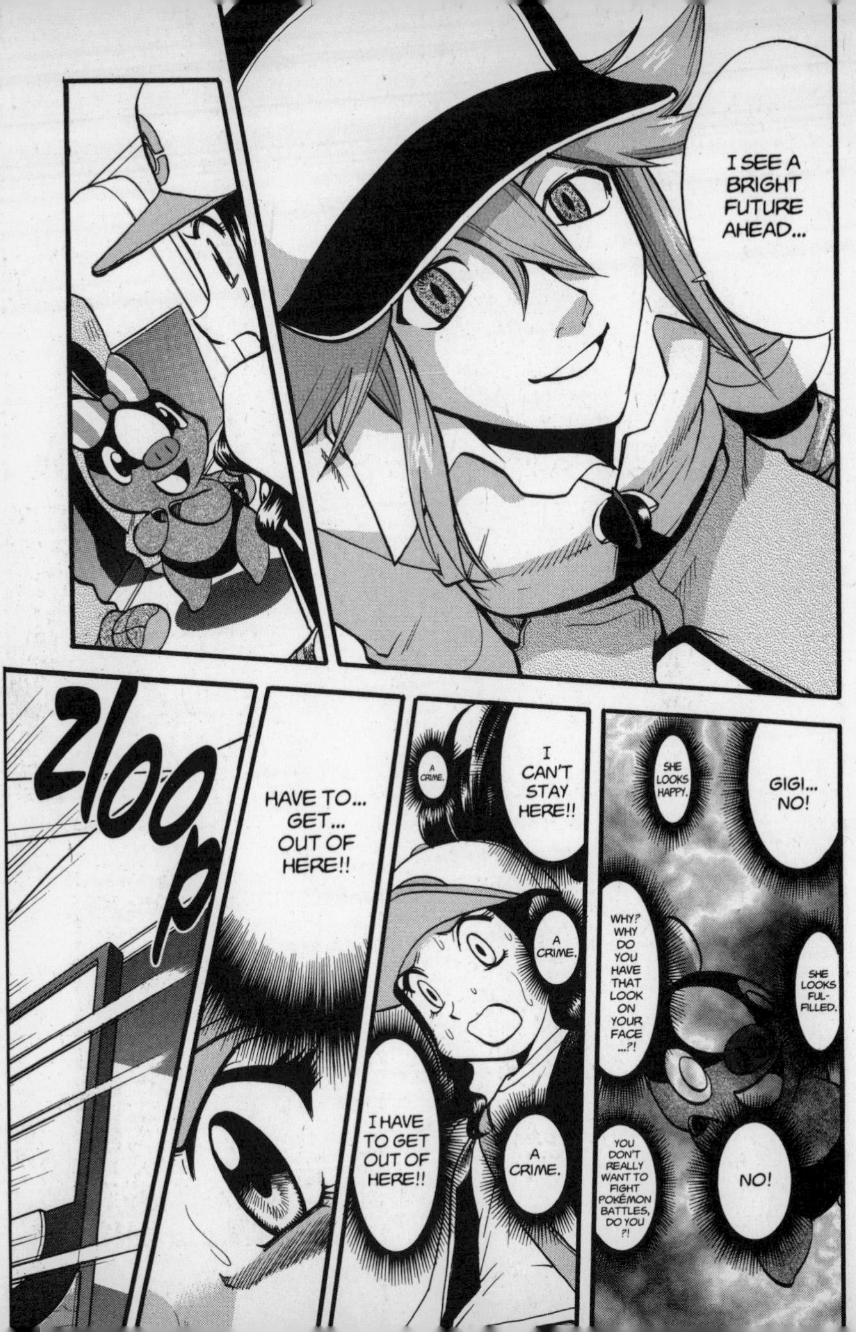
I SEE A BRIGHT FUTURE AHEAD...
GIGI... NO!
SHE LOOKS HAPPY.
SHE LOOKS FUL-FILLED.
WHY? WHY DO YOU HAVE THAT LOOK ON YOUR FACE ...?!
NO!
YOU DON'T REALLY WANT TO FIGHT POKÉMON BATTLES, DO YOU ?!
I CAN'T STAY HERE!!
A CRIME.
A CRIME.
A CRIME.
I HAVE TO GET OUT OF HERE!!
HAVE TO... GET... OUT OF HERE!!
ZOOOP

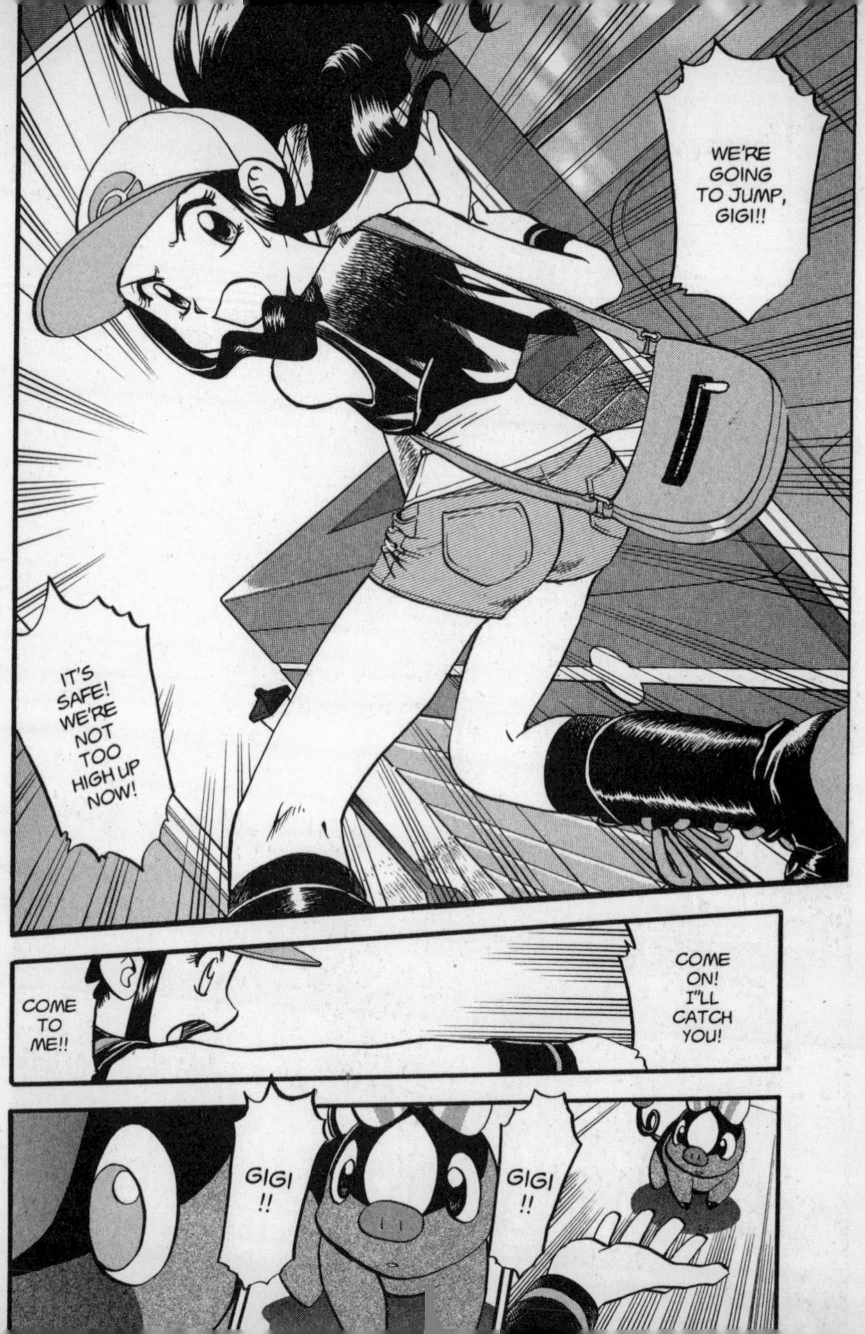
WE'RE GOING TO JUMP, GIGI!!
IT'S SAFE! WE'RE NOT TOO HIGH UP NOW!
COME ON! I'LL CATCH YOU!
COME TO ME!!
GIGI !!
GIGI !!

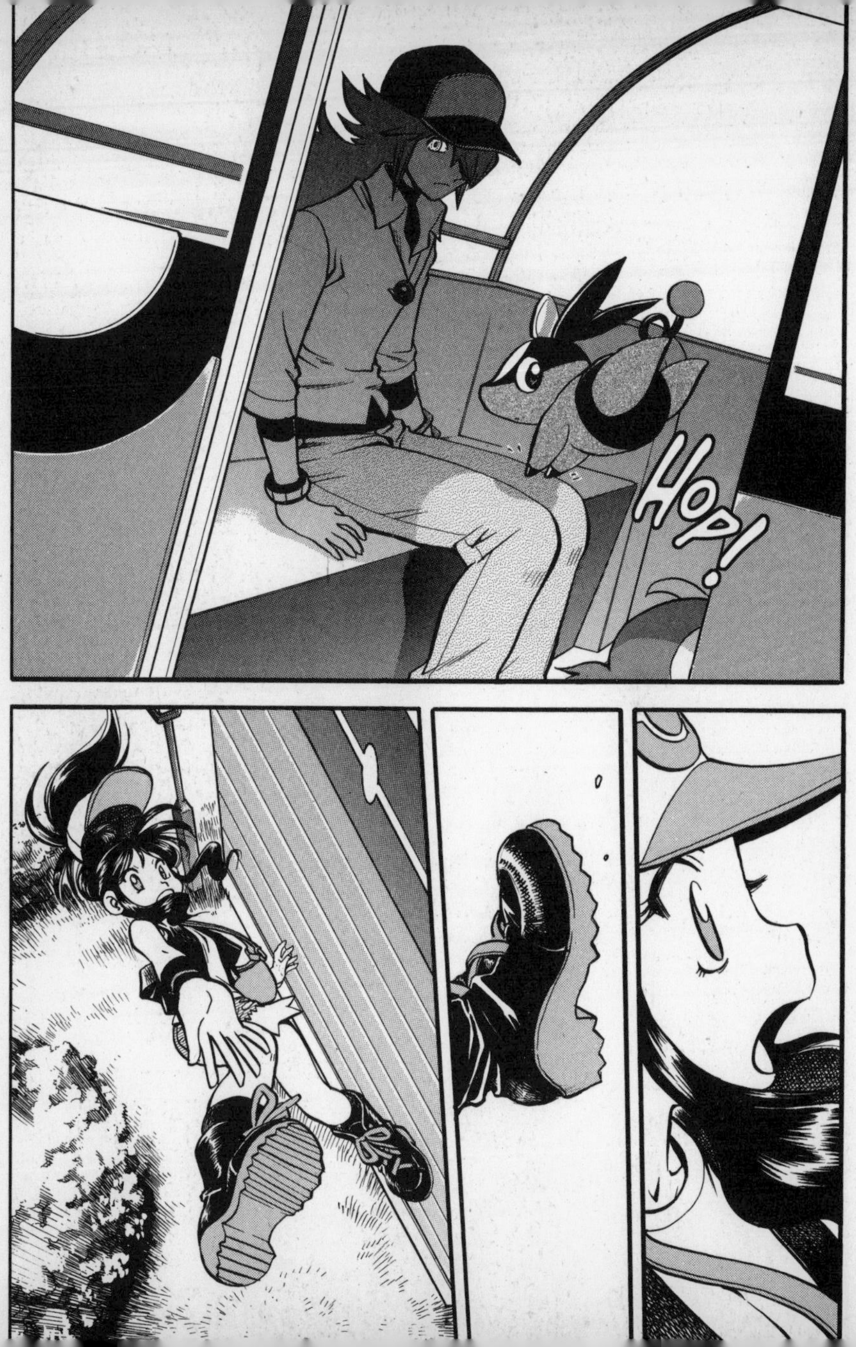
HOP!

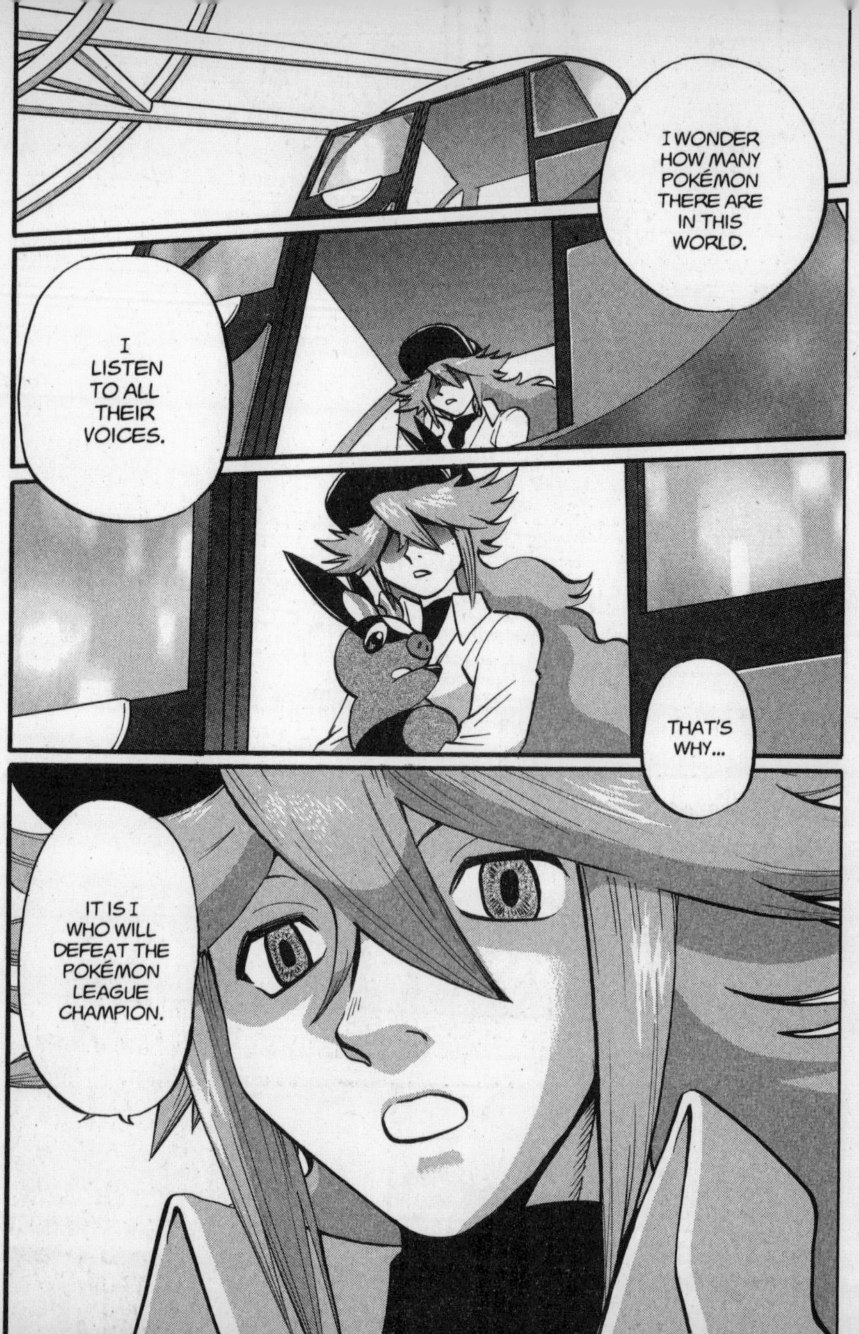
I WONDER HOW MANY POKÉMON THERE ARE IN THIS WORLD.
I LISTEN TO ALL THEIR VOICES.
THAT'S WHY...
IT IS I WHO WILL DEFEAT THE POKÉMON LEAGUE CHAMPION.

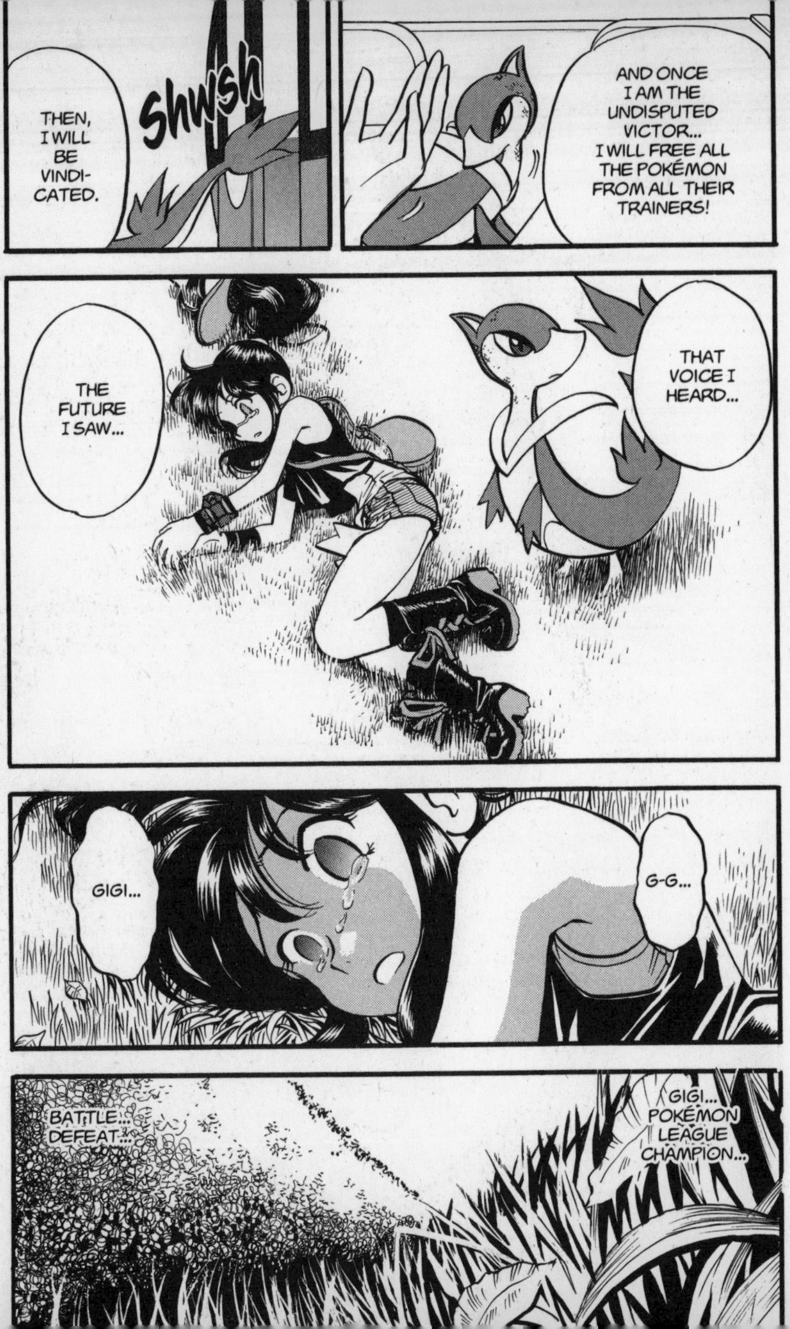
AND ONCE I AM THE UNDISPUTED VICTOR... I WILL FREE ALL THE POKÉMON FROM ALL THEIR TRAINERS!
Shwsh
THEN, I WILL BE VINDI-CATED.
THAT VOICE I HEARD...
THE FUTURE I SAW...
G-G...
GIGI...
GIGI... POKÉMON LEAGUE CHAMPION...
BATTLE... DEFEAT...

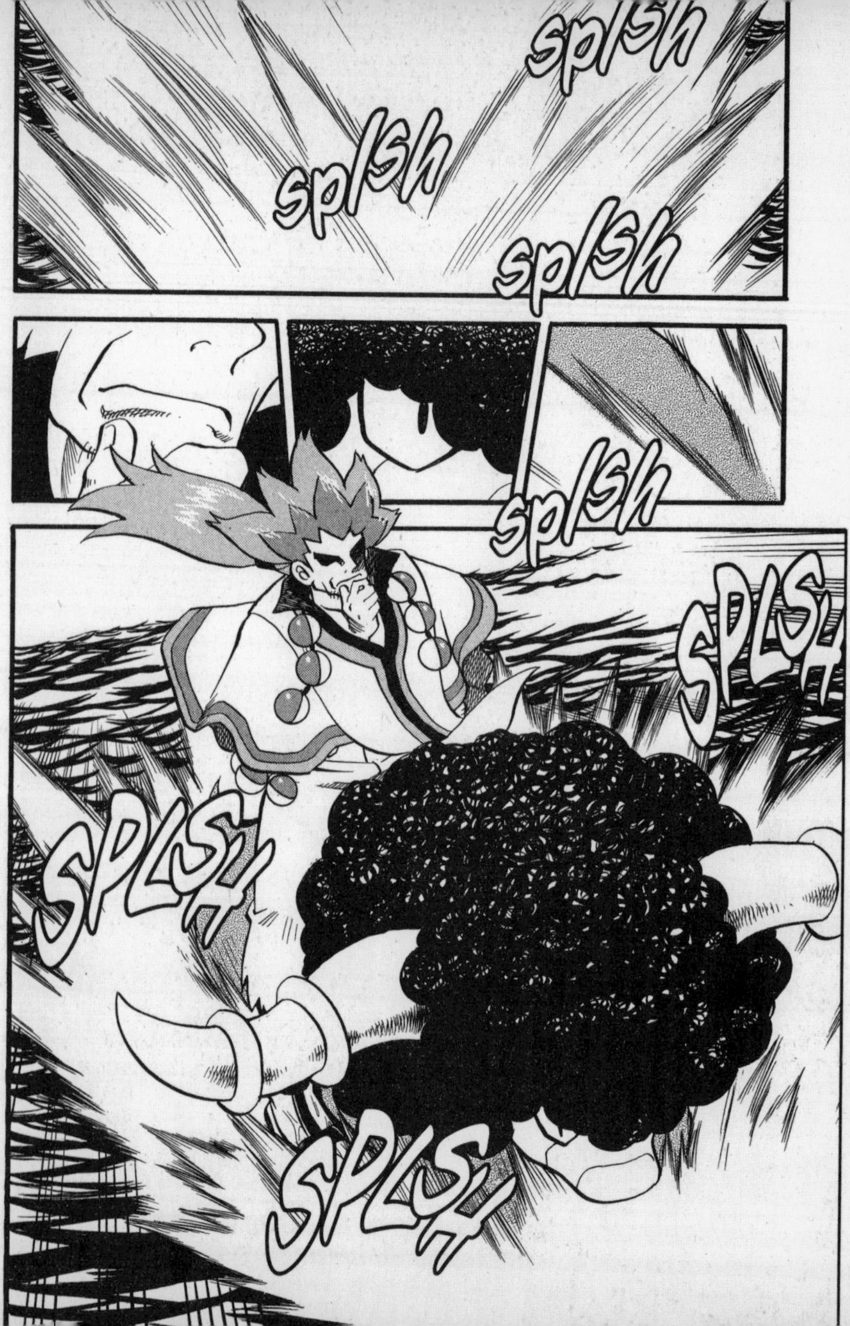
splsh
splsh
splsh
splsh
SPLSH
SPLSH
SPLSH

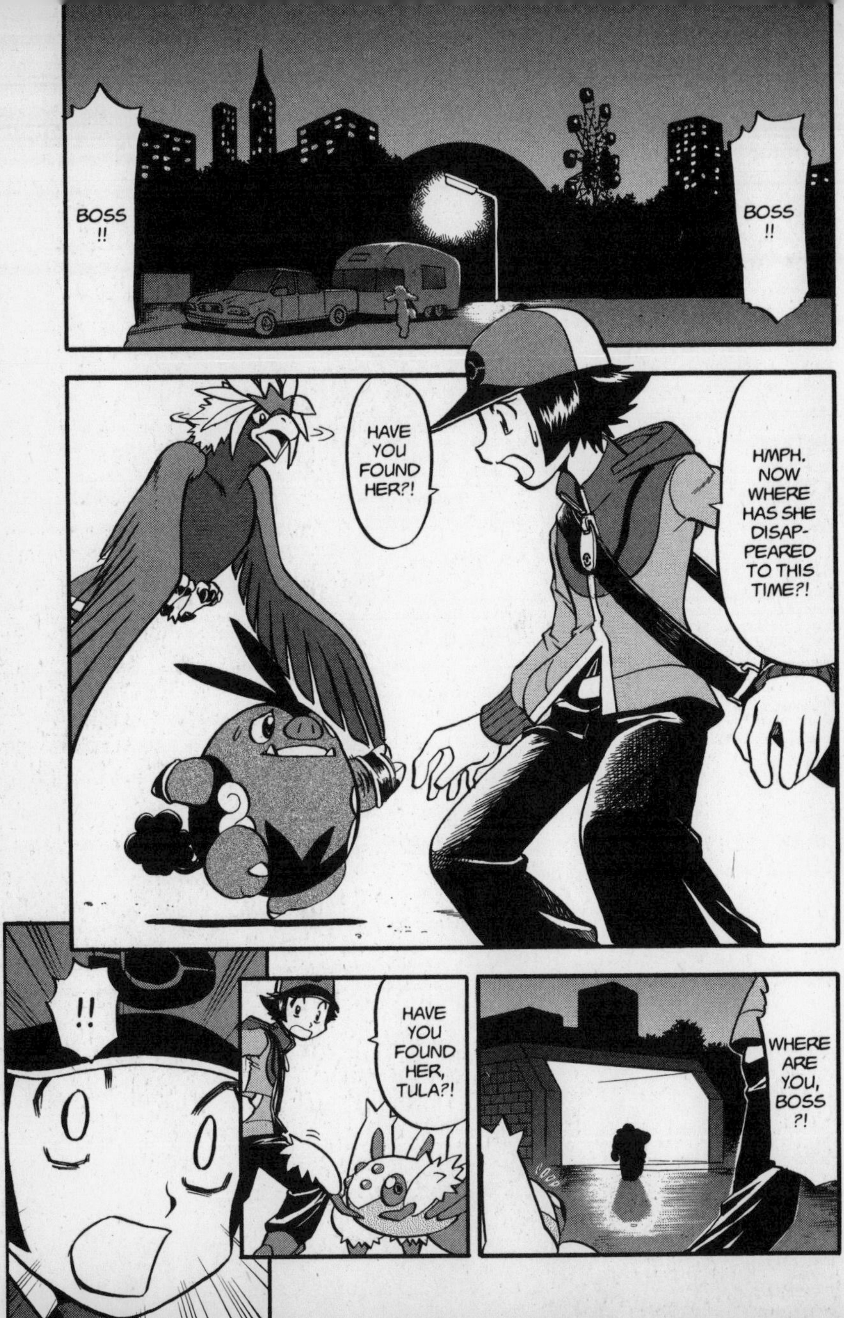
BOSS !!
BOSS !!
HMPH. NOW WHERE HAS SHE DISAP-PEARED TO THIS TIME?!
HAVE YOU FOUND HER?!
WHERE ARE YOU, BOSS ?!
HAVE YOU FOUND HER, TULA?!
!!

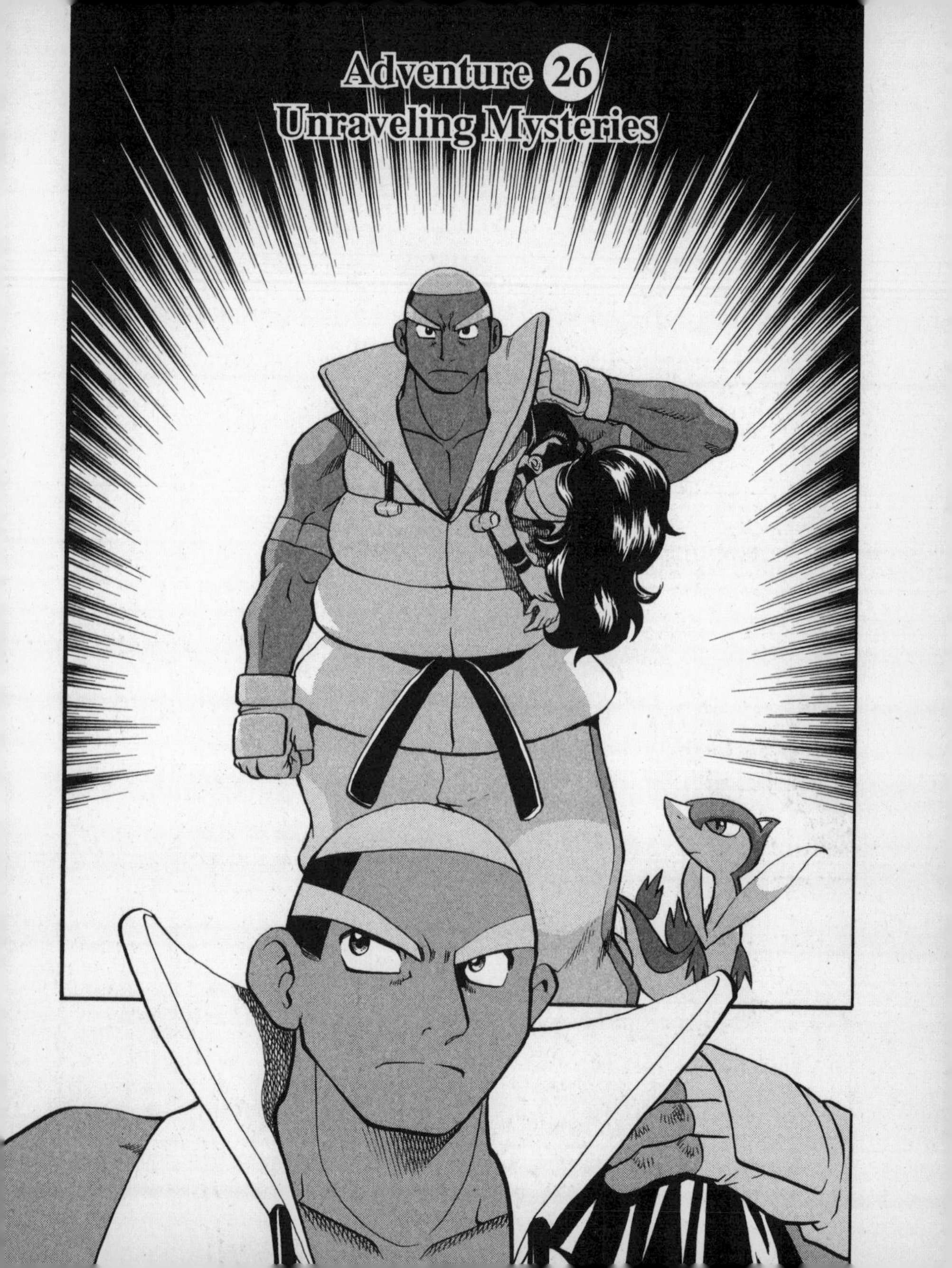
Adventure 26
Unraveling Mysteries

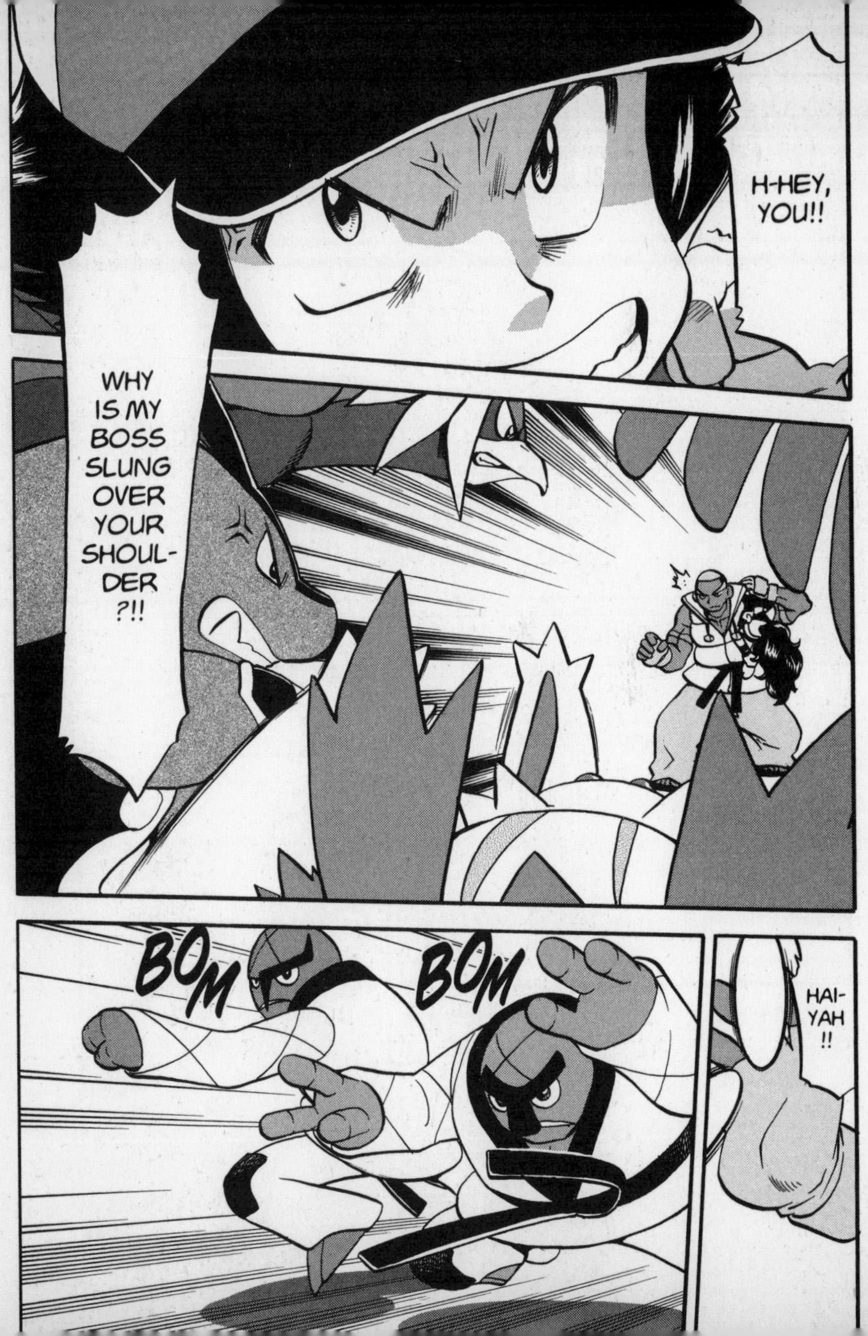
H-HEY, YOU!!
WHY IS MY BOSS SLUNG OVER YOUR SHOULDER ?!!
HAI-YAH !!
BOM BOM

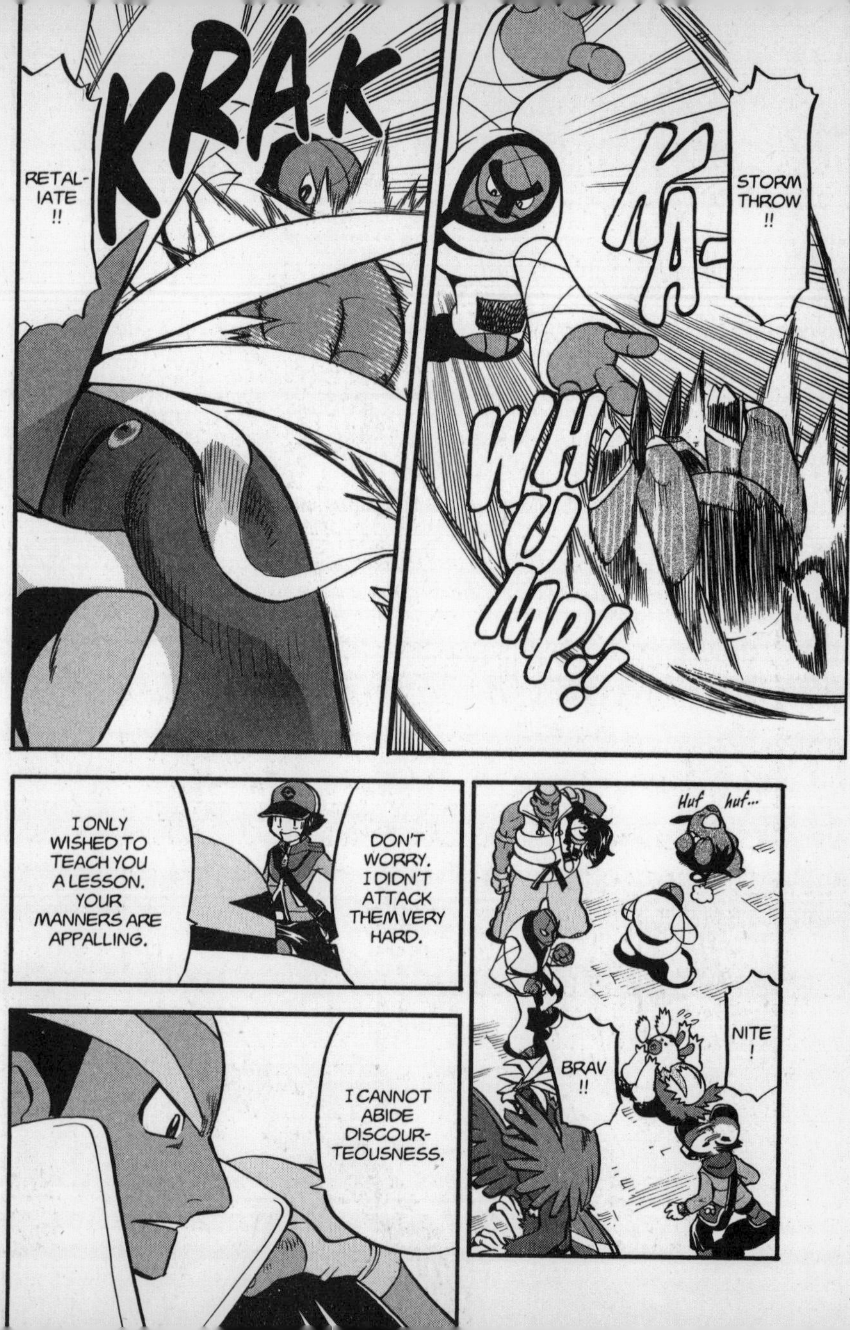
STORM THROW !!
KA-
WH U MP!!
KRAK
RETAL- IATE !!
Huf huf...
NITE !
BRAV !!
DON'T WORRY. I DIDN'T ATTACK THEM VERY HARD.
I ONLY WISHED TO TEACH YOU A LESSON. YOUR MANNERS ARE APPALLING.
I CANNOT ABIDE DISCOUR- TEOUSNESS.

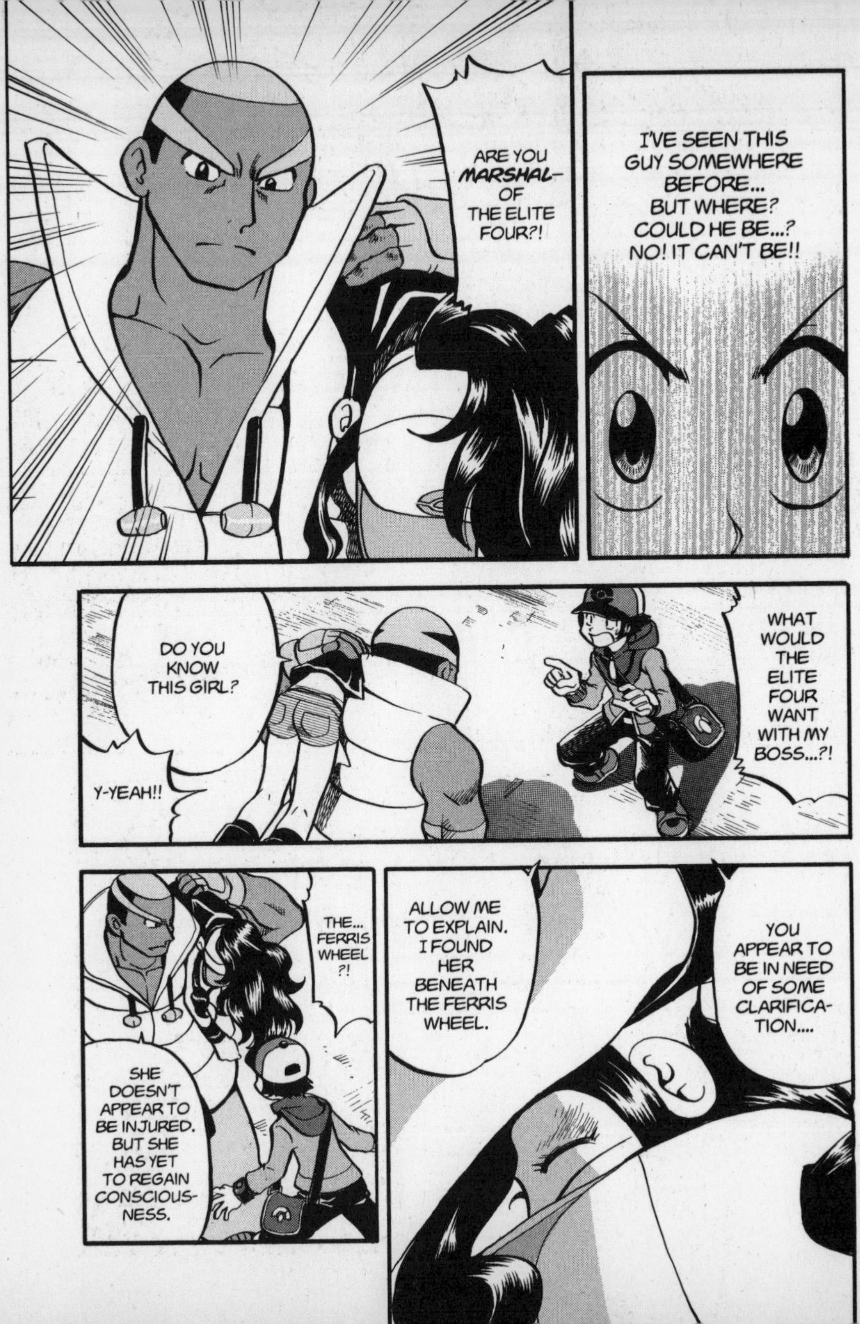
I'VE SEEN THIS GUY SOMEWHERE BEFORE... BUT WHERE? COULD HE BE...? NO! IT CAN'T BE!!
ARE YOU *MARSHAL*- OF THE ELITE FOUR?!
WHAT WOULD THE ELITE FOUR WANT WITH MY BOSS...?!
DO YOU KNOW THIS GIRL?
Y-YEAH!!
YOU APPEAR TO BE IN NEED OF SOME CLARIFICA-TION....
ALLOW ME TO EXPLAIN. I FOUND HER BENEATH THE FERRIS WHEEL.
THE... FERRIS WHEEL ?!
SHE DOESN'T APPEAR TO BE INJURED. BUT SHE HAS YET TO REGAIN CONSCIOUS-NESS.

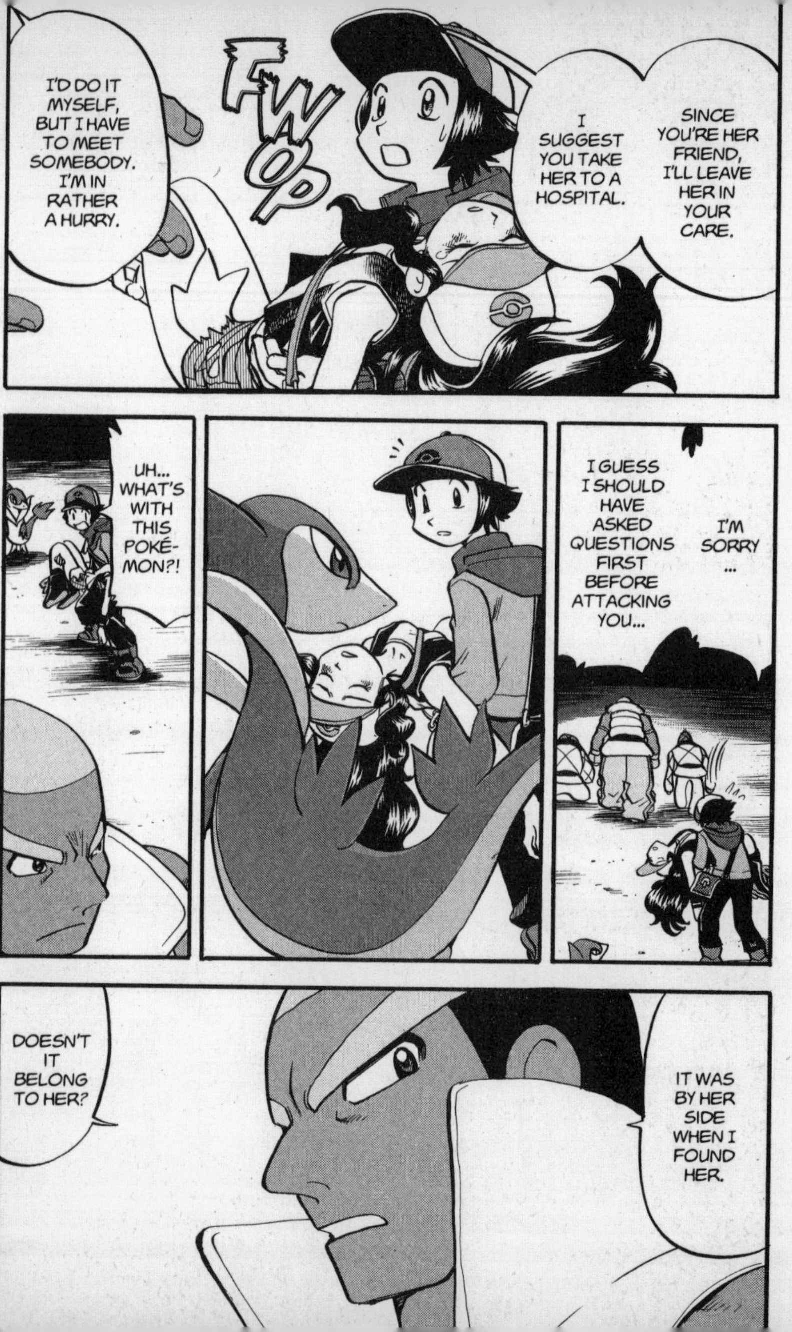
SINCE YOU'RE HER FRIEND, I'LL LEAVE HER IN YOUR CARE.
I SUGGEST YOU TAKE HER TO A HOSPITAL.
FWOOP
I'D DO IT MYSELF, BUT I HAVE TO MEET SOMEBODY. I'M IN RATHER A HURRY.
I'M SORRY...
I GUESS I SHOULD HAVE ASKED QUESTIONS FIRST BEFORE ATTACKING YOU...
UH... WHAT'S WITH THIS POKÉMON?!
IT WAS BY HER SIDE WHEN I FOUND HER.
DOESN'T IT BELONG TO HER?

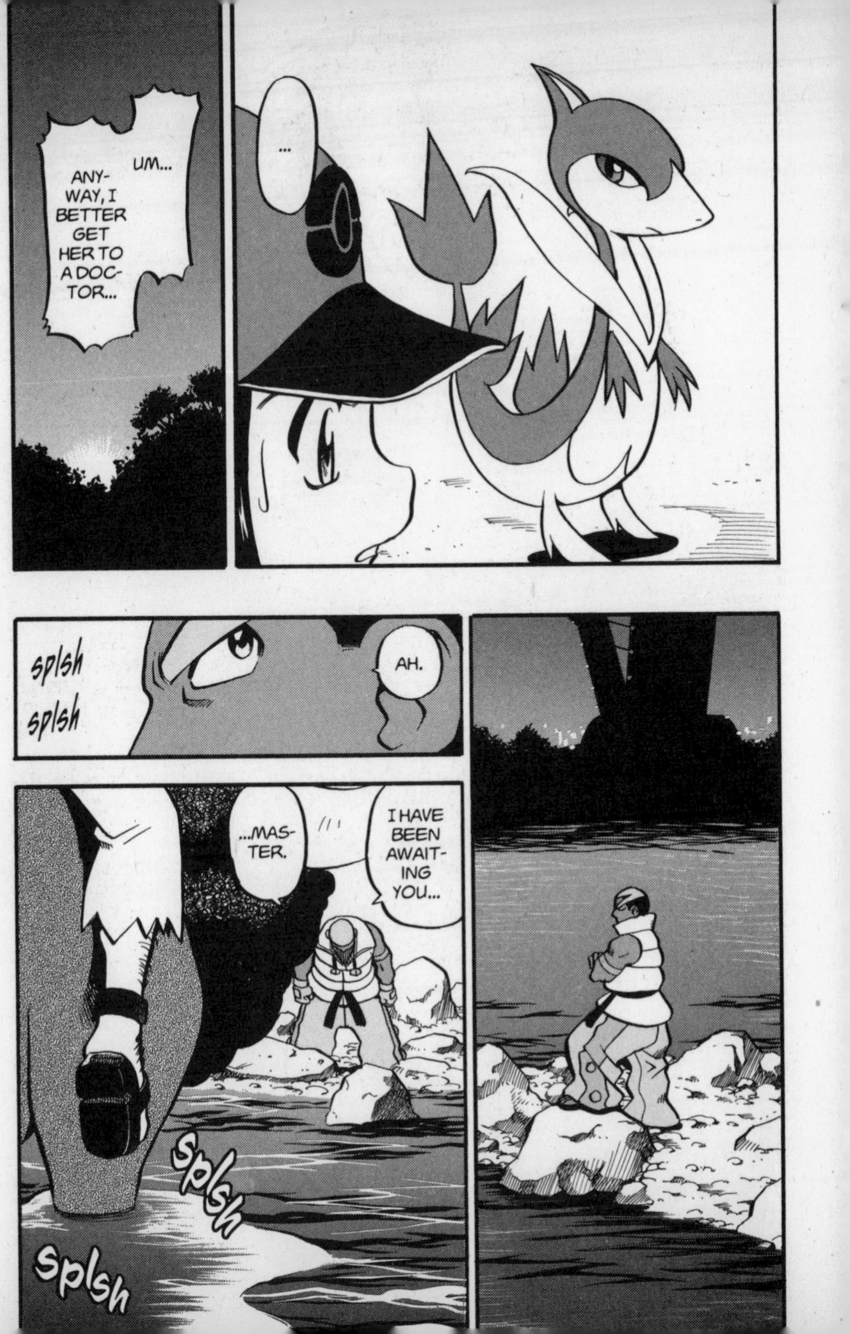
...
UM... ANYWAY, I BETTER GET HER TO A DOCTOR...
AH.
splsh splsh
I HAVE BEEN AWAITING YOU...
...MASTER.
splsh
splsh

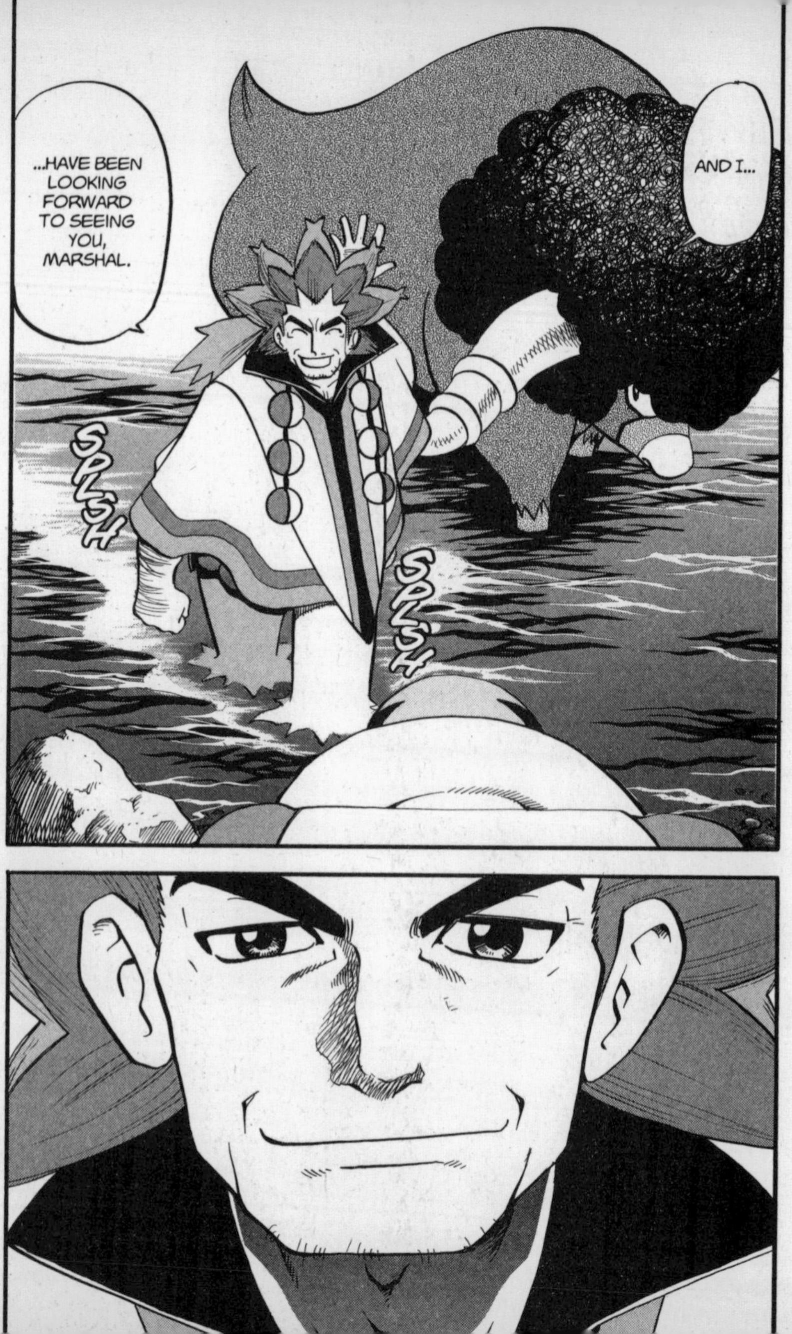
AND I...
...HAVE BEEN LOOKING FORWARD TO SEEING YOU, MARSHAL.
SPLSH
SPLSH

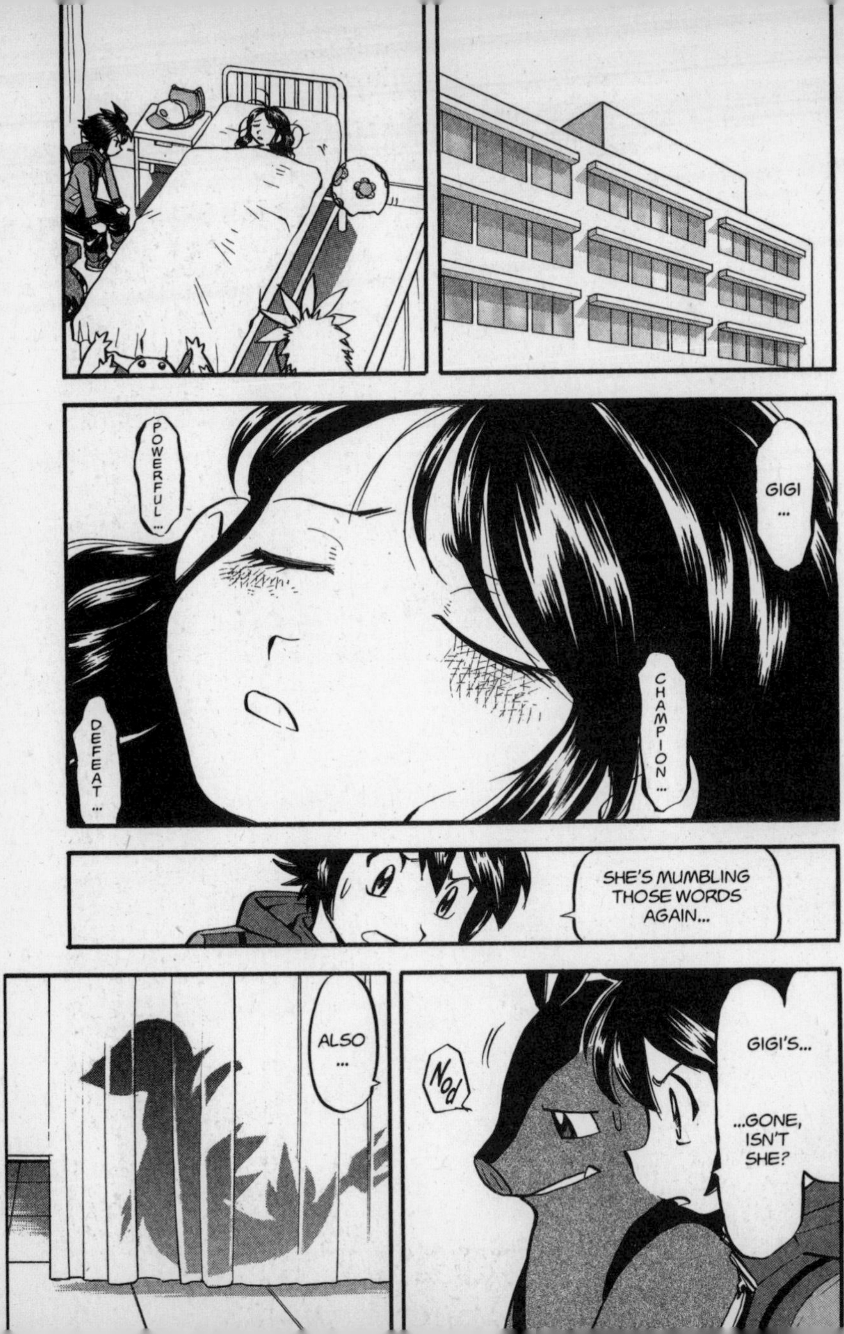
GIGI...
POWERFUL...
CHAMPION...
DEFEAT...
SHE'S MUMBLING THOSE WORDS AGAIN...
GIGI'S...
...GONE, ISN'T SHE?
Nod
ALSO...

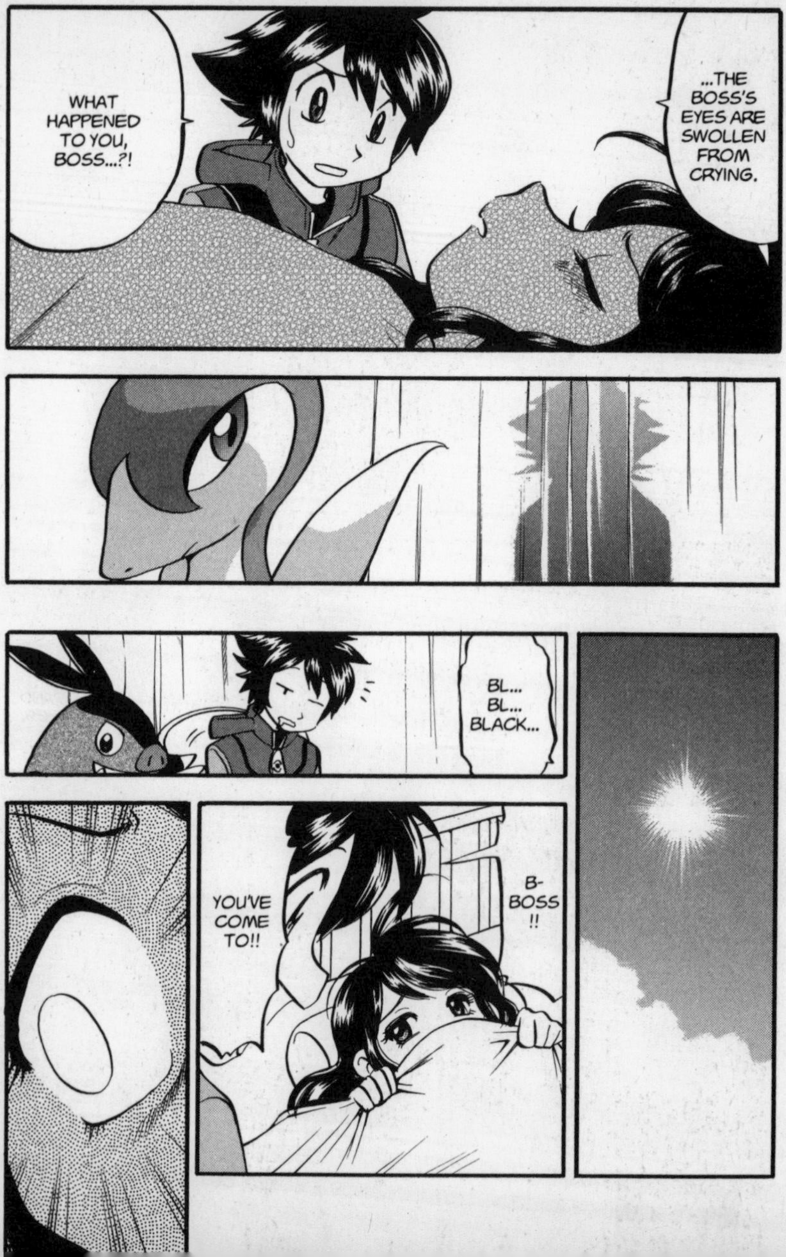
...THE BOSS'S EYES ARE SWOLLEN FROM CRYING.
WHAT HAPPENED TO YOU, BOSS...?!
BL... BL... BLACK...
B-BOSS!!
YOU'VE COME TO!!

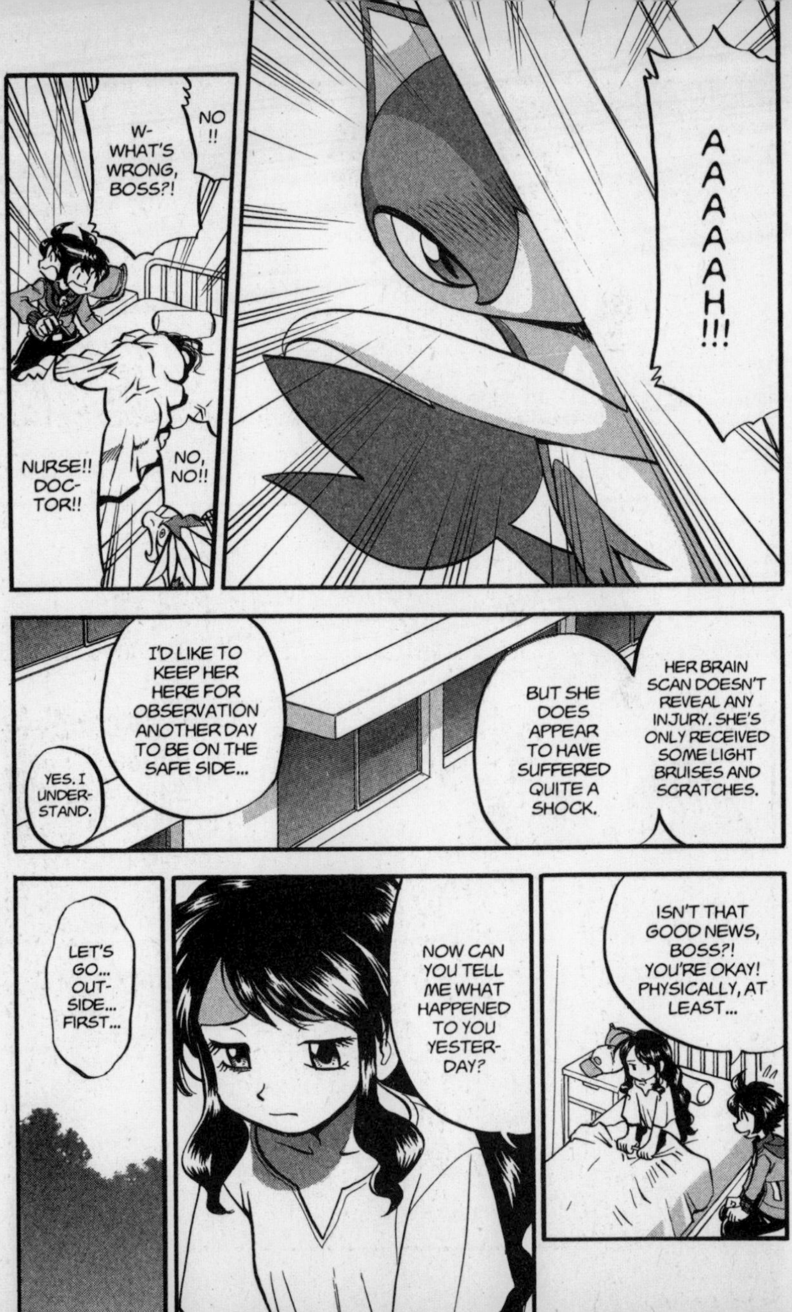
AAAAAH!!!
NO!!
W-WHAT'S WRONG, BOSS?!
NO, NO!!
NURSE!! DOCTOR!!
HER BRAIN SCAN DOESN'T REVEAL ANY INJURY. SHE'S ONLY RECEIVED SOME LIGHT BRUISES AND SCRATCHES.
BUT SHE DOES APPEAR TO HAVE SUFFERED QUITE A SHOCK.
I'D LIKE TO KEEP HER HERE FOR OBSERVATION ANOTHER DAY TO BE ON THE SAFE SIDE...
YES. I UNDERSTAND.
ISN'T THAT GOOD NEWS, BOSS?! YOU'RE OKAY! PHYSICALLY, AT LEAST...
NOW CAN YOU TELL ME WHAT HAPPENED TO YOU YESTERDAY?
LET'S GO... OUTSIDE... FIRST...

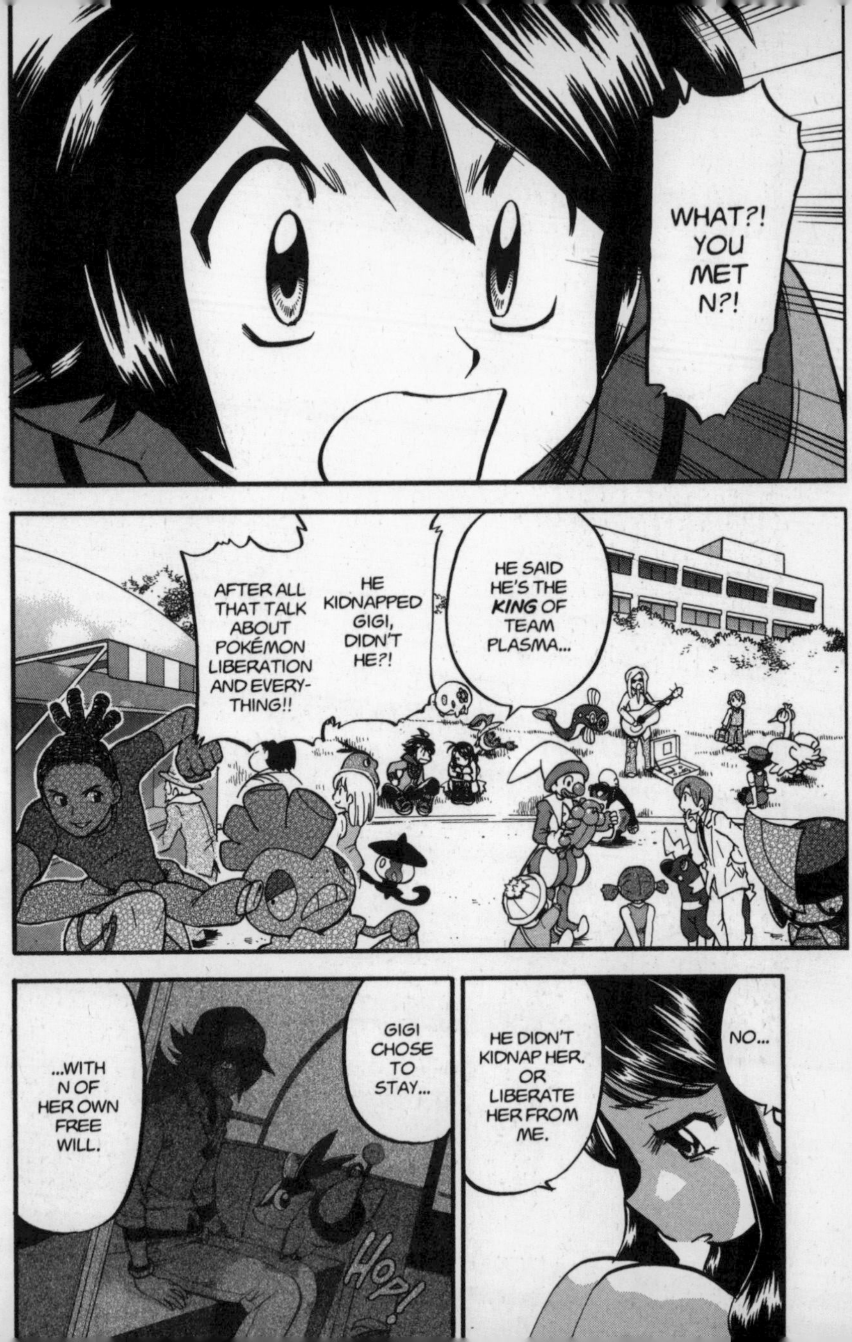
WHAT?! YOU MET N?!
HE SAID HE'S THE *KING* OF TEAM PLASMA...
HE KIDNAPPED GIGI, DIDN'T HE?!
AFTER ALL THAT TALK ABOUT POKÉMON LIBERATION AND EVERYTHING!!
NO...
HE DIDN'T KIDNAP HER. OR LIBERATE HER FROM ME.
GIGI CHOSE TO STAY...
...WITH N OF HER OWN FREE WILL.
HOP!

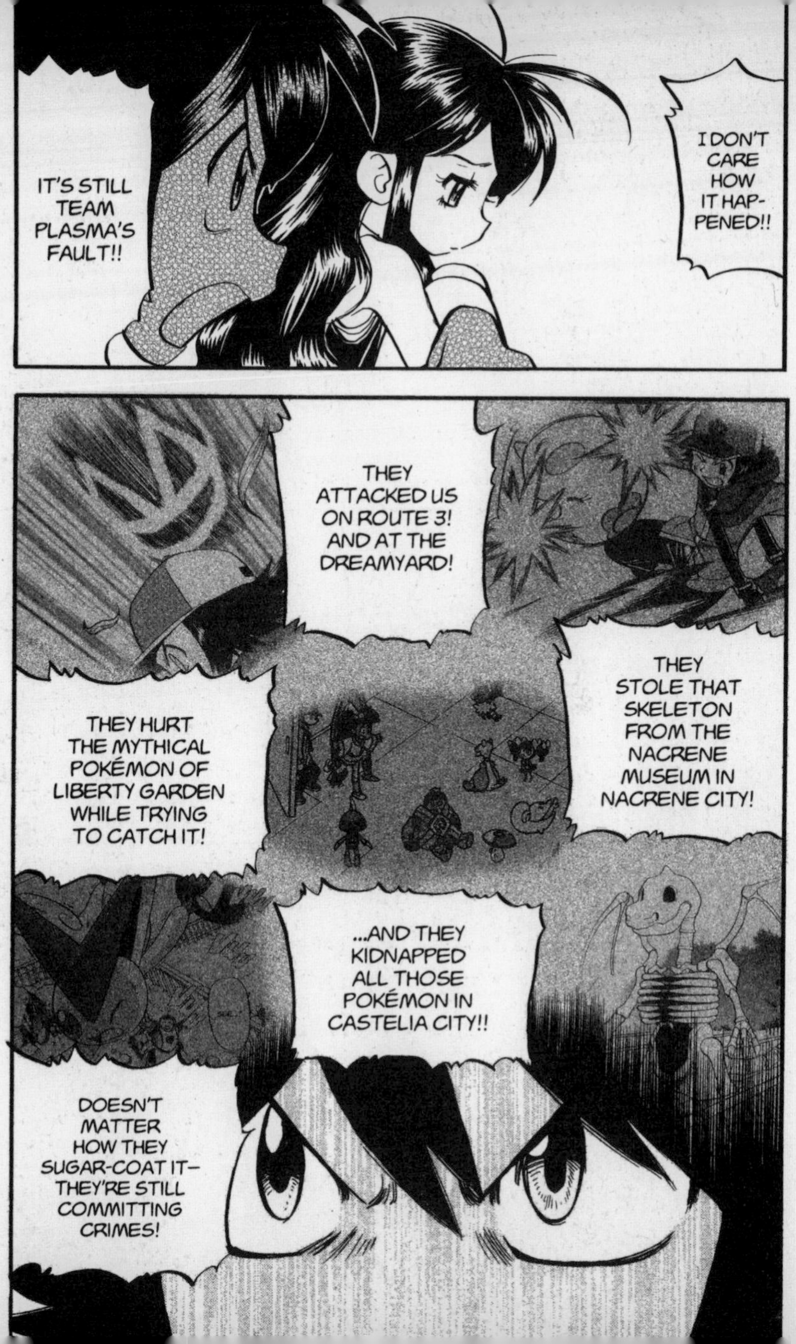
I DON'T CARE HOW IT HAP-PENED!!
IT'S STILL TEAM PLASMA'S FAULT!!
THEY ATTACKED US ON ROUTE 3! AND AT THE DREAMYARD!
THEY STOLE THAT SKELETON FROM THE NACRENE MUSEUM IN NACRENE CITY!
THEY HURT THE MYTHICAL POKÉMON OF LIBERTY GARDEN WHILE TRYING TO CATCH IT!
...AND THEY KIDNAPPED ALL THOSE POKÉMON IN CASTELIA CITY!!
DOESN'T MATTER HOW THEY SUGAR-COAT IT— THEY'RE STILL COMMITTING CRIMES!

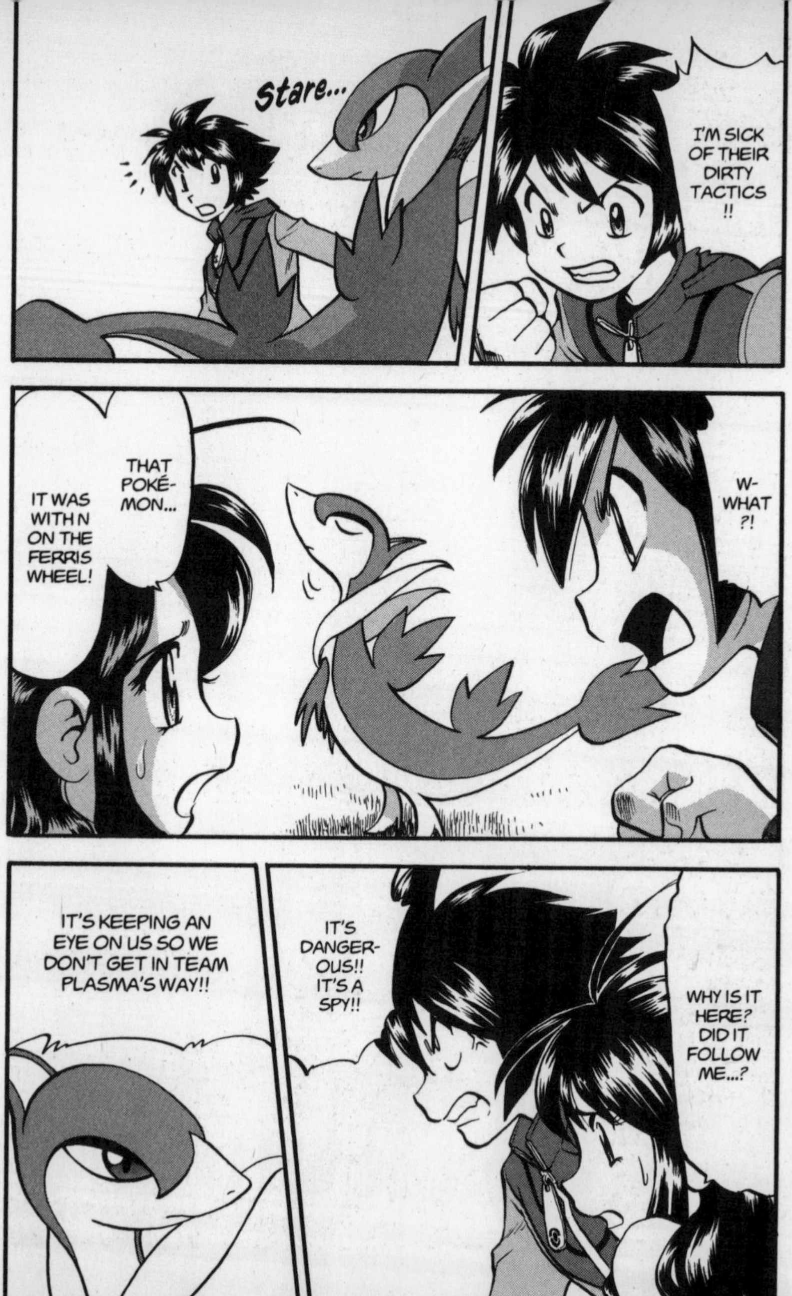
I'M SICK OF THEIR DIRTY TACTICS!!
Stare...
W-WHAT?!
THAT POKÉMON...
IT WAS WITH N ON THE FERRIS WHEEL!
WHY IS IT HERE? DID IT FOLLOW ME...?
IT'S DANGEROUS!! IT'S A SPY!!
IT'S KEEPING AN EYE ON US SO WE DON'T GET IN TEAM PLASMA'S WAY!!

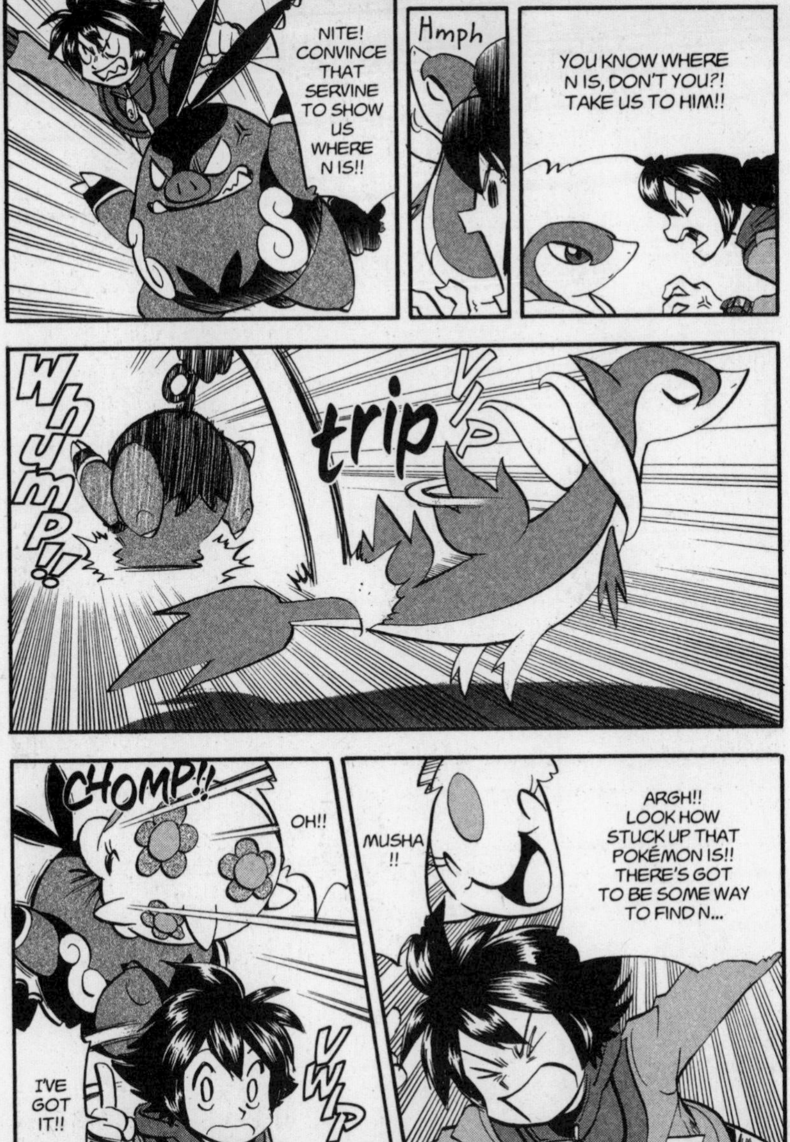
YOU KNOW WHERE N IS, DON'T YOU?! TAKE US TO HIM!!
Hmph
NITE! CONVINCE THAT SERVINE TO SHOW US WHERE N IS!!
VIP
trip
WHUMP!!
ARGH!! LOOK HOW STUCK UP THAT POKÉMON IS!! THERE'S GOT TO BE SOME WAY TO FIND N...
MUSHA !!
OH!!
CHOMP!!
VWIP
I'VE GOT IT!!

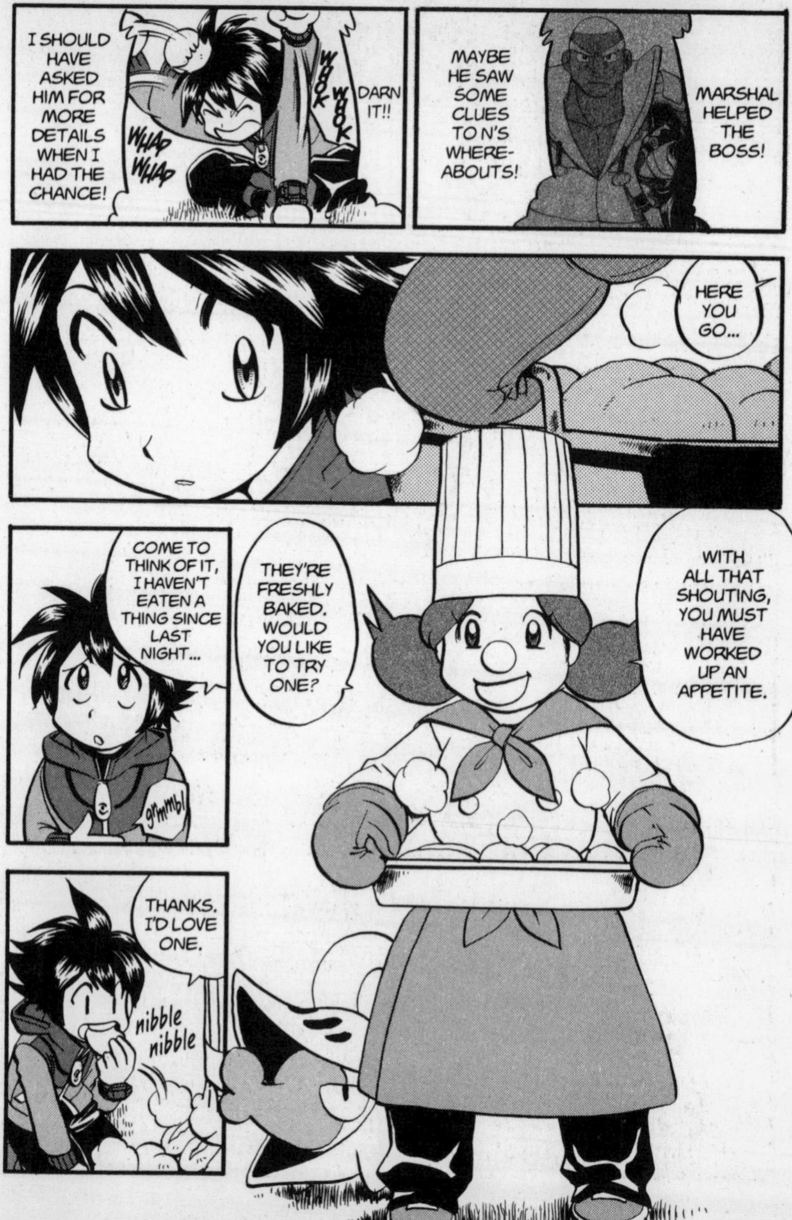
MARSHAL HELPED THE BOSS!
MAYBE HE SAW SOME CLUES TO N'S WHERE-ABOUTS!
DARN IT!!
WHOK WHOK
I SHOULD HAVE ASKED HIM FOR MORE DETAILS WHEN I HAD THE CHANCE!
WHAP WHAP
HERE YOU GO...
WITH ALL THAT SHOUTING, YOU MUST HAVE WORKED UP AN APPETITE.
THEY'RE FRESHLY BAKED. WOULD YOU LIKE TO TRY ONE?
COME TO THINK OF IT, I HAVEN'T EATEN A THING SINCE LAST NIGHT...
grmmbl
THANKS. I'D LOVE ONE.
nibble nibble

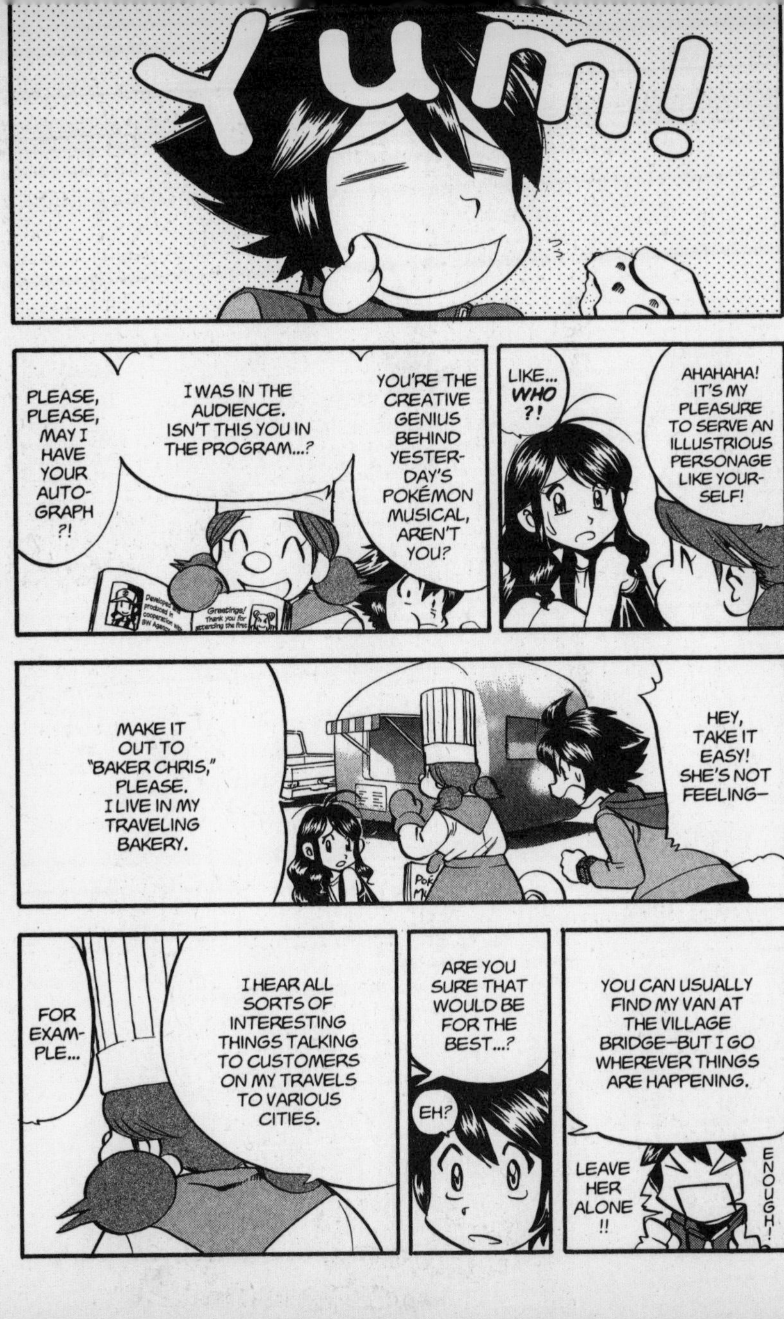

YUM!
AHAHAHA! IT'S MY PLEASURE TO SERVE AN ILLUSTRIOUS PERSONAGE LIKE YOURSELF!
LIKE... WHO?!
YOU'RE THE CREATIVE GENIUS BEHIND YESTERDAY'S POKÉMON MUSICAL, AREN'T YOU?
I WAS IN THE AUDIENCE. ISN'T THIS YOU IN THE PROGRAM...?
PLEASE, PLEASE, MAY I HAVE YOUR AUTOGRAPH?!
HEY, TAKE IT EASY! SHE'S NOT FEELING—
MAKE IT OUT TO "BAKER CHRIS," PLEASE. I LIVE IN MY TRAVELING BAKERY.
YOU CAN USUALLY FIND MY VAN AT THE VILLAGE BRIDGE—BUT I GO WHEREVER THINGS ARE HAPPENING.
ENOUGH!
LEAVE HER ALONE!!
ARE YOU SURE THAT WOULD BE FOR THE BEST...?
EH?
I HEAR ALL SORTS OF INTERESTING THINGS TALKING TO CUSTOMERS ON MY TRAVELS TO VARIOUS CITIES.
FOR EXAMPLE...

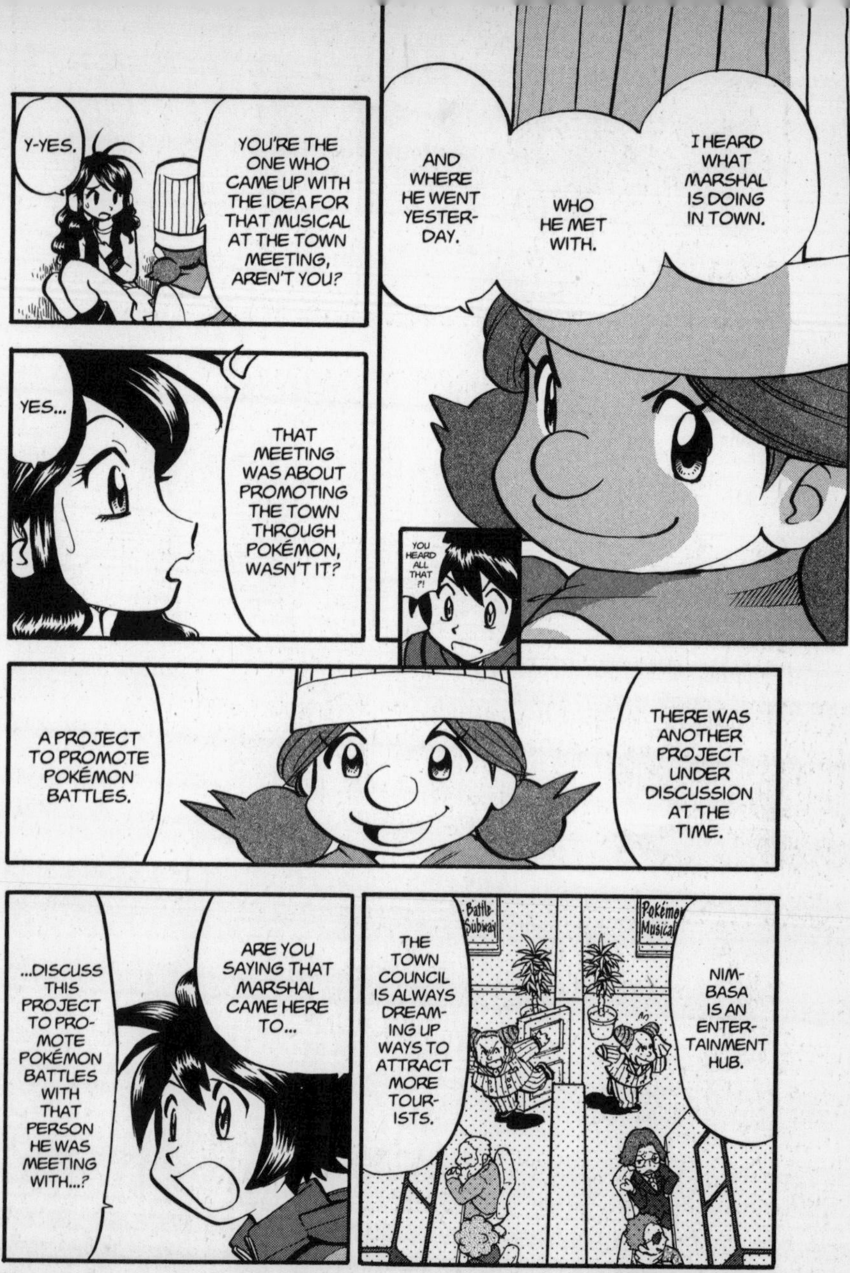
I HEARD WHAT MARSHAL IS DOING IN TOWN.
WHO HE MET WITH.
AND WHERE HE WENT YESTER-DAY.
YOU HEARD ALL THAT ?!
YOU'RE THE ONE WHO CAME UP WITH THE IDEA FOR THAT MUSICAL AT THE TOWN MEETING, AREN'T YOU?
Y-YES.
THAT MEETING WAS ABOUT PROMOTING THE TOWN THROUGH POKÉMON, WASN'T IT?
YES...
THERE WAS ANOTHER PROJECT UNDER DISCUSSION AT THE TIME.
A PROJECT TO PROMOTE POKÉMON BATTLES.
NIM-BASA IS AN ENTER-TAINMENT HUB.
Pokémon Musical
Battle Subway
THE TOWN COUNCIL IS ALWAYS DREAM-ING UP WAYS TO ATTRACT MORE TOUR-ISTS.
ARE YOU SAYING THAT MARSHAL CAME HERE TO...
...DISCUSS THIS PROJECT TO PRO-MOTE POKÉMON BATTLES WITH THAT PERSON HE WAS MEETING WITH...?

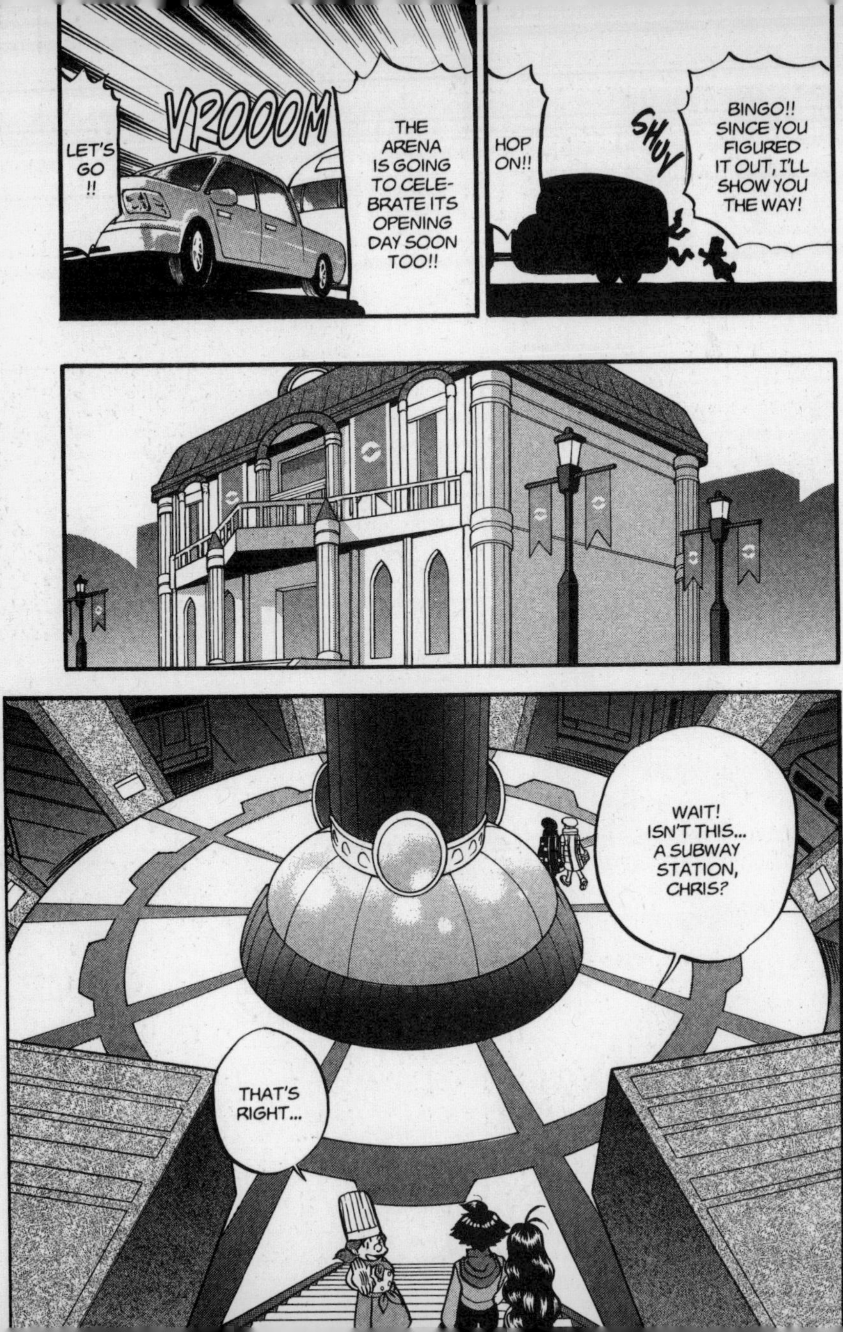
BINGO!! SINCE YOU FIGURED IT OUT, I'LL SHOW YOU THE WAY!
SHUV
HOP ON!!
THE ARENA IS GOING TO CELE-BRATE ITS OPENING DAY SOON TOO!!
VROOOM
LET'S GO !!
WAIT! ISN'T THIS... A SUBWAY STATION, CHRIS?
THAT'S RIGHT...

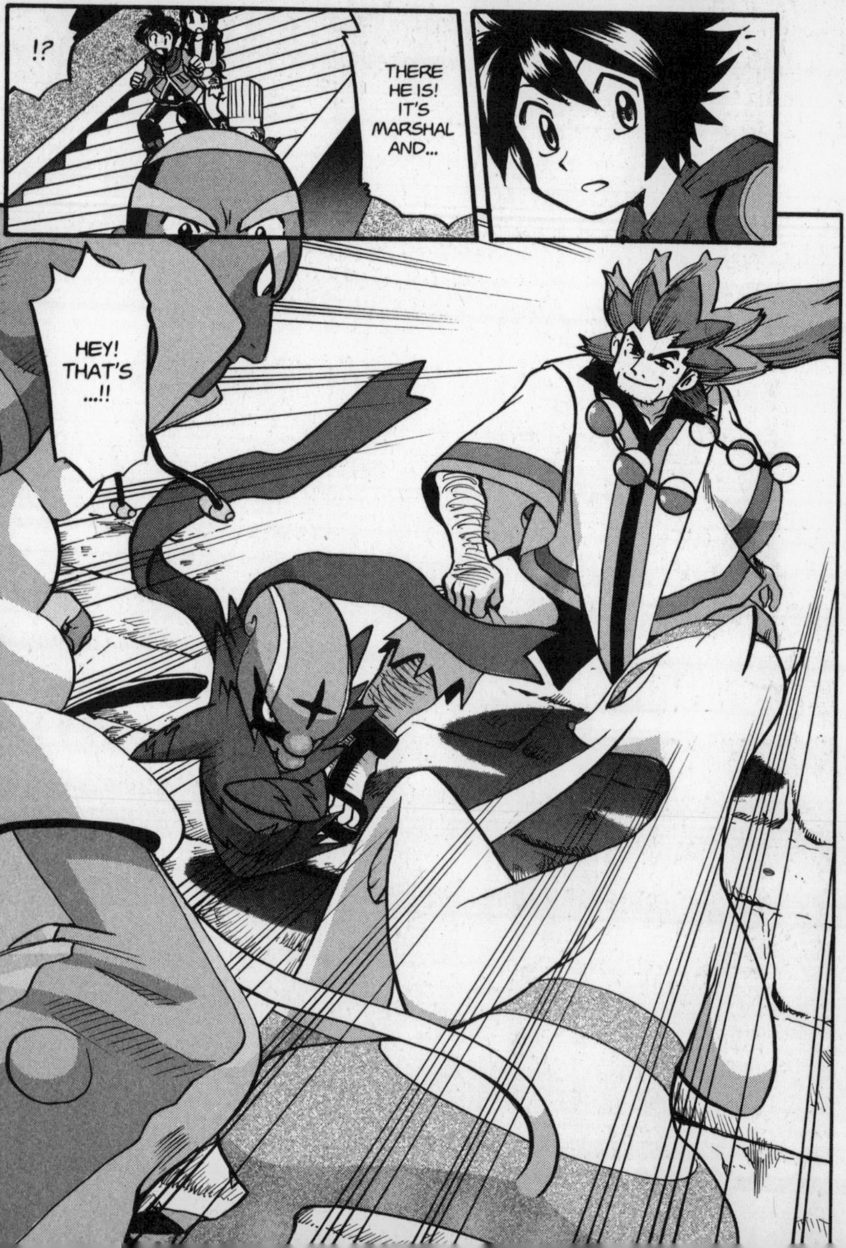
THERE HE IS! IT'S MARSHAL AND...
!?
HEY! THAT'S ...!!

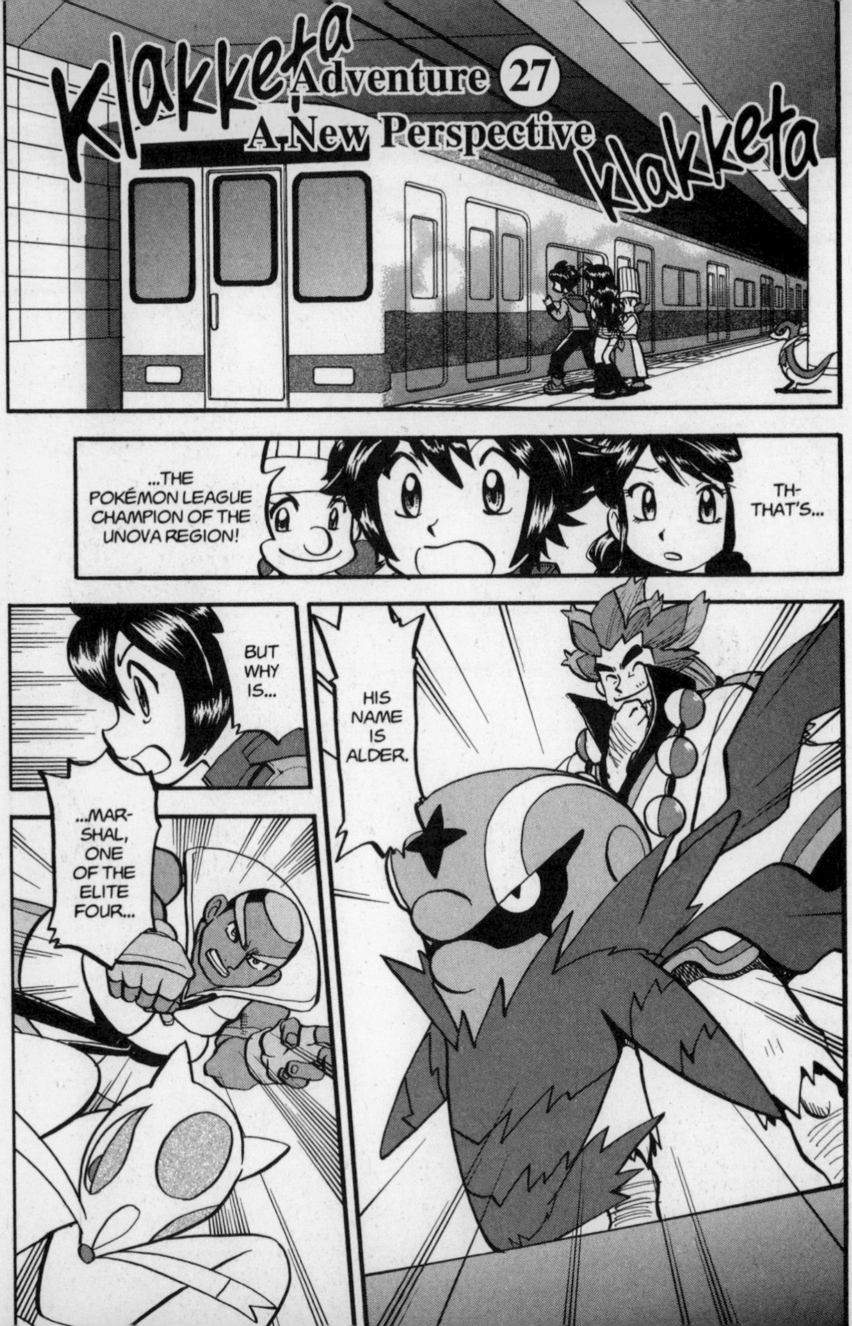
klakketa
Adventure 27
A New Perspective
klakketa
TH-THAT'S...
...THE POKÉMON LEAGUE CHAMPION OF THE UNOVA REGION!
HIS NAME IS ALDER.
BUT WHY IS...
...MAR-SHAL, ONE OF THE ELITE FOUR...

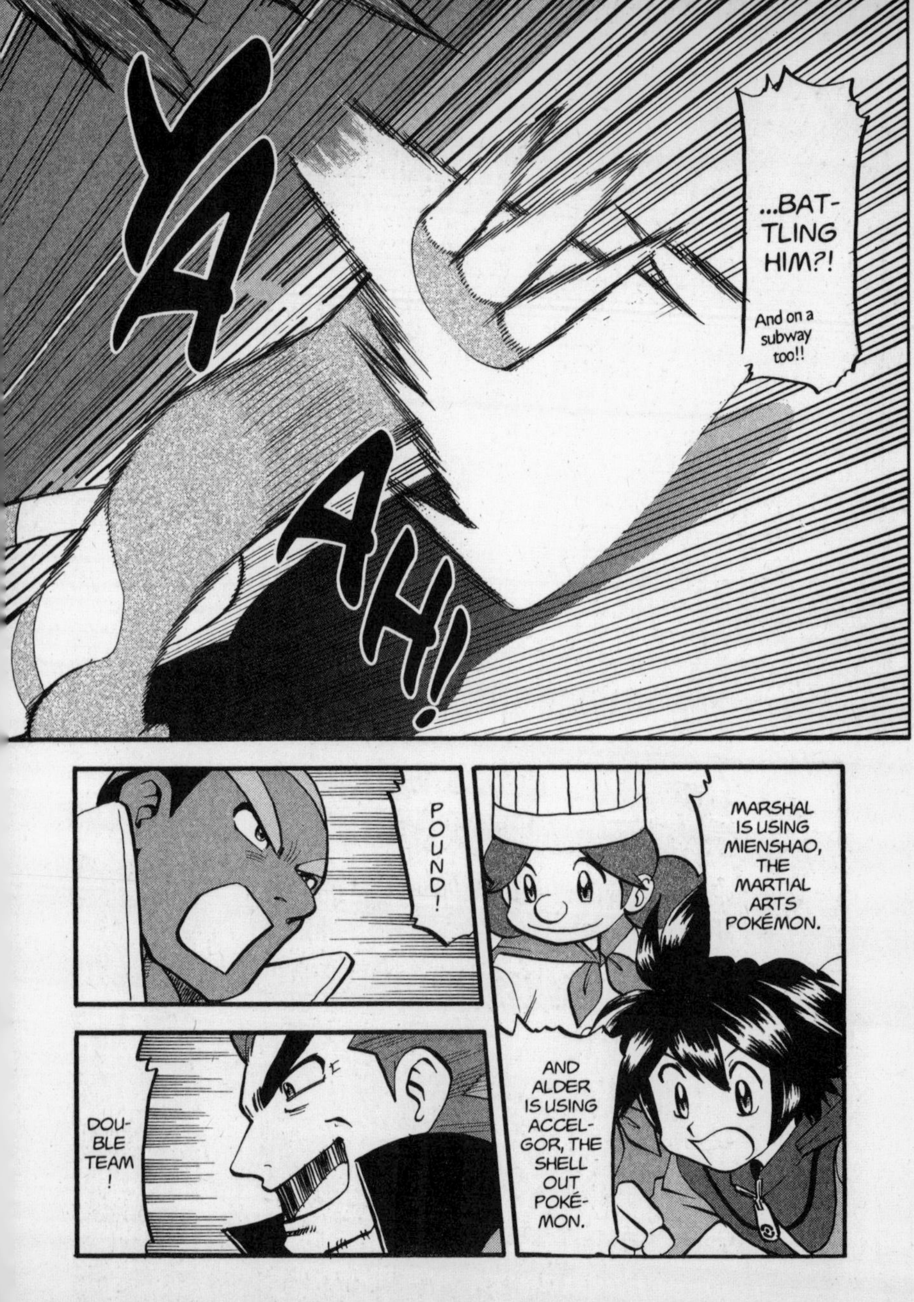
...BATTLING HIM?!
And on a subway too!!
YA
AH!
MARSHAL IS USING MIENSHAO, THE MARTIAL ARTS POKÉMON.
AND ALDER IS USING ACCELGOR, THE SHELL OUT POKÉMON.
POUND!
DOUBLE TEAM!

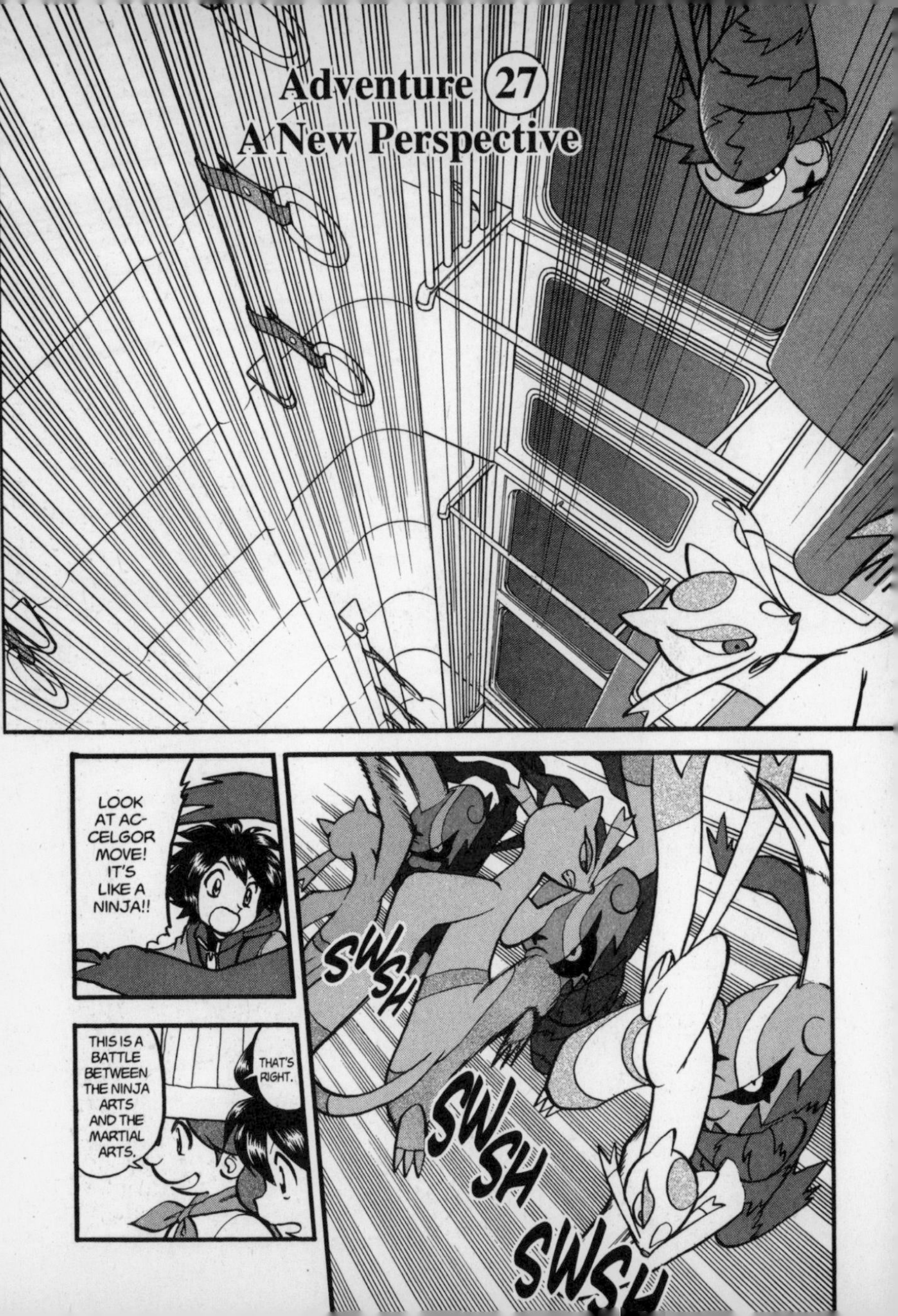
Adventure 27
A New Perspective
SWSH
SWSH
SWSH
LOOK AT AC-CELGOR MOVE! IT'S LIKE A NINJA!!
THIS IS A BATTLE BETWEEN THE NINJA ARTS AND THE MARTIAL ARTS.
THAT'S RIGHT.

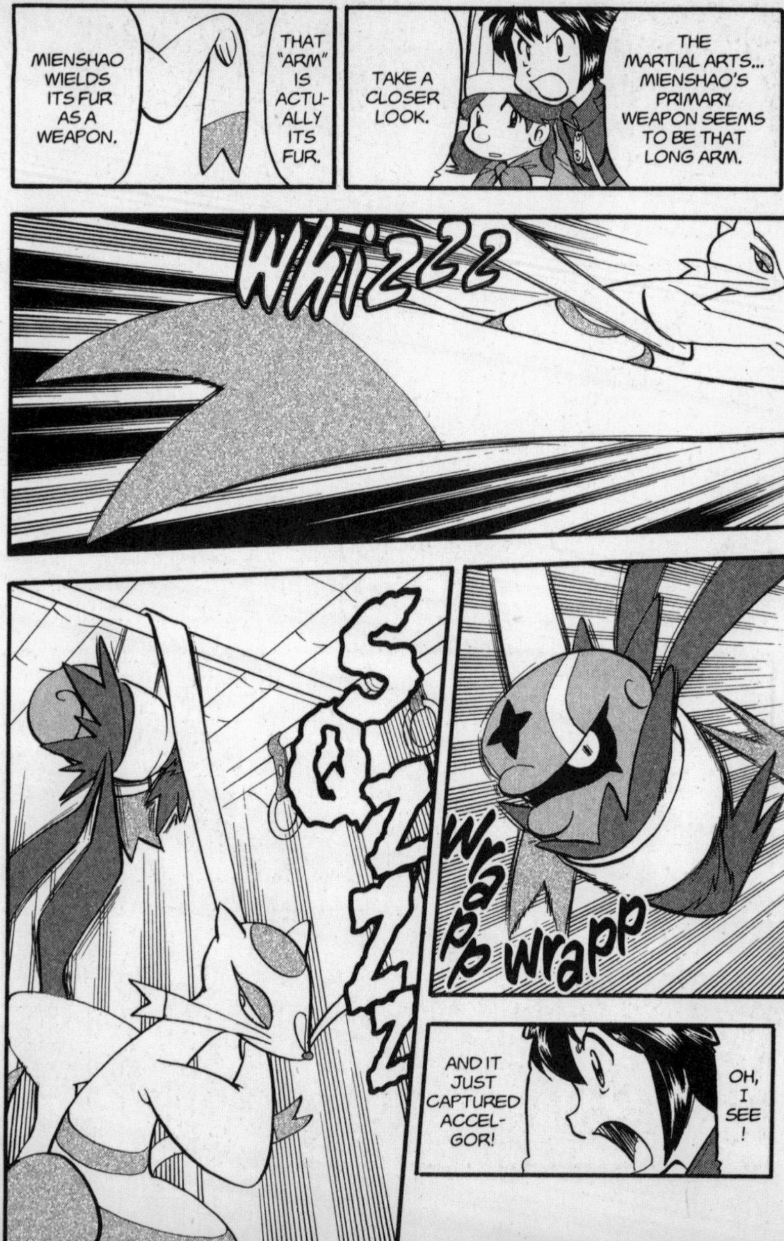
THE MARTIAL ARTS... MIENSHAO'S PRIMARY WEAPON SEEMS TO BE THAT LONG ARM.
TAKE A CLOSER LOOK.
THAT "ARM" IS ACTU-ALLY ITS FUR.
MIENSHAO WIELDS ITS FUR AS A WEAPON.
WHIZZZ
wrapp wrapp
OH, I SEE!
AND IT JUST CAPTURED ACCEL-GOR!
SQZZZ

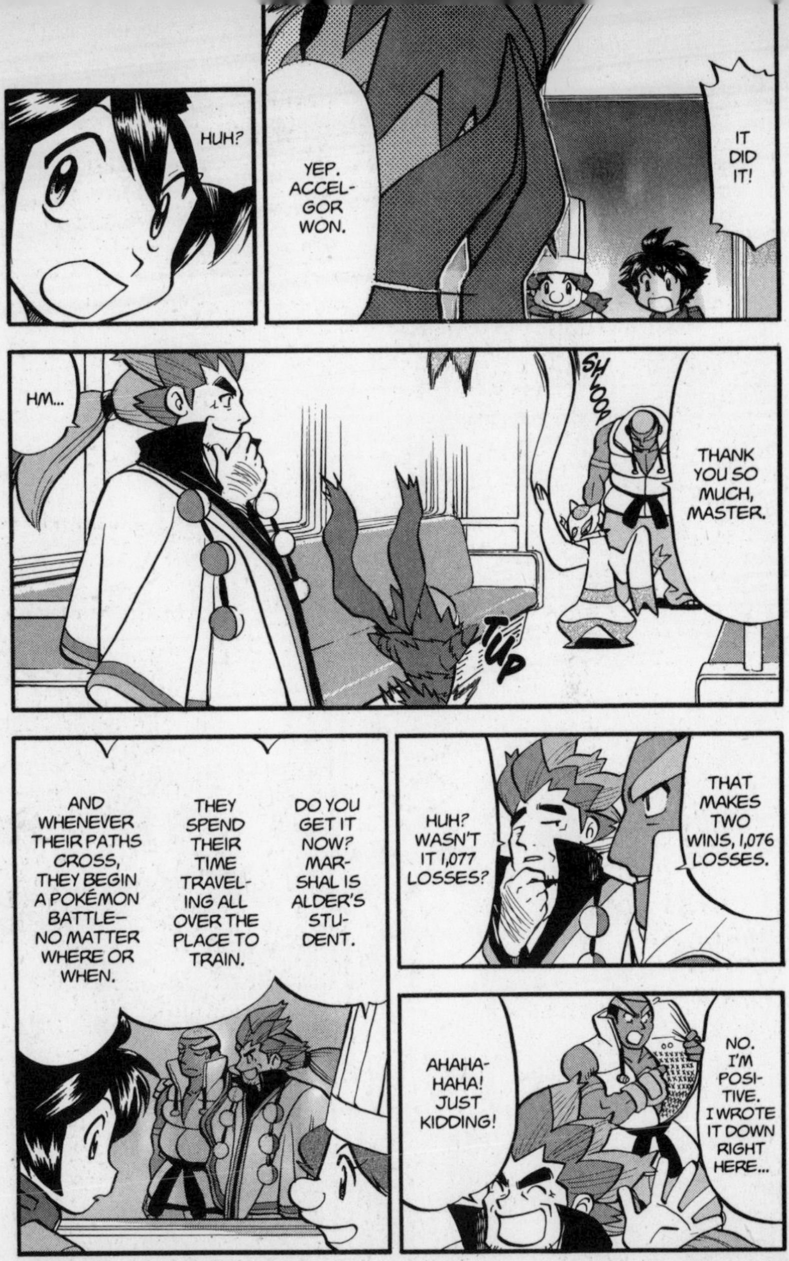
IT DID IT!
YEP. ACCELGOR WON.
HUH?
THANK YOU SO MUCH, MASTER.
SHLOOP
TUP
HM...
THAT MAKES TWO WINS, 1,076 LOSSES.
HUH? WASN'T IT 1,077 LOSSES?
NO. I'M POSITIVE. I WROTE IT DOWN RIGHT HERE...
AHAHAHAHA! JUST KIDDING!
DO YOU GET IT NOW? MARSHAL IS ALDER'S STUDENT.
THEY SPEND THEIR TIME TRAVELING ALL OVER THE PLACE TO TRAIN.
AND WHENEVER THEIR PATHS CROSS, THEY BEGIN A POKÉMON BATTLE—NO MATTER WHERE OR WHEN.

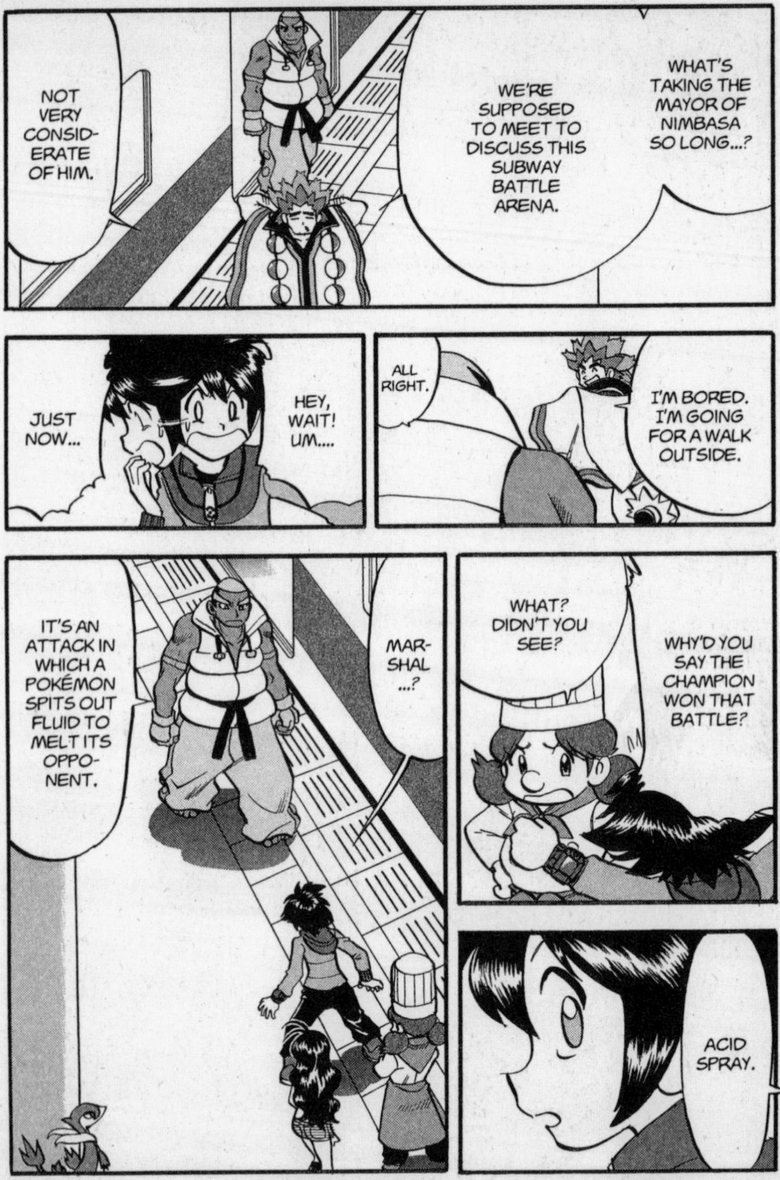
WHAT'S TAKING THE MAYOR OF NIMBASA SO LONG...?
WE'RE SUPPOSED TO MEET TO DISCUSS THIS SUBWAY BATTLE ARENA.
NOT VERY CONSID-ERATE OF HIM.
I'M BORED. I'M GOING FOR A WALK OUTSIDE.
ALL RIGHT.
HEY, WAIT! UM....
JUST NOW...
WHY'D YOU SAY THE CHAMPION WON THAT BATTLE?
WHAT? DIDN'T YOU SEE?
ACID SPRAY.
MAR-SHAL ...?
IT'S AN ATTACK IN WHICH A POKÉMON SPITS OUT FLUID TO MELT ITS OPPO-NENT.

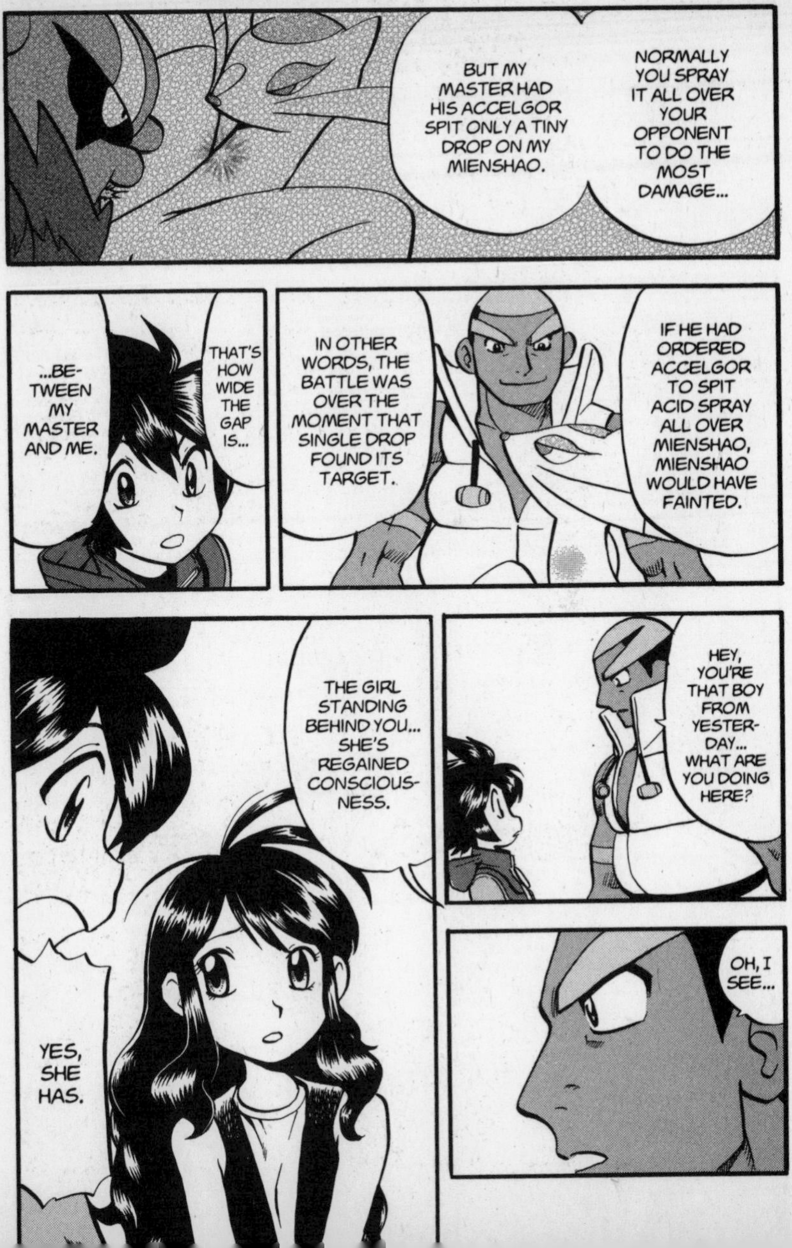
NORMALLY YOU SPRAY IT ALL OVER YOUR OPPONENT TO DO THE MOST DAMAGE...
BUT MY MASTER HAD HIS ACCELGOR SPIT ONLY A TINY DROP ON MY MIENSHAO.
IF HE HAD ORDERED ACCELGOR TO SPIT ACID SPRAY ALL OVER MIENSHAO, MIENSHAO WOULD HAVE FAINTED.
IN OTHER WORDS, THE BATTLE WAS OVER THE MOMENT THAT SINGLE DROP FOUND ITS TARGET.
THAT'S HOW WIDE THE GAP IS...
...BE-TWEEN MY MASTER AND ME.
HEY, YOU'RE THAT BOY FROM YESTER-DAY... WHAT ARE YOU DOING HERE?
OH, I SEE...
THE GIRL STANDING BEHIND YOU... SHE'S REGAINED CONSCIOUS-NESS.
YES, SHE HAS.

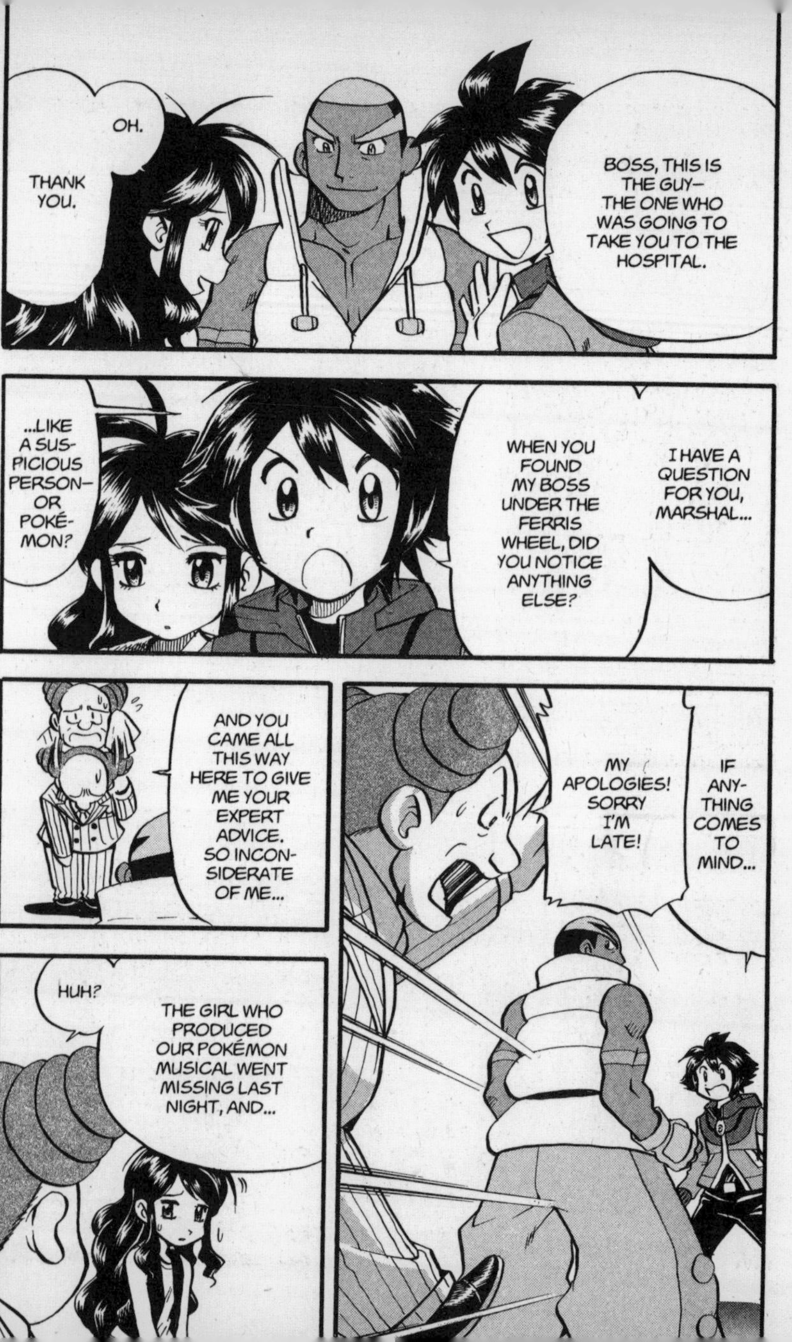

BOSS, THIS IS THE GUY— THE ONE WHO WAS GOING TO TAKE YOU TO THE HOSPITAL.
OH.
THANK YOU.
I HAVE A QUESTION FOR YOU, MARSHAL...
WHEN YOU FOUND MY BOSS UNDER THE FERRIS WHEEL, DID YOU NOTICE ANYTHING ELSE?
...LIKE A SUS-PICIOUS PERSON— OR POKÉ-MON?
IF ANY-THING COMES TO MIND...
MY APOLOGIES! SORRY I'M LATE!
AND YOU CAME ALL THIS WAY HERE TO GIVE ME YOUR EXPERT ADVICE. SO INCON-SIDERATE OF ME...
THE GIRL WHO PRODUCED OUR POKÉMON MUSICAL WENT MISSING LAST NIGHT, AND...
HUH?

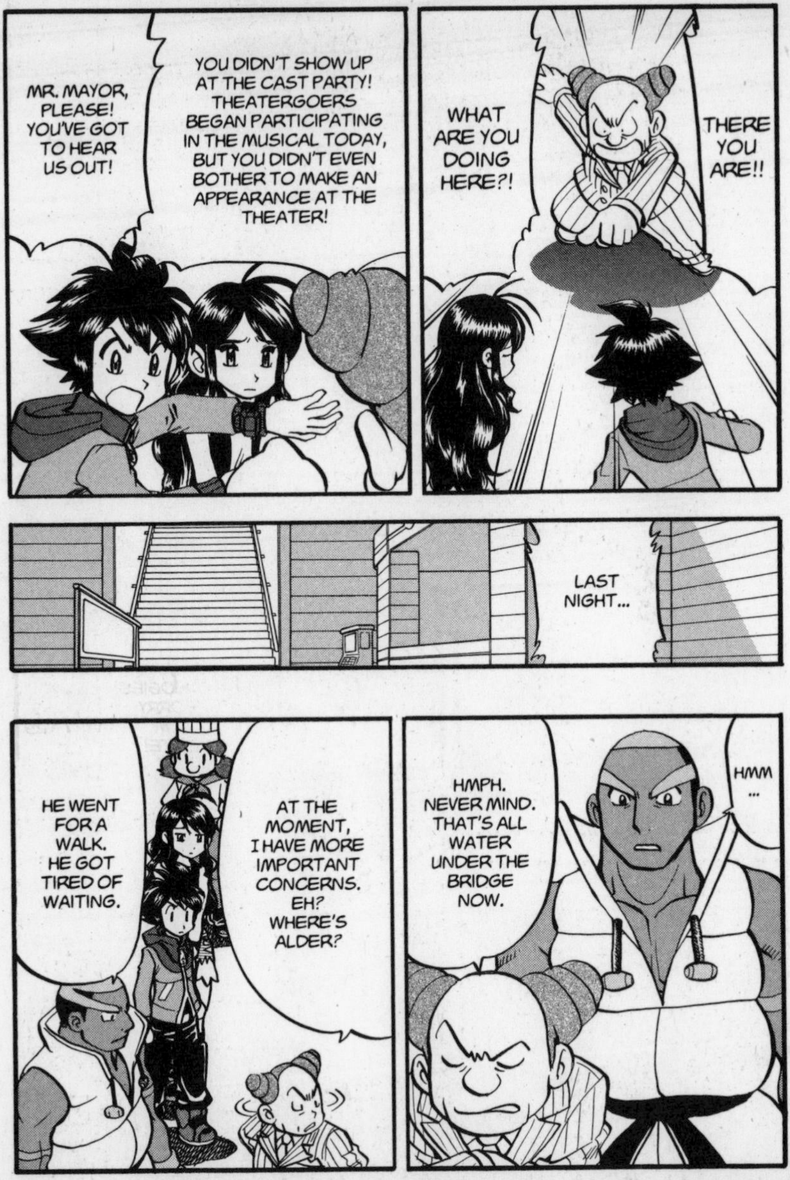
THERE YOU ARE!!
WHAT ARE YOU DOING HERE?!
YOU DIDN'T SHOW UP AT THE CAST PARTY! THEATERGOERS BEGAN PARTICIPATING IN THE MUSICAL TODAY, BUT YOU DIDN'T EVEN BOTHER TO MAKE AN APPEARANCE AT THE THEATER!
MR. MAYOR, PLEASE! YOU'VE GOT TO HEAR US OUT!
LAST NIGHT...
HMM ...
HMPH. NEVER MIND. THAT'S ALL WATER UNDER THE BRIDGE NOW.
AT THE MOMENT, I HAVE MORE IMPORTANT CONCERNS. EH? WHERE'S ALDER?
HE WENT FOR A WALK. HE GOT TIRED OF WAITING.

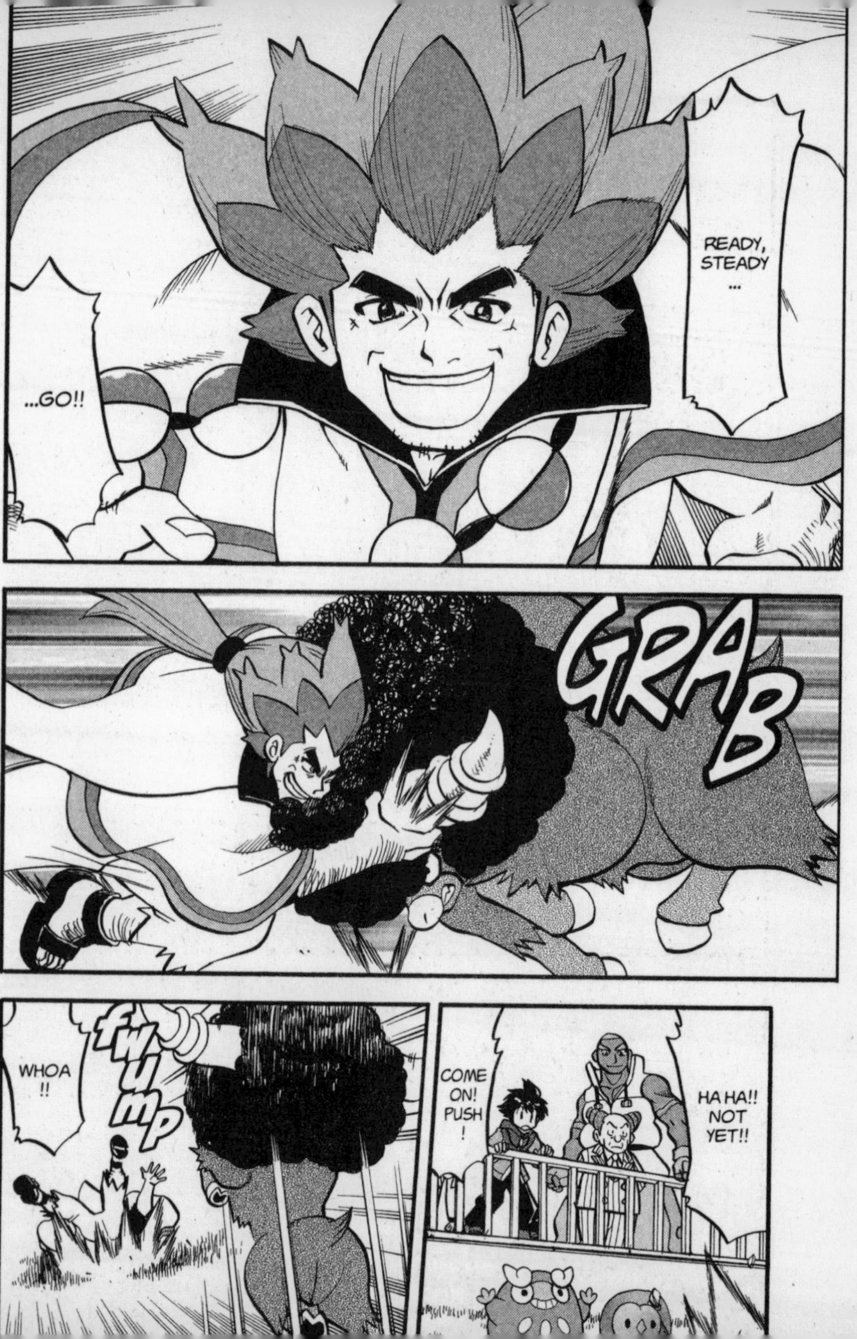
READY, STEADY ...
...GO!!
GRAB
HA HA!! NOT YET!!
COME ON! PUSH!
fwump
WHOA!!

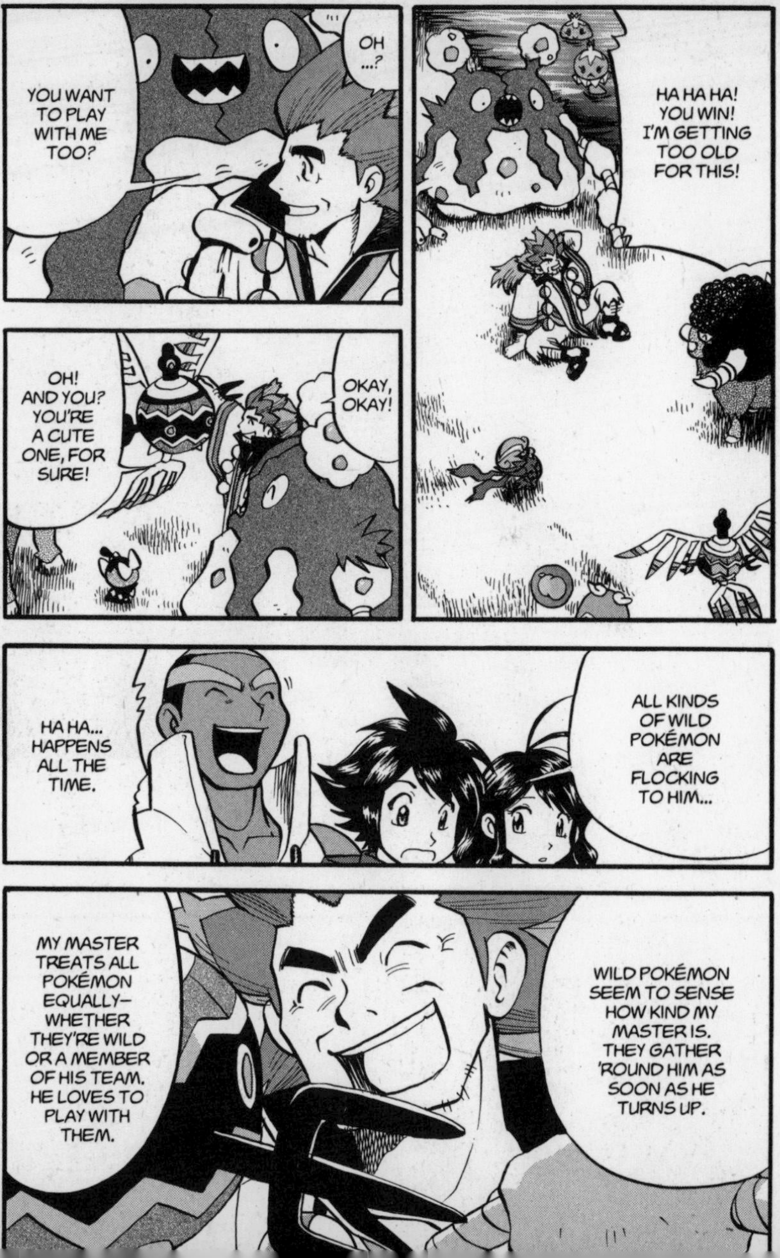
HA HA HA! YOU WIN! I'M GETTING TOO OLD FOR THIS!
OH ...?
YOU WANT TO PLAY WITH ME TOO?
OKAY, OKAY!
OH! AND YOU? YOU'RE A CUTE ONE, FOR SURE!
ALL KINDS OF WILD POKÉMON ARE FLOCKING TO HIM...
HA HA... HAPPENS ALL THE TIME.
WILD POKÉMON SEEM TO SENSE HOW KIND MY MASTER IS. THEY GATHER 'ROUND HIM AS SOON AS HE TURNS UP.
MY MASTER TREATS ALL POKÉMON EQUALLY— WHETHER THEY'RE WILD OR A MEMBER OF HIS TEAM. HE LOVES TO PLAY WITH THEM.

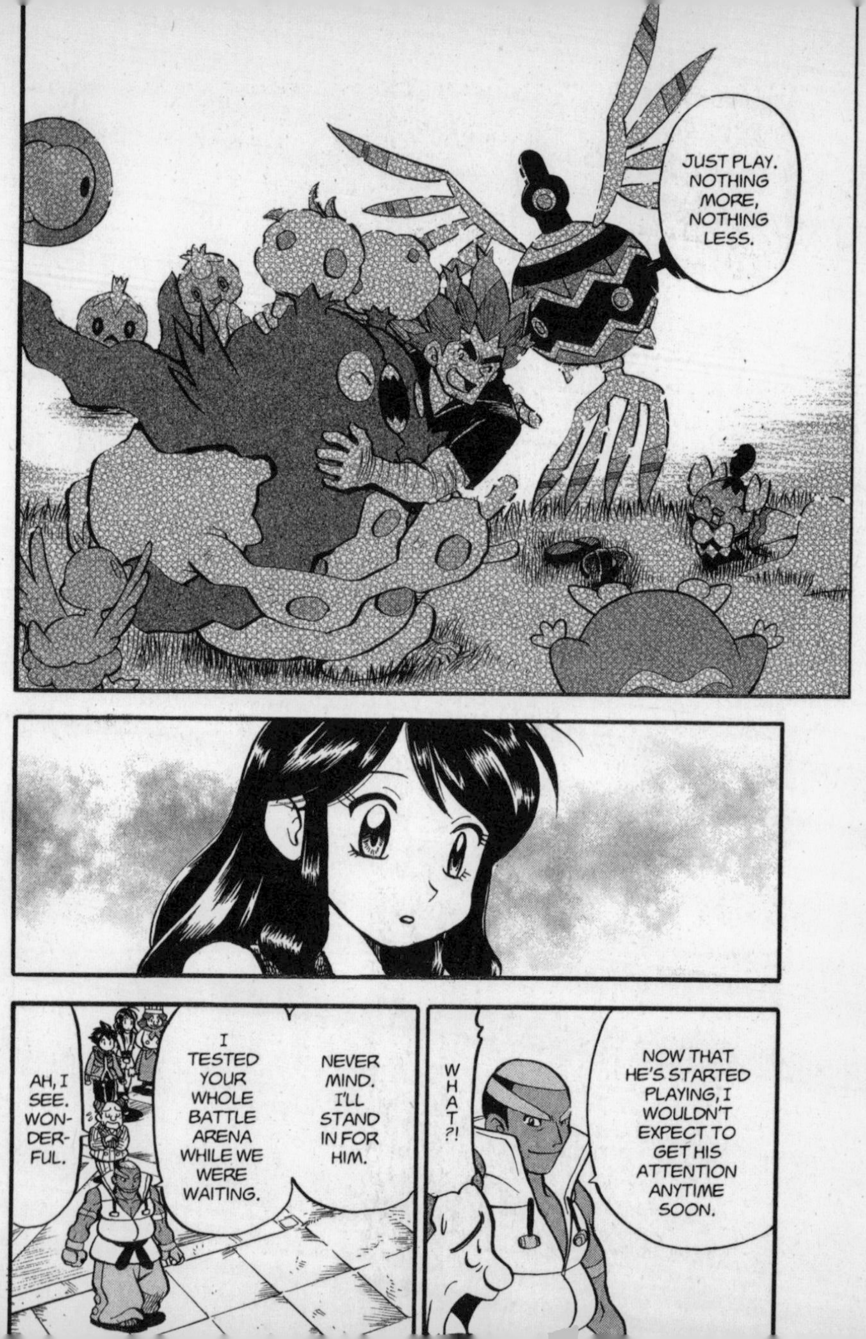
JUST PLAY. NOTHING MORE, NOTHING LESS.
NOW THAT HE'S STARTED PLAYING, I WOULDN'T EXPECT TO GET HIS ATTENTION ANYTIME SOON.
WHAT?!
NEVER MIND. I'LL STAND IN FOR HIM.
I TESTED YOUR WHOLE BATTLE ARENA WHILE WE WERE WAITING.
AH, I SEE. WONDERFUL.

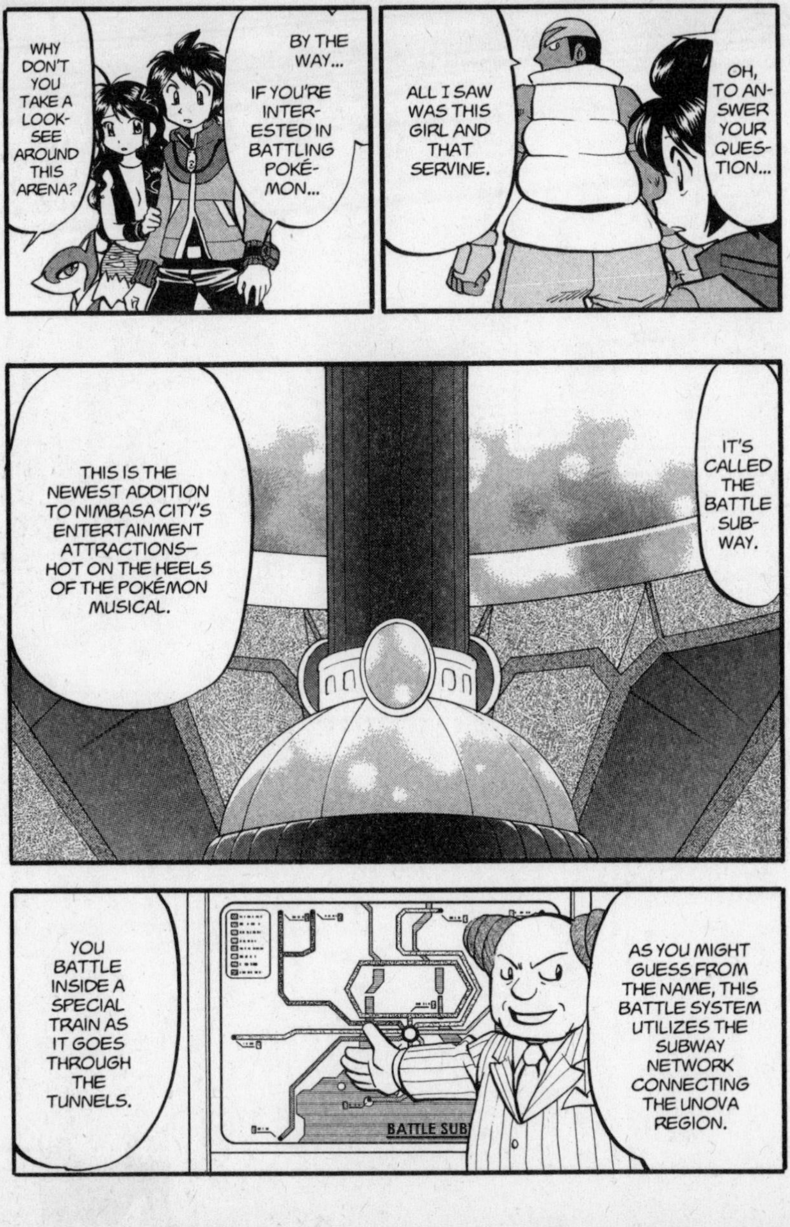
OH, TO AN-SWER YOUR QUES-TION...
ALL I SAW WAS THIS GIRL AND THAT SERVINE.
BY THE WAY...
IF YOU'RE INTER-ESTED IN BATTLING POKÉ-MON...
WHY DON'T YOU TAKE A LOOK-SEE AROUND THIS ARENA?
IT'S CALLED THE BATTLE SUB-WAY.
THIS IS THE NEWEST ADDITION TO NIMBASA CITY'S ENTERTAINMENT ATTRACTIONS— HOT ON THE HEELS OF THE POKÉMON MUSICAL.
AS YOU MIGHT GUESS FROM THE NAME, THIS BATTLE SYSTEM UTILIZES THE SUBWAY NETWORK CONNECTING THE UNOVA REGION.
BATTLE SUB
YOU BATTLE INSIDE A SPECIAL TRAIN AS IT GOES THROUGH THE TUNNELS.

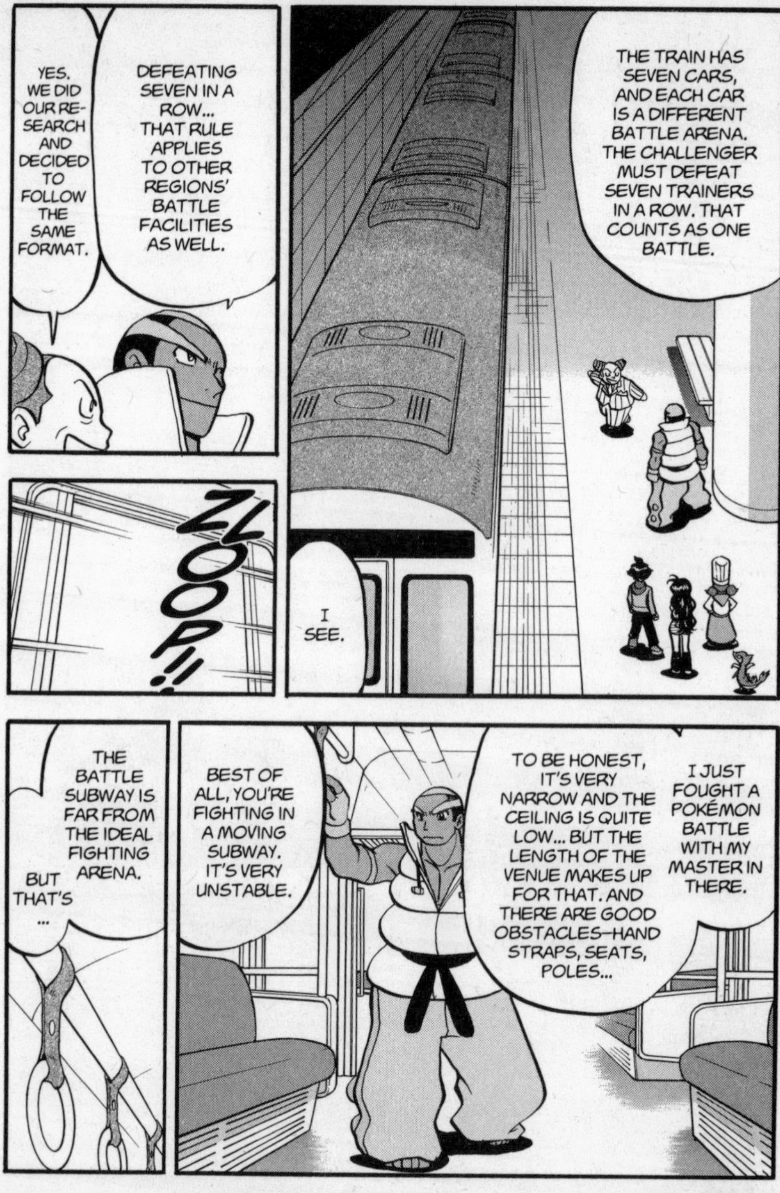
THE TRAIN HAS SEVEN CARS, AND EACH CAR IS A DIFFERENT BATTLE ARENA. THE CHALLENGER MUST DEFEAT SEVEN TRAINERS IN A ROW. THAT COUNTS AS ONE BATTLE.
I SEE.
DEFEATING SEVEN IN A ROW... THAT RULE APPLIES TO OTHER REGIONS' BATTLE FACILITIES AS WELL.
YES. WE DID OUR RE-SEARCH AND DECIDED TO FOLLOW THE SAME FORMAT.
ZLOOP!!
I JUST FOUGHT A POKÉMON BATTLE WITH MY MASTER IN THERE.
TO BE HONEST, IT'S VERY NARROW AND THE CEILING IS QUITE LOW... BUT THE LENGTH OF THE VENUE MAKES UP FOR THAT. AND THERE ARE GOOD OBSTACLES—HAND STRAPS, SEATS, POLES...
BEST OF ALL, YOU'RE FIGHTING IN A MOVING SUBWAY. IT'S VERY UNSTABLE.
THE BATTLE SUBWAY IS FAR FROM THE IDEAL FIGHTING ARENA.
BUT THAT'S ...

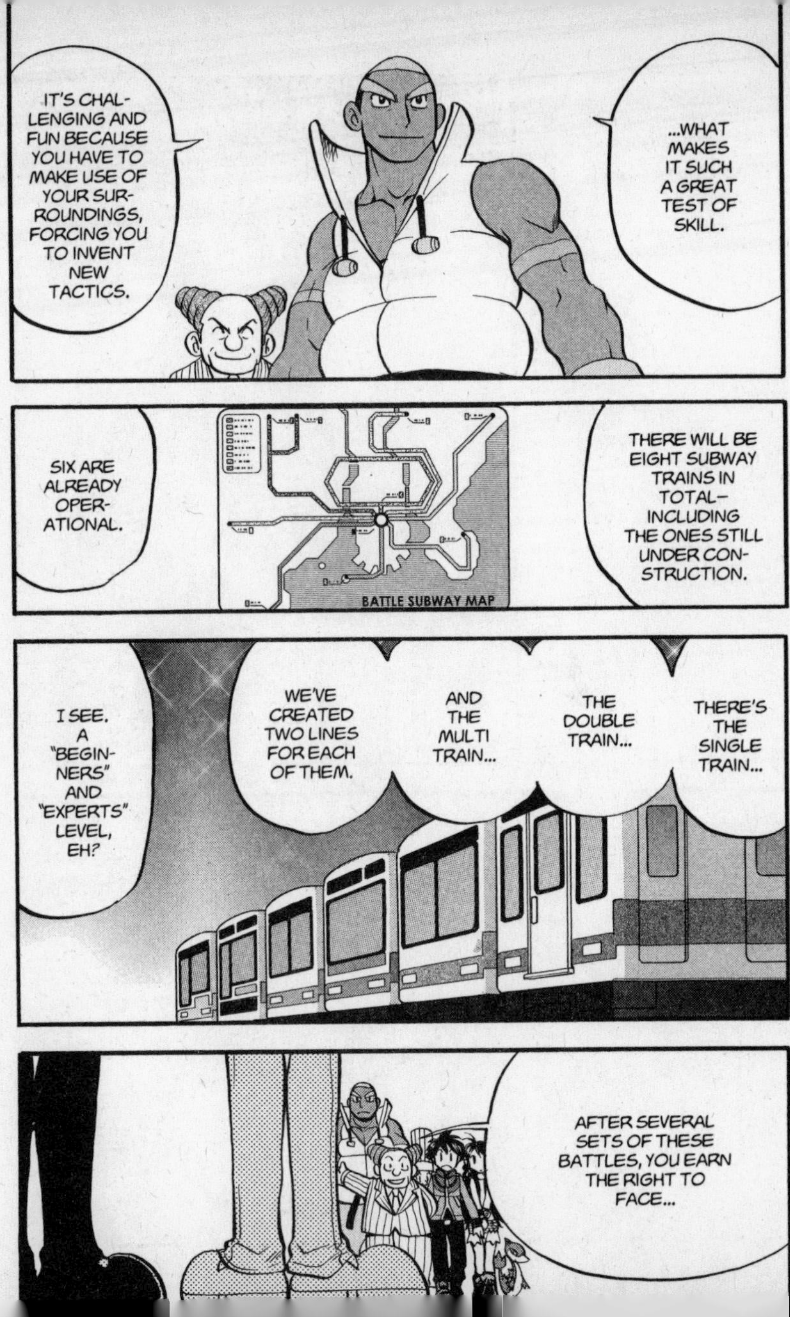
...WHAT MAKES IT SUCH A GREAT TEST OF SKILL.
IT'S CHAL-LENGING AND FUN BECAUSE YOU HAVE TO MAKE USE OF YOUR SUR-ROUNDINGS, FORCING YOU TO INVENT NEW TACTICS.
THERE WILL BE EIGHT SUBWAY TRAINS IN TOTAL—INCLUDING THE ONES STILL UNDER CON-STRUCTION.
BATTLE SUBWAY MAP
SIX ARE ALREADY OPER-ATIONAL.
THERE'S THE SINGLE TRAIN...
THE DOUBLE TRAIN...
AND THE MULTI TRAIN...
WE'VE CREATED TWO LINES FOR EACH OF THEM.
I SEE. A "BEGIN-NERS" AND "EXPERTS" LEVEL, EH?
AFTER SEVERAL SETS OF THESE BATTLES, YOU EARN THE RIGHT TO FACE...

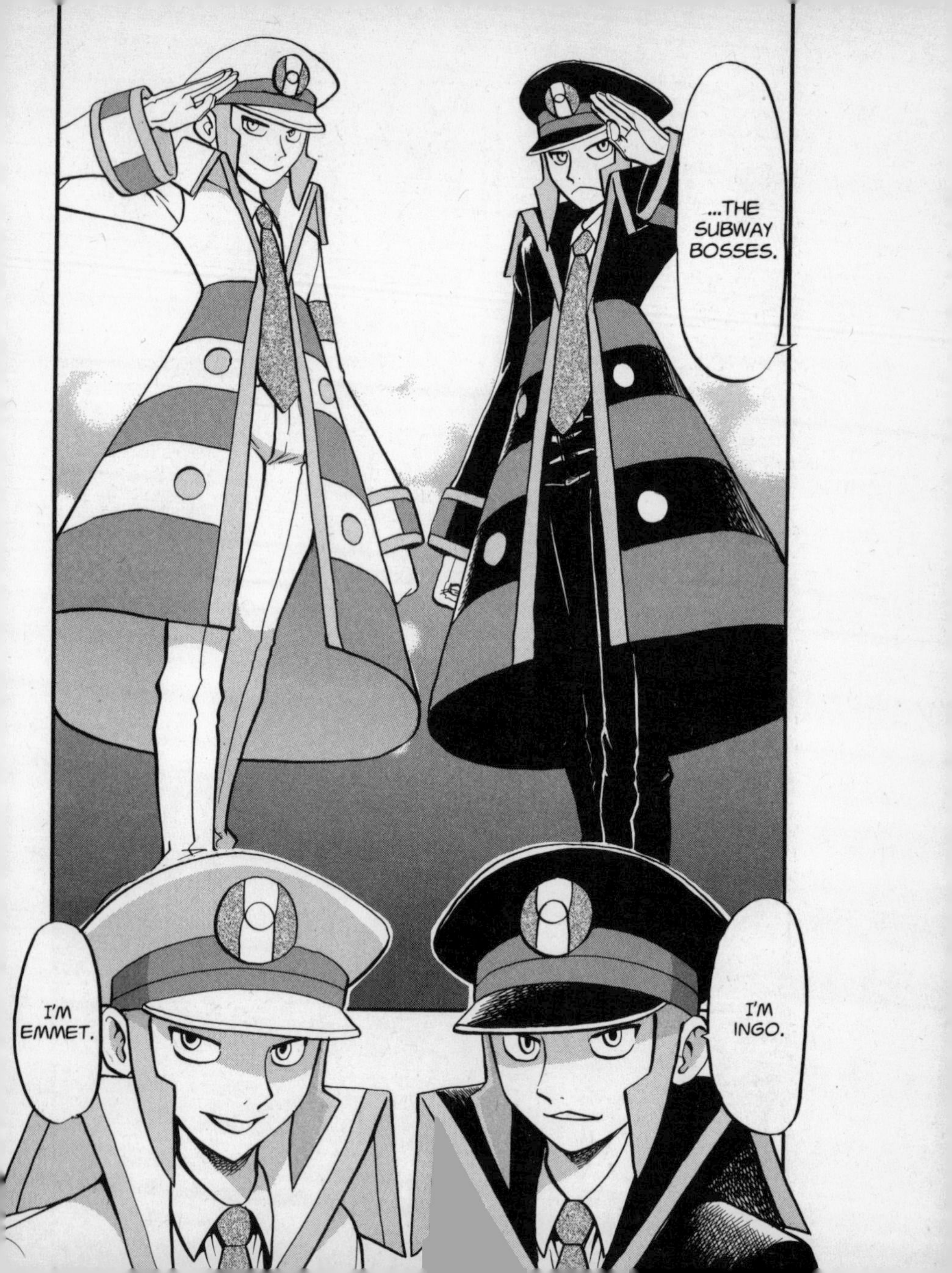
...THE SUBWAY BOSSES.
I'M INGO.
I'M EMMET.

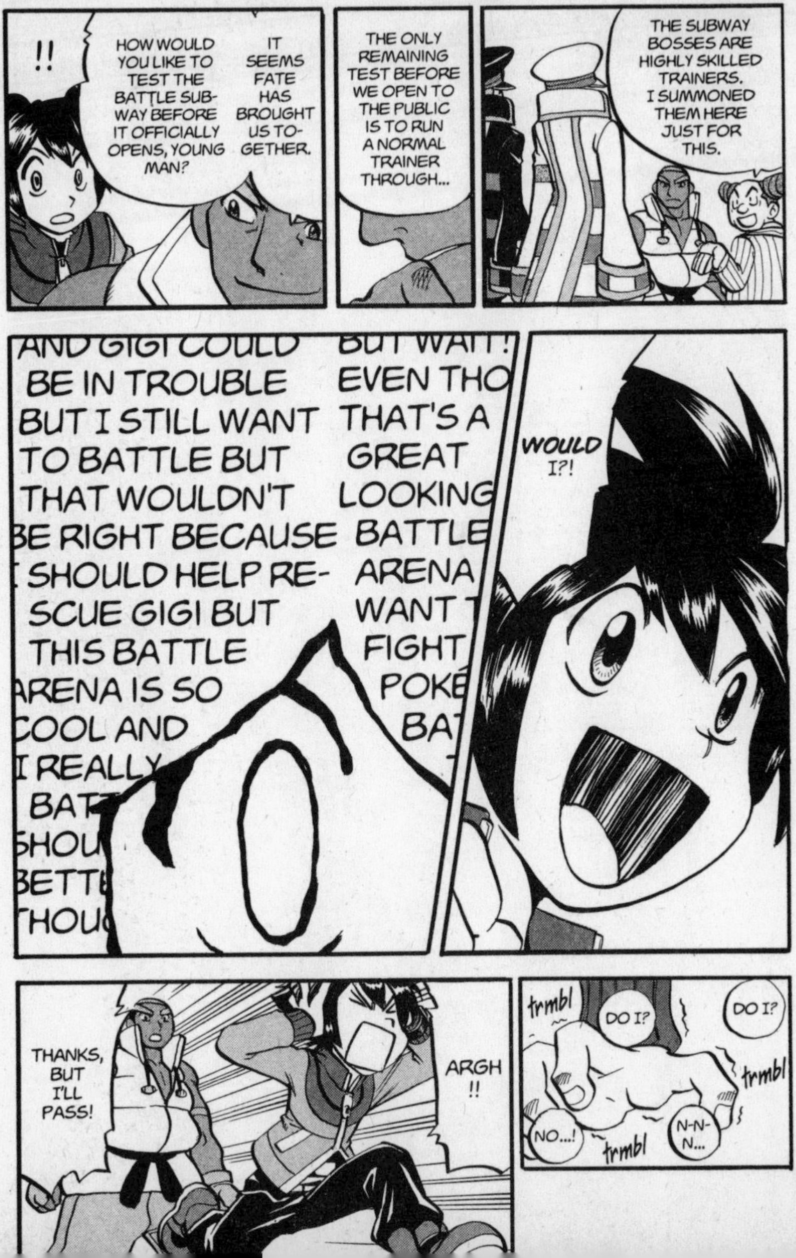
THE SUBWAY BOSSES ARE HIGHLY SKILLED TRAINERS. I SUMMONED THEM HERE JUST FOR THIS.
THE ONLY REMAINING TEST BEFORE WE OPEN TO THE PUBLIC IS TO RUN A NORMAL TRAINER THROUGH...
IT SEEMS FATE HAS BROUGHT US TO-GETHER.
HOW WOULD YOU LIKE TO TEST THE BATTLE SUB-WAY BEFORE IT OFFICIALLY OPENS, YOUNG MAN?
!!
WOULD I?!
AND GIGI COULD BE IN TROUBLE BUT I STILL WANT TO BATTLE BUT THAT WOULDN'T BE RIGHT BECAUSE I SHOULD HELP RE-SCUE GIGI BUT THIS BATTLE ARENA IS SO COOL AND I REALLY
BUT WAIT! EVEN THO THAT'S A GREAT LOOKING BATTLE ARENA
DO I?
DO I?
trmbl
trmbl
N-N-N...
NO...!
trmbl
ARGH !!
THANKS, BUT I'LL PASS!

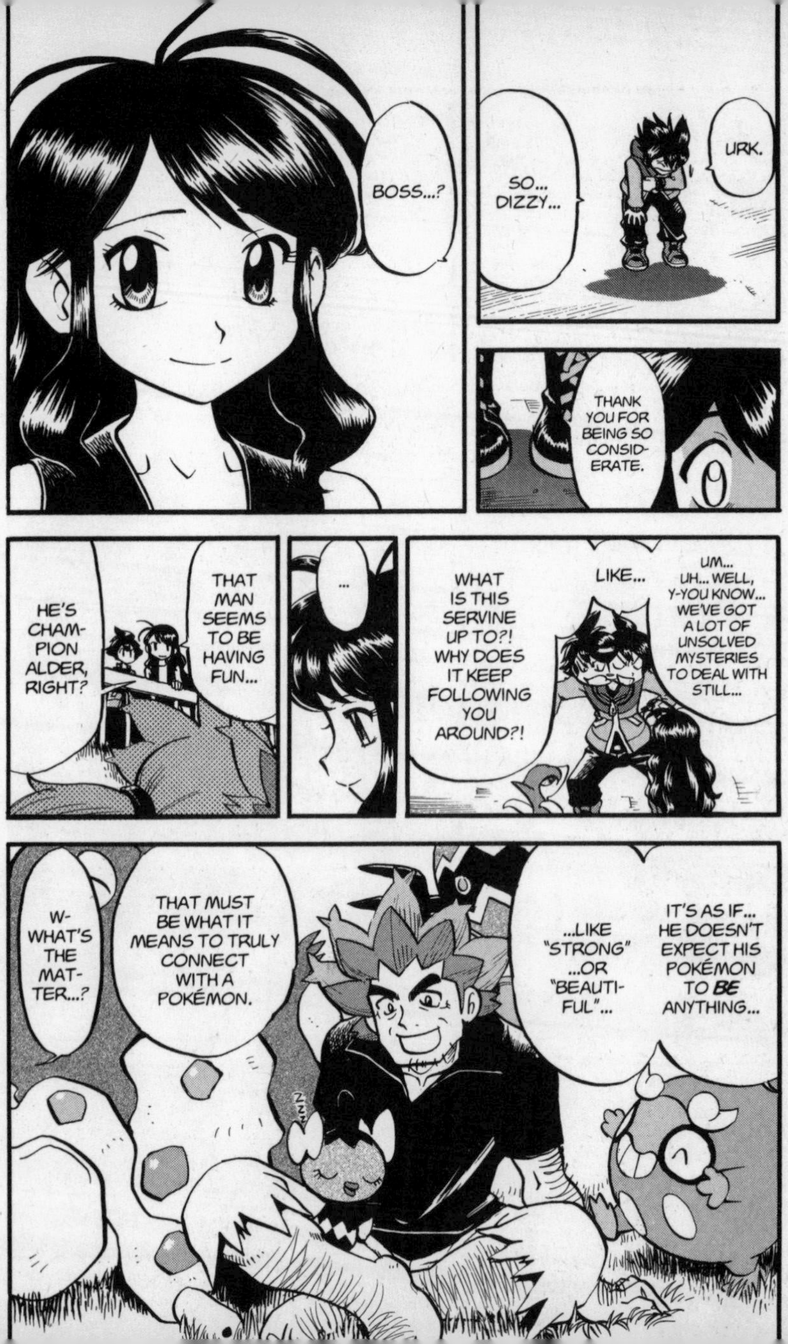
URK.
SO... DIZZY...
THANK YOU FOR BEING SO CONSIDERATE.
BOSS...?
UM... UH... WELL, Y-YOU KNOW... WE'VE GOT A LOT OF UNSOLVED MYSTERIES TO DEAL WITH STILL...
LIKE...
WHAT IS THIS SERVINE UP TO?! WHY DOES IT KEEP FOLLOWING YOU AROUND?!
...
THAT MAN SEEMS TO BE HAVING FUN...
HE'S CHAMPION ALDER, RIGHT?
IT'S AS IF... HE DOESN'T EXPECT HIS POKÉMON TO *BE* ANYTHING...
...LIKE "STRONG" ...OR "BEAUTIFUL"...
THAT MUST BE WHAT IT MEANS TO TRULY CONNECT WITH A POKÉMON.
W-WHAT'S THE MATTER...?
ZZZ

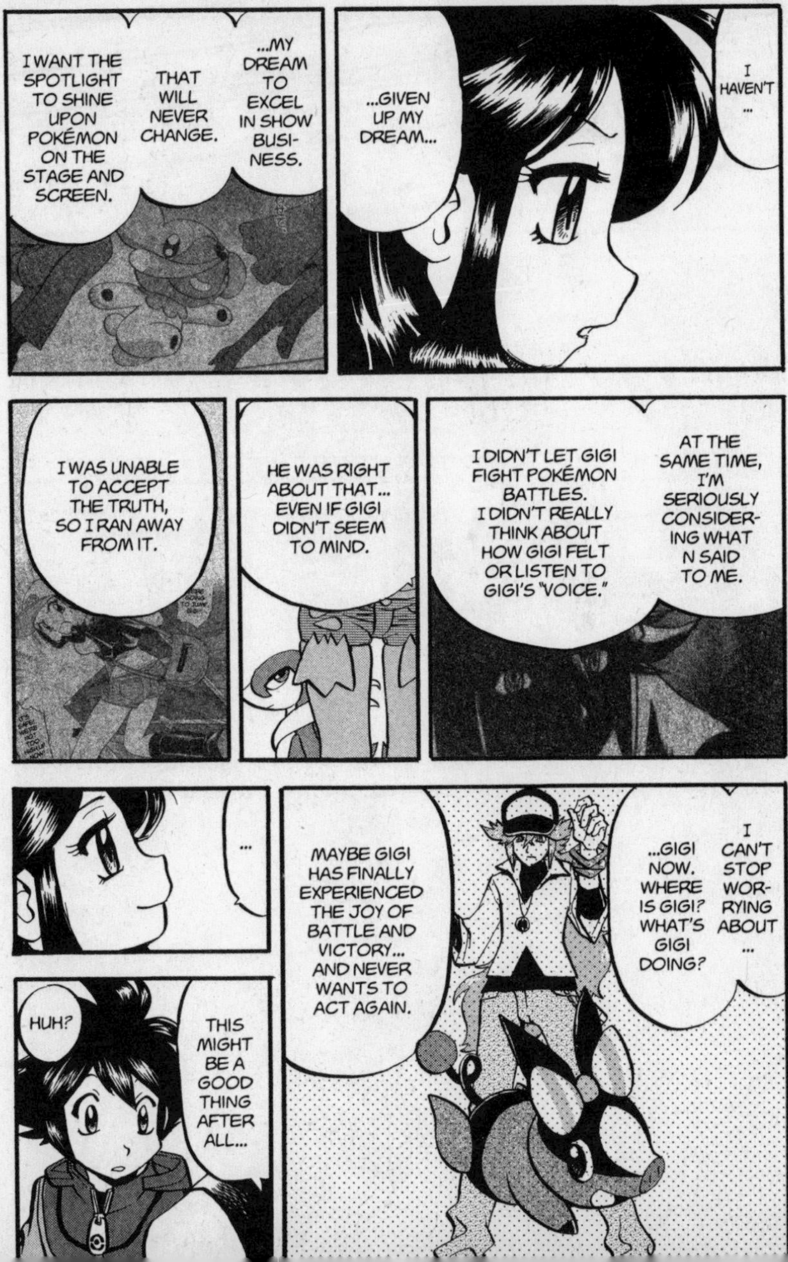
I HAVEN'T ...
...GIVEN UP MY DREAM...
...MY DREAM TO EXCEL IN SHOW BUSI-NESS.
THAT WILL NEVER CHANGE.
I WANT THE SPOTLIGHT TO SHINE UPON POKÉMON ON THE STAGE AND SCREEN.
AT THE SAME TIME, I'M SERIOUSLY CONSIDER-ING WHAT N SAID TO ME.
I DIDN'T LET GIGI FIGHT POKÉMON BATTLES. I DIDN'T REALLY THINK ABOUT HOW GIGI FELT OR LISTEN TO GIGI'S "VOICE."
HE WAS RIGHT ABOUT THAT... EVEN IF GIGI DIDN'T SEEM TO MIND.
I WAS UNABLE TO ACCEPT THE TRUTH, SO I RAN AWAY FROM IT.
I CAN'T STOP WOR-RYING ABOUT ...
...GIGI NOW. WHERE IS GIGI? WHAT'S GIGI DOING?
MAYBE GIGI HAS FINALLY EXPERIENCED THE JOY OF BATTLE AND VICTORY... AND NEVER WANTS TO ACT AGAIN.
...
THIS MIGHT BE A GOOD THING AFTER ALL...
HUH?

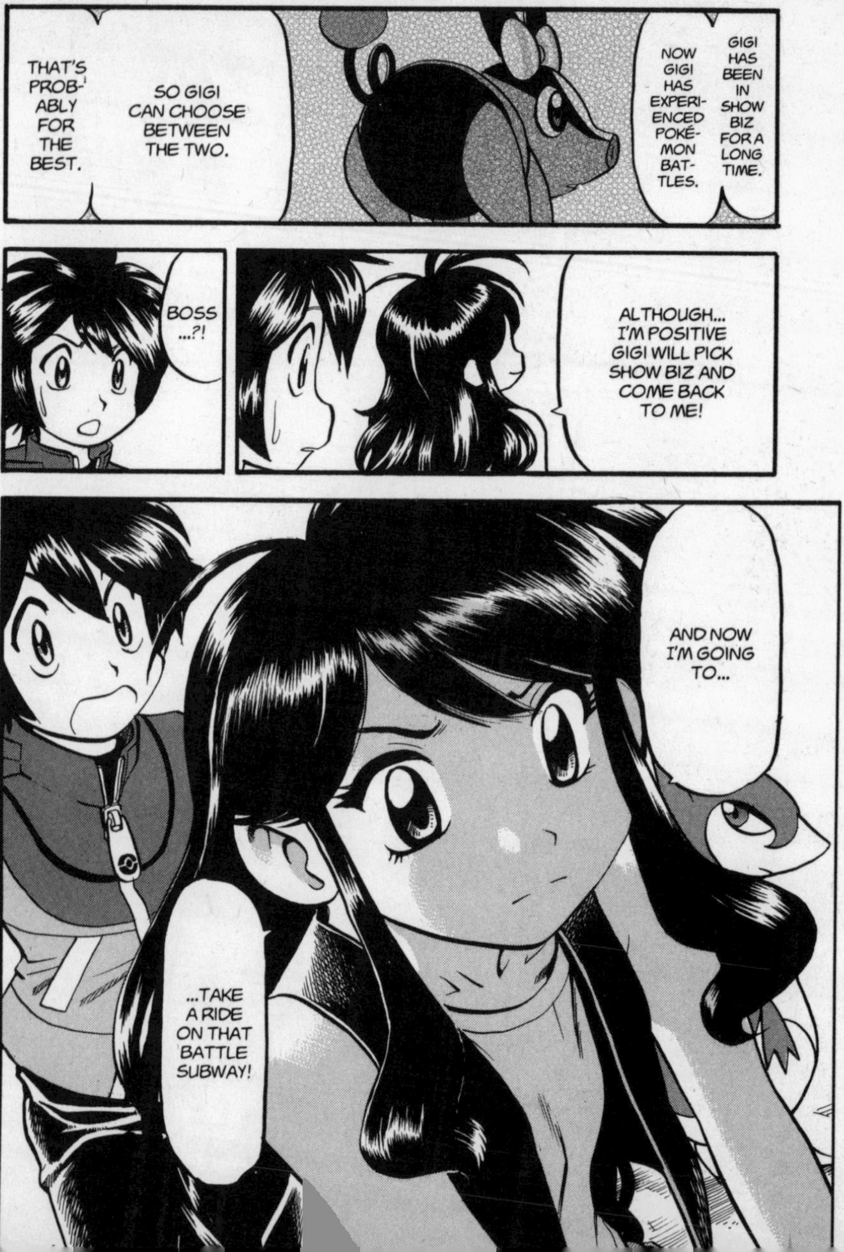
GIGI HAS BEEN IN SHOW BIZ FOR A LONG TIME.
NOW GIGI HAS EXPERIENCED POKÉMON BATTLES.
SO GIGI CAN CHOOSE BETWEEN THE TWO.
THAT'S PROBABLY FOR THE BEST.
ALTHOUGH... I'M POSITIVE GIGI WILL PICK SHOW BIZ AND COME BACK TO ME!
BOSS ...?!
AND NOW I'M GOING TO...
...TAKE A RIDE ON THAT BATTLE SUBWAY!

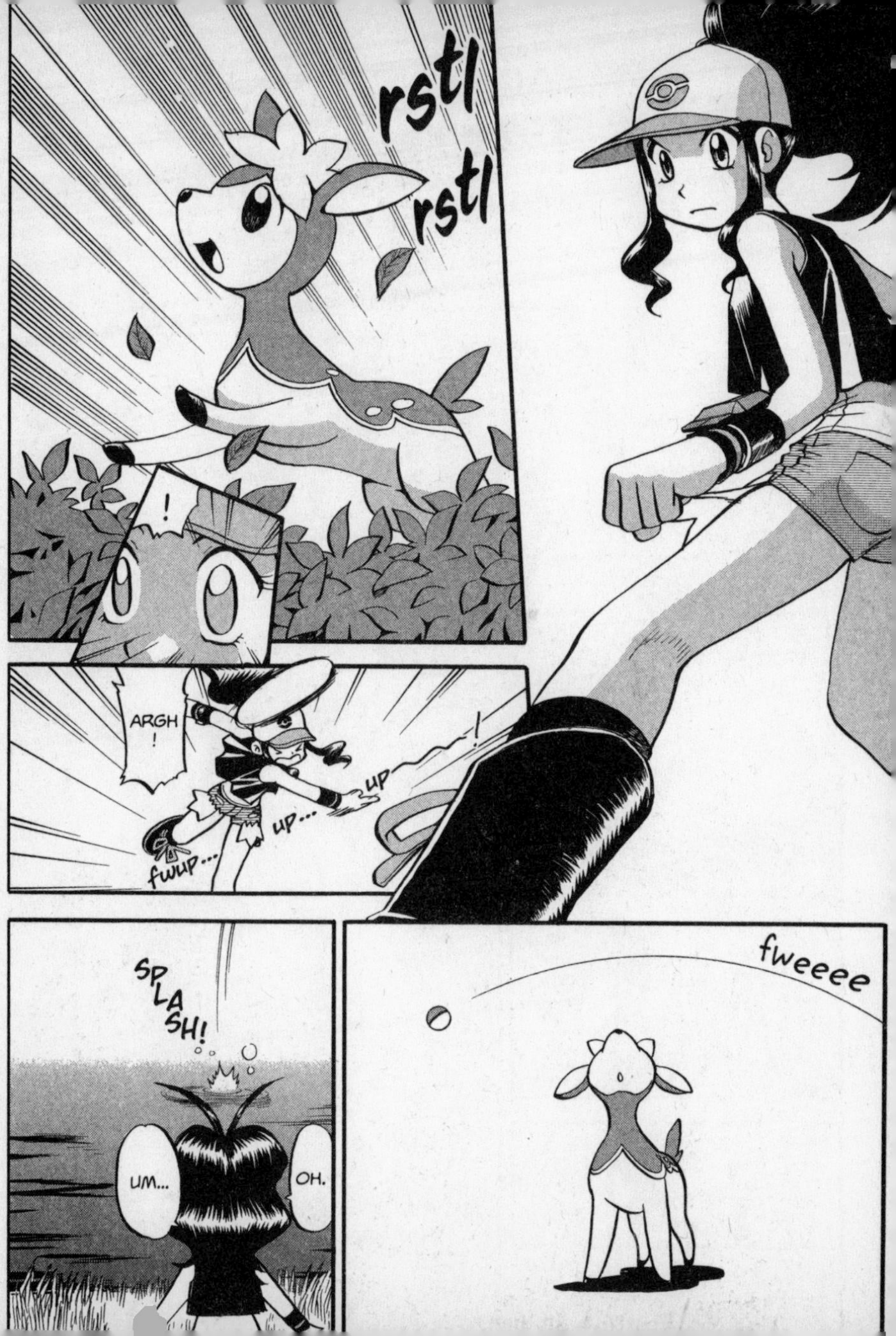
rstl
rstl
!
up~!
ARGH!
up...
fwuup...
fweeee
SPLASH!
OH.
UM...

Adventure ㉘ Growing Pains

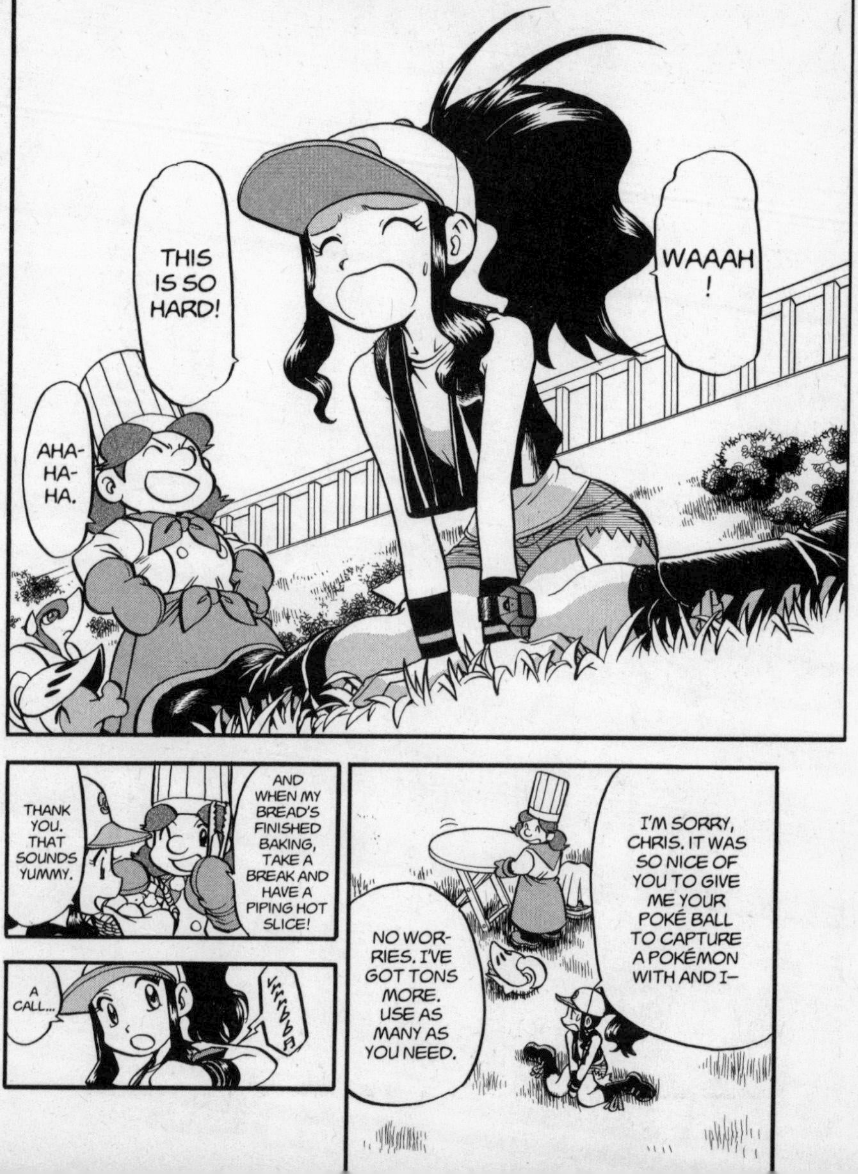
WAAAH!
THIS IS SO HARD!
AHA-HA-HA.
I'M SORRY, CHRIS. IT WAS SO NICE OF YOU TO GIVE ME YOUR POKÉ BALL TO CAPTURE A POKÉMON WITH AND I–
NO WORRIES. I'VE GOT TONS MORE. USE AS MANY AS YOU NEED.
AND WHEN MY BREAD'S FINISHED BAKING, TAKE A BREAK AND HAVE A PIPING HOT SLICE!
THANK YOU. THAT SOUNDS YUMMY.
Vrrrbb♫
A CALL...

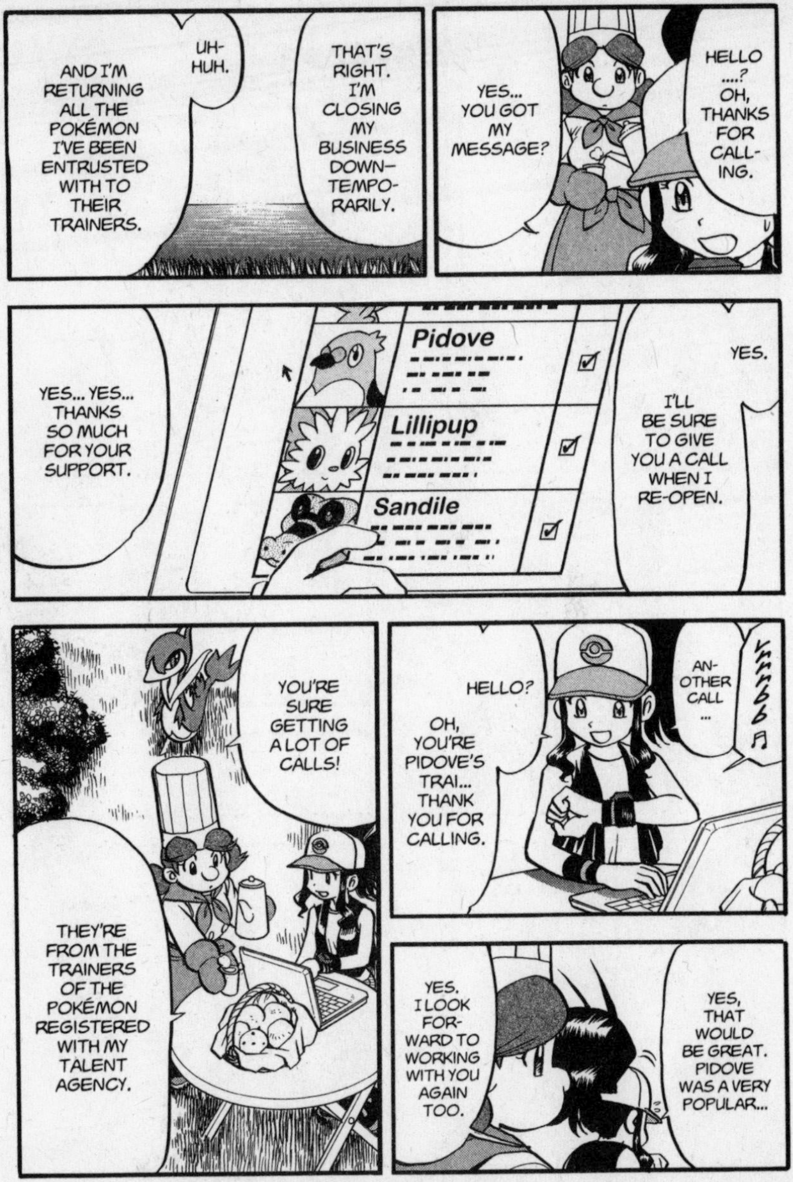
HELLO ....? OH, THANKS FOR CALLING.
YES... YOU GOT MY MESSAGE?
THAT'S RIGHT. I'M CLOSING MY BUSINESS DOWN— TEMPORARILY.
UH-HUH.
AND I'M RETURNING ALL THE POKÉMON I'VE BEEN ENTRUSTED WITH TO THEIR TRAINERS.
YES.
I'LL BE SURE TO GIVE YOU A CALL WHEN I RE-OPEN.
Pidove
Lillipup
Sandile
YES... YES... THANKS SO MUCH FOR YOUR SUPPORT.
ANOTHER CALL ...
HELLO?
OH, YOU'RE PIDOVE'S TRAI... THANK YOU FOR CALLING.
YES, THAT WOULD BE GREAT. PIDOVE WAS A VERY POPULAR...
YES. I LOOK FORWARD TO WORKING WITH YOU AGAIN TOO.
YOU'RE SURE GETTING A LOT OF CALLS!
THEY'RE FROM THE TRAINERS OF THE POKÉMON REGISTERED WITH MY TALENT AGENCY.

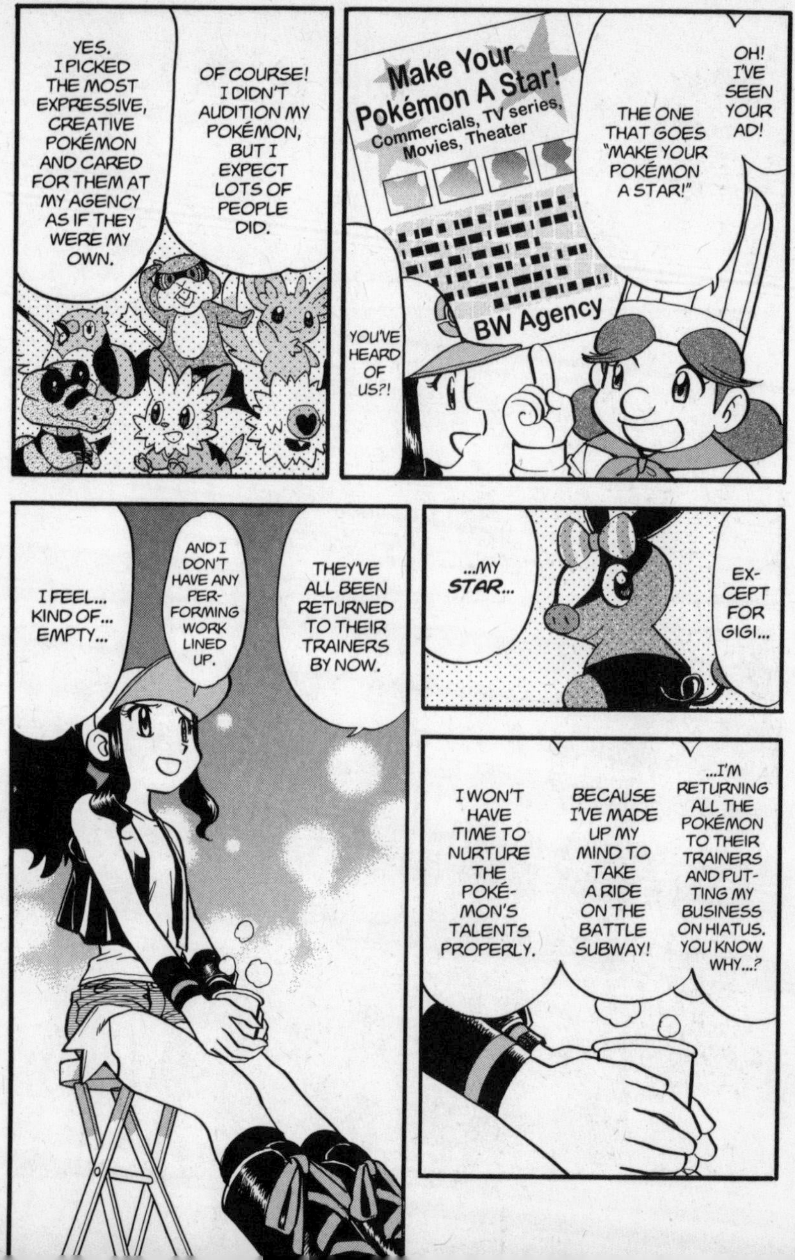
OH! I'VE SEEN YOUR AD!
THE ONE THAT GOES "MAKE YOUR POKÉMON A STAR!"
Make Your Pokémon A Star!
Commercials, TV series, Movies, Theater
BW Agency
YOU'VE HEARD OF US?!
OF COURSE! I DIDN'T AUDITION MY POKÉMON, BUT I EXPECT LOTS OF PEOPLE DID.
YES. I PICKED THE MOST EXPRESSIVE, CREATIVE POKÉMON AND CARED FOR THEM AT MY AGENCY AS IF THEY WERE MY OWN.
EX-CEPT FOR GIGI...
...MY STAR...
...I'M RETURNING ALL THE POKÉMON TO THEIR TRAINERS AND PUT-TING MY BUSINESS ON HIATUS. YOU KNOW WHY...?
BECAUSE I'VE MADE UP MY MIND TO TAKE A RIDE ON THE BATTLE SUBWAY!
I WON'T HAVE TIME TO NURTURE THE POKÉ-MON'S TALENTS PROPERLY.
THEY'VE ALL BEEN RETURNED TO THEIR TRAINERS BY NOW.
AND I DON'T HAVE ANY PER-FORMING WORK LINED UP.
I FEEL... KIND OF... EMPTY...

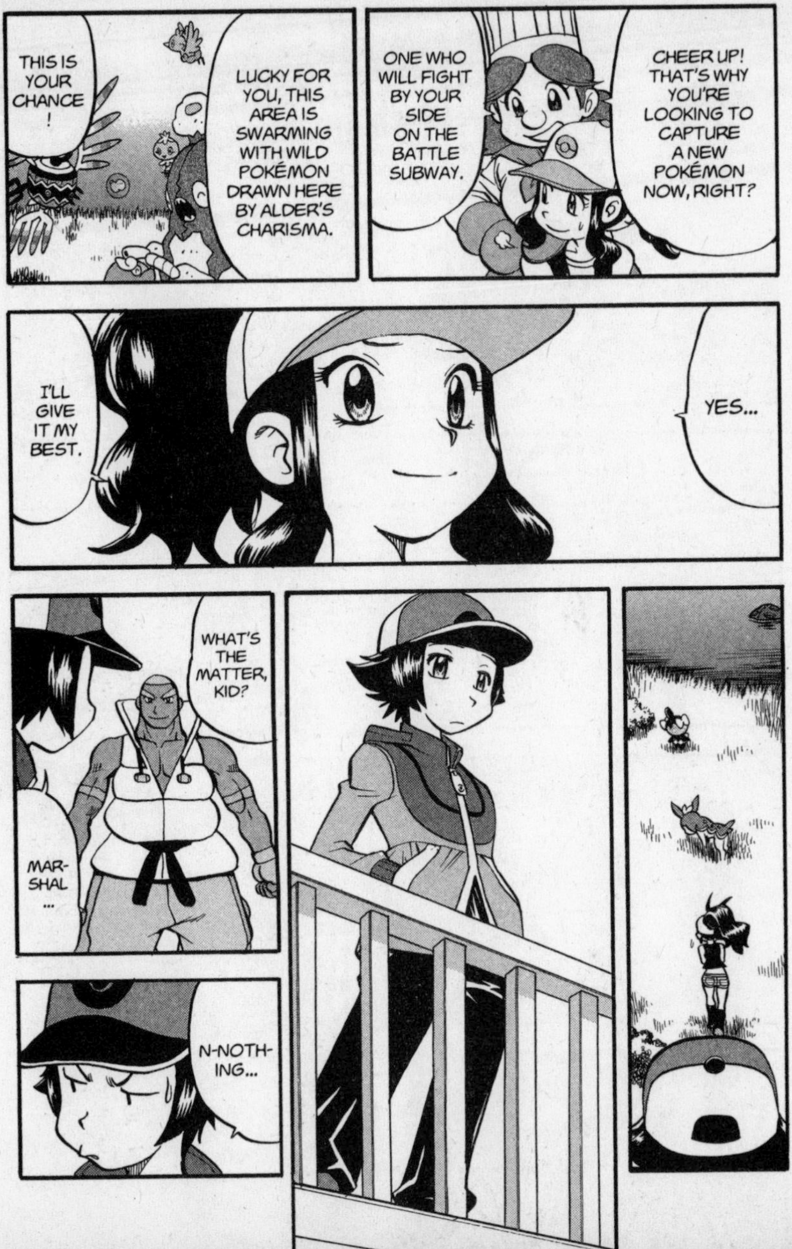
CHEER UP! THAT'S WHY YOU'RE LOOKING TO CAPTURE A NEW POKÉMON NOW, RIGHT?
ONE WHO WILL FIGHT BY YOUR SIDE ON THE BATTLE SUBWAY.
LUCKY FOR YOU, THIS AREA IS SWARMING WITH WILD POKÉMON DRAWN HERE BY ALDER'S CHARISMA.
THIS IS YOUR CHANCE!
YES...
I'LL GIVE IT MY BEST.
WHAT'S THE MATTER, KID?
MARSHAL...
N-NOTHING...

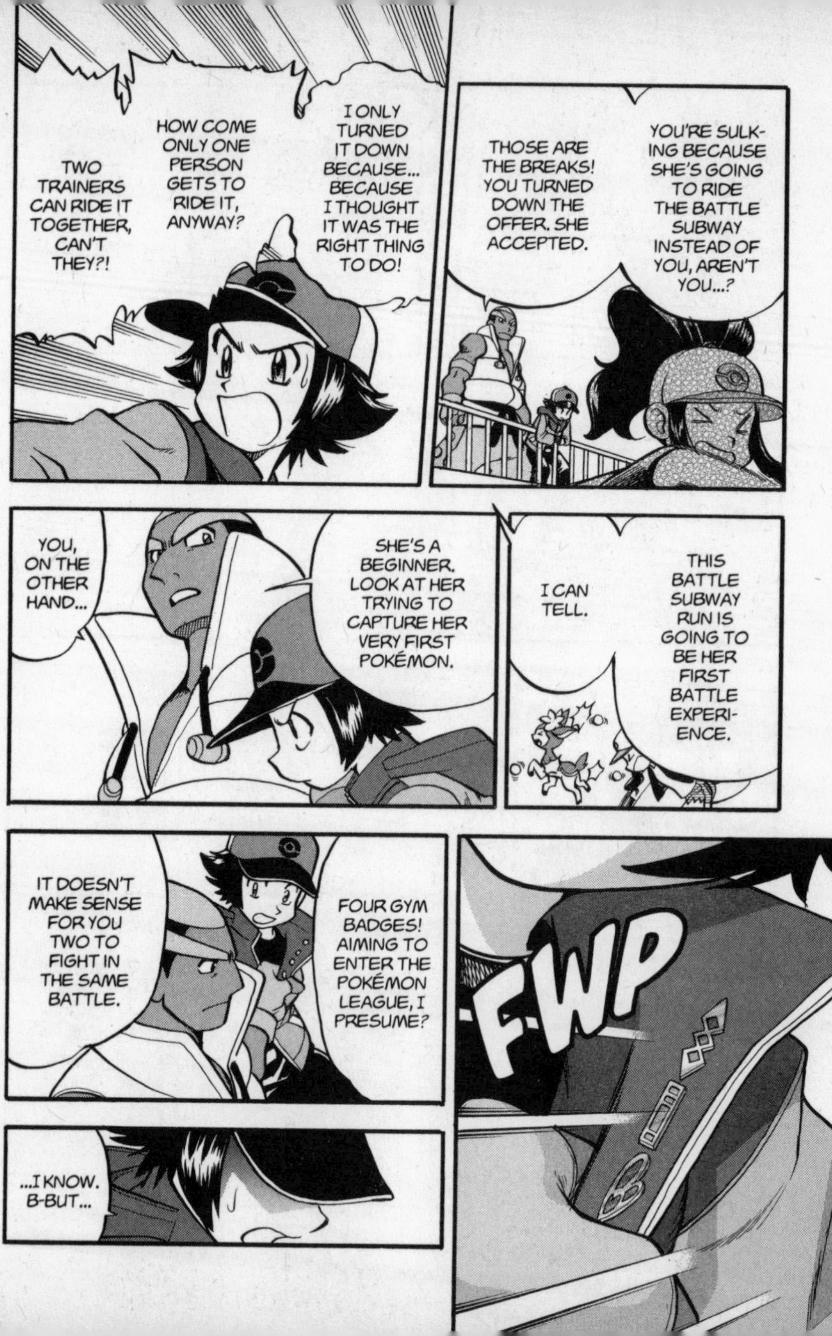
YOU'RE SULKING BECAUSE SHE'S GOING TO RIDE THE BATTLE SUBWAY INSTEAD OF YOU, AREN'T YOU...?
THOSE ARE THE BREAKS! YOU TURNED DOWN THE OFFER. SHE ACCEPTED.
I ONLY TURNED IT DOWN BECAUSE... BECAUSE I THOUGHT IT WAS THE RIGHT THING TO DO!
HOW COME ONLY ONE PERSON GETS TO RIDE IT, ANYWAY?
TWO TRAINERS CAN RIDE IT TOGETHER, CAN'T THEY?!
THIS BATTLE SUBWAY RUN IS GOING TO BE HER FIRST BATTLE EXPERIENCE.
I CAN TELL.
SHE'S A BEGINNER. LOOK AT HER TRYING TO CAPTURE HER VERY FIRST POKÉMON.
YOU, ON THE OTHER HAND...
FWP
FOUR GYM BADGES! AIMING TO ENTER THE POKÉMON LEAGUE, I PRESUME?
IT DOESN'T MAKE SENSE FOR YOU TWO TO FIGHT IN THE SAME BATTLE.
...I KNOW. B-BUT...

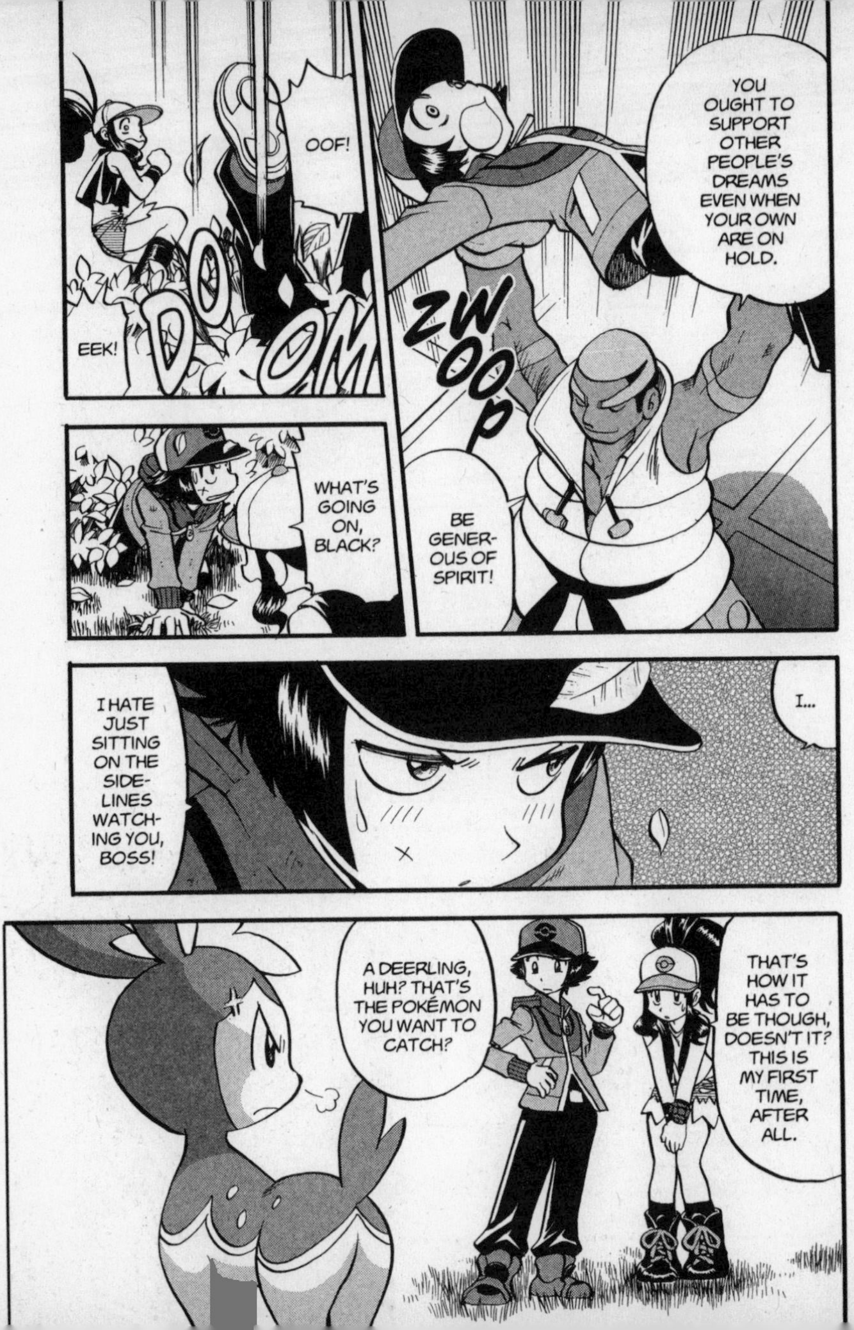
YOU OUGHT TO SUPPORT OTHER PEOPLE'S DREAMS EVEN WHEN YOUR OWN ARE ON HOLD.
ZWOOOP
BE GENEROUS OF SPIRIT!
OOF!
DOOM
EEK!
WHAT'S GOING ON, BLACK?
I...
I HATE JUST SITTING ON THE SIDELINES WATCHING YOU, BOSS!
THAT'S HOW IT HAS TO BE THOUGH, DOESN'T IT? THIS IS MY FIRST TIME, AFTER ALL.
A DEERLING, HUH? THAT'S THE POKéMON YOU WANT TO CATCH?

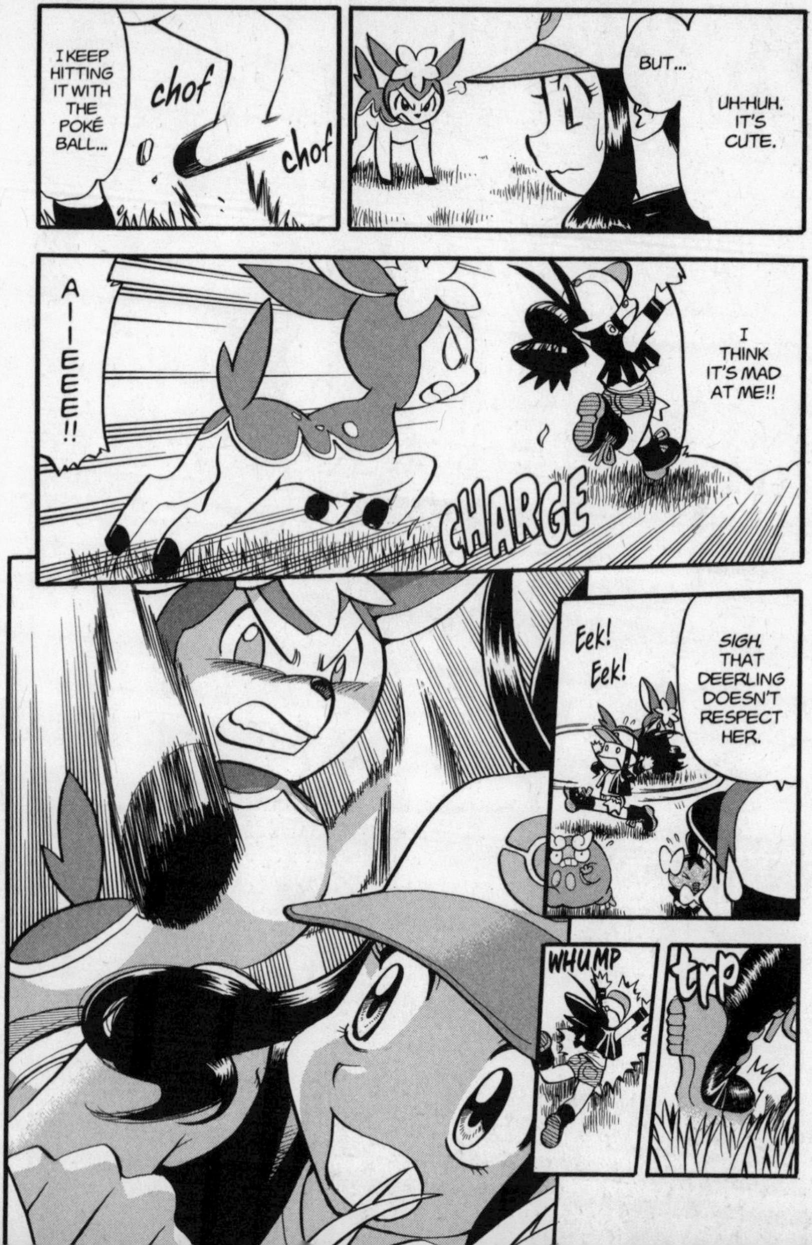
UH-HUH. IT'S CUTE.
BUT...
I KEEP HITTING IT WITH THE POKÉ BALL...
chof
chof
I THINK IT'S MAD AT ME!!
AIIEEE!!
CHARGE
SIGH. THAT DEERLING DOESN'T RESPECT HER.
Eek! Eek!
trp
WHUMP

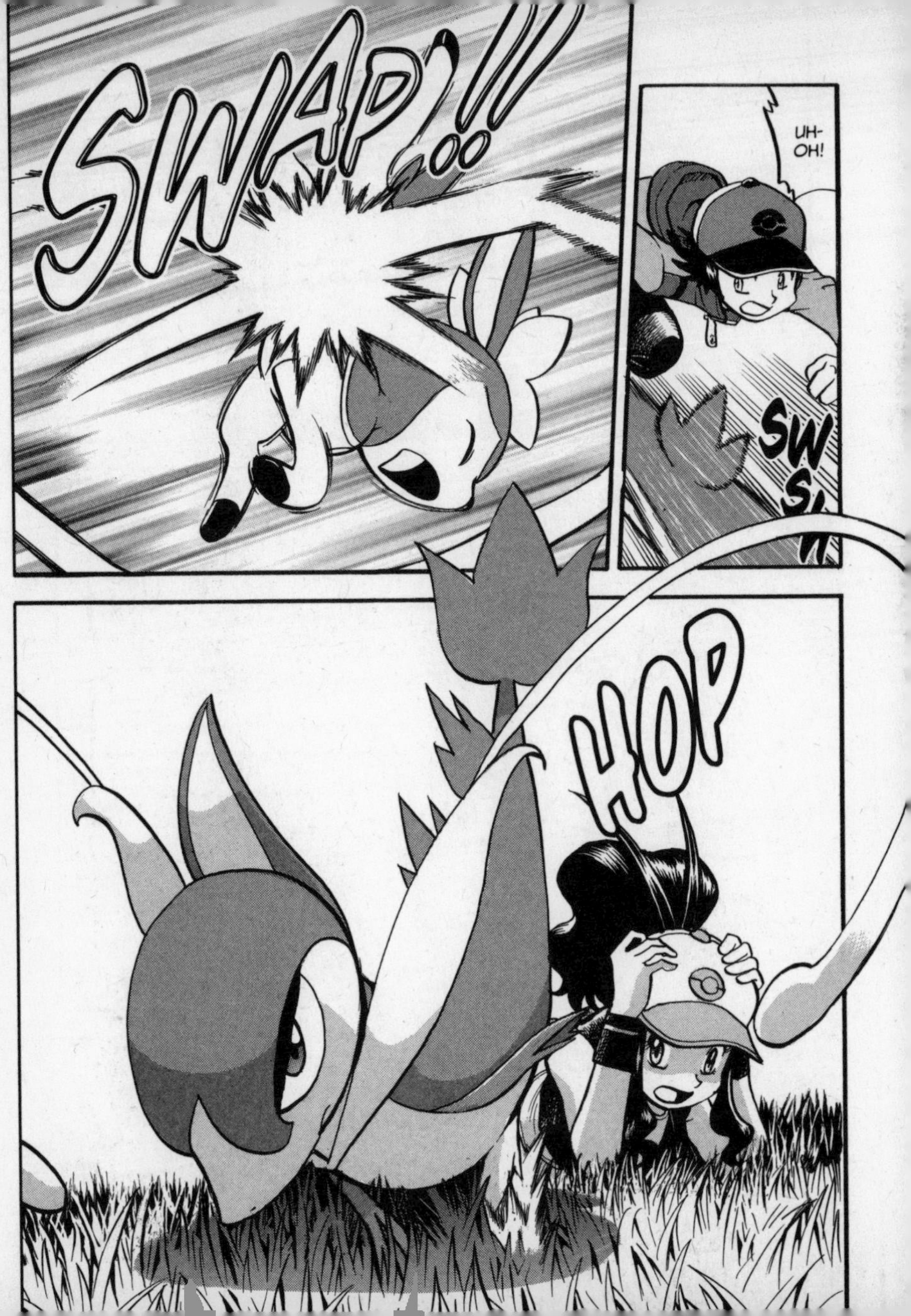
UH-OH!
SWSH
SWAP!!
HOP

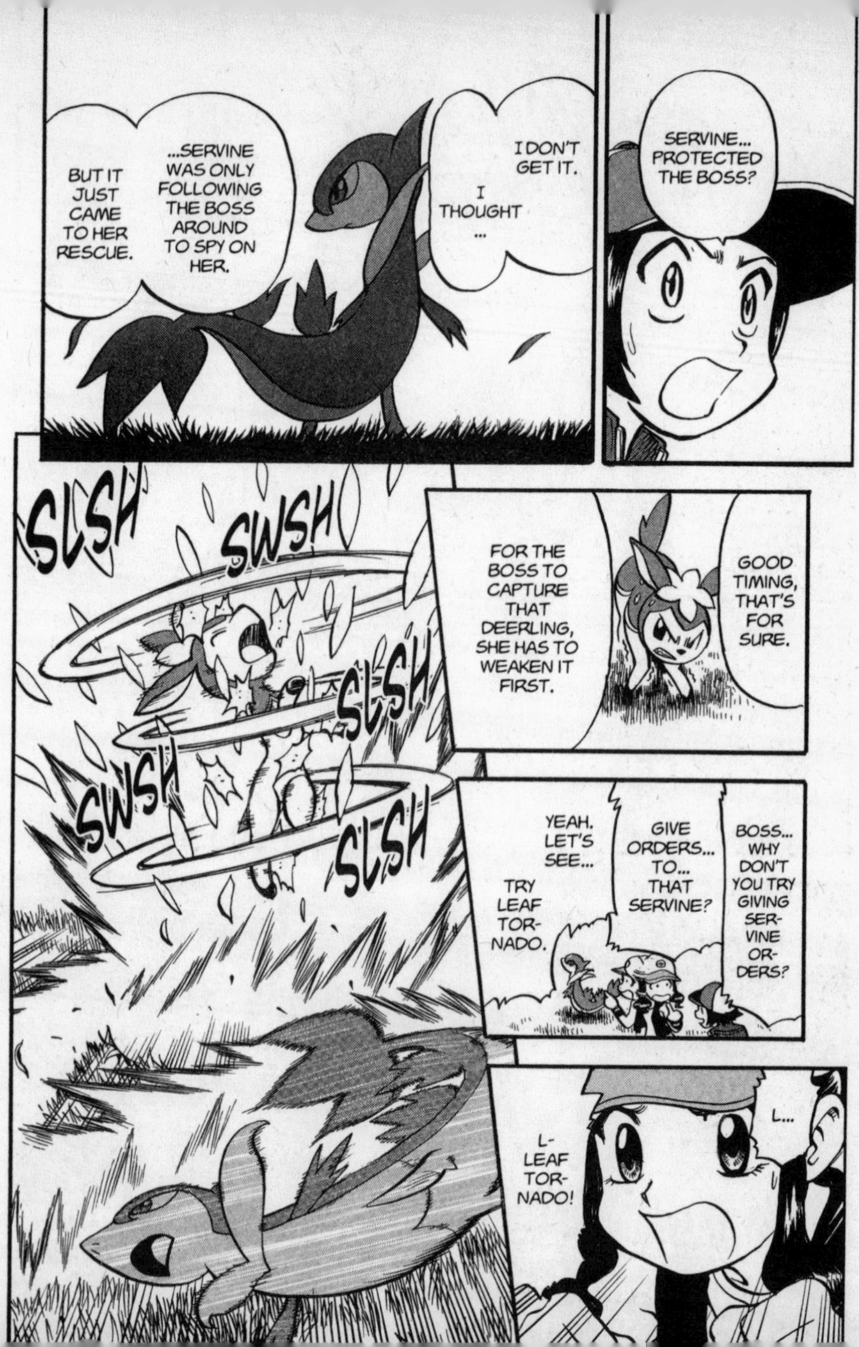
SERVINE... PROTECTED THE BOSS?
I DON'T GET IT.
I THOUGHT ...
...SERVINE WAS ONLY FOLLOWING THE BOSS AROUND TO SPY ON HER.
BUT IT JUST CAME TO HER RESCUE.
GOOD TIMING, THAT'S FOR SURE.
FOR THE BOSS TO CAPTURE THAT DEERLING, SHE HAS TO WEAKEN IT FIRST.
BOSS... WHY DON'T YOU TRY GIVING SER-VINE OR-DERS?
GIVE ORDERS... TO... THAT SERVINE?
YEAH. LET'S SEE...
TRY LEAF TOR-NADO.
L...
L-LEAF TOR-NADO!
SLSH
SWSH
SLSH
SWSH
SLSH

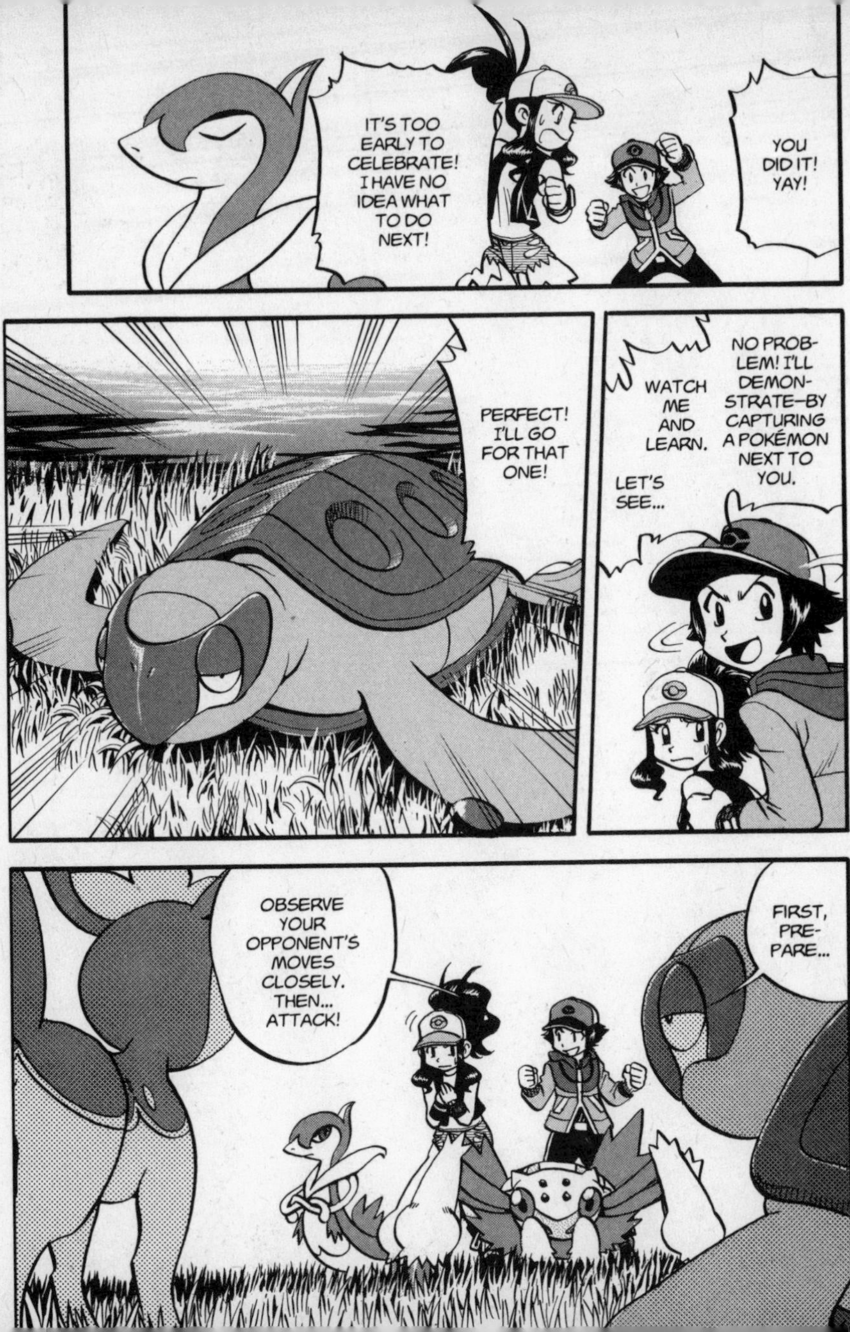

YOU DID IT! YAY!
IT'S TOO EARLY TO CELEBRATE! I HAVE NO IDEA WHAT TO DO NEXT!
NO PROB-LEM! I'LL DEMON-STRATE—BY CAPTURING A POKÉMON NEXT TO YOU.
WATCH ME AND LEARN.
LET'S SEE...
PERFECT! I'LL GO FOR THAT ONE!
FIRST, PRE-PARE...
OBSERVE YOUR OPPONENT'S MOVES CLOSELY. THEN... ATTACK!

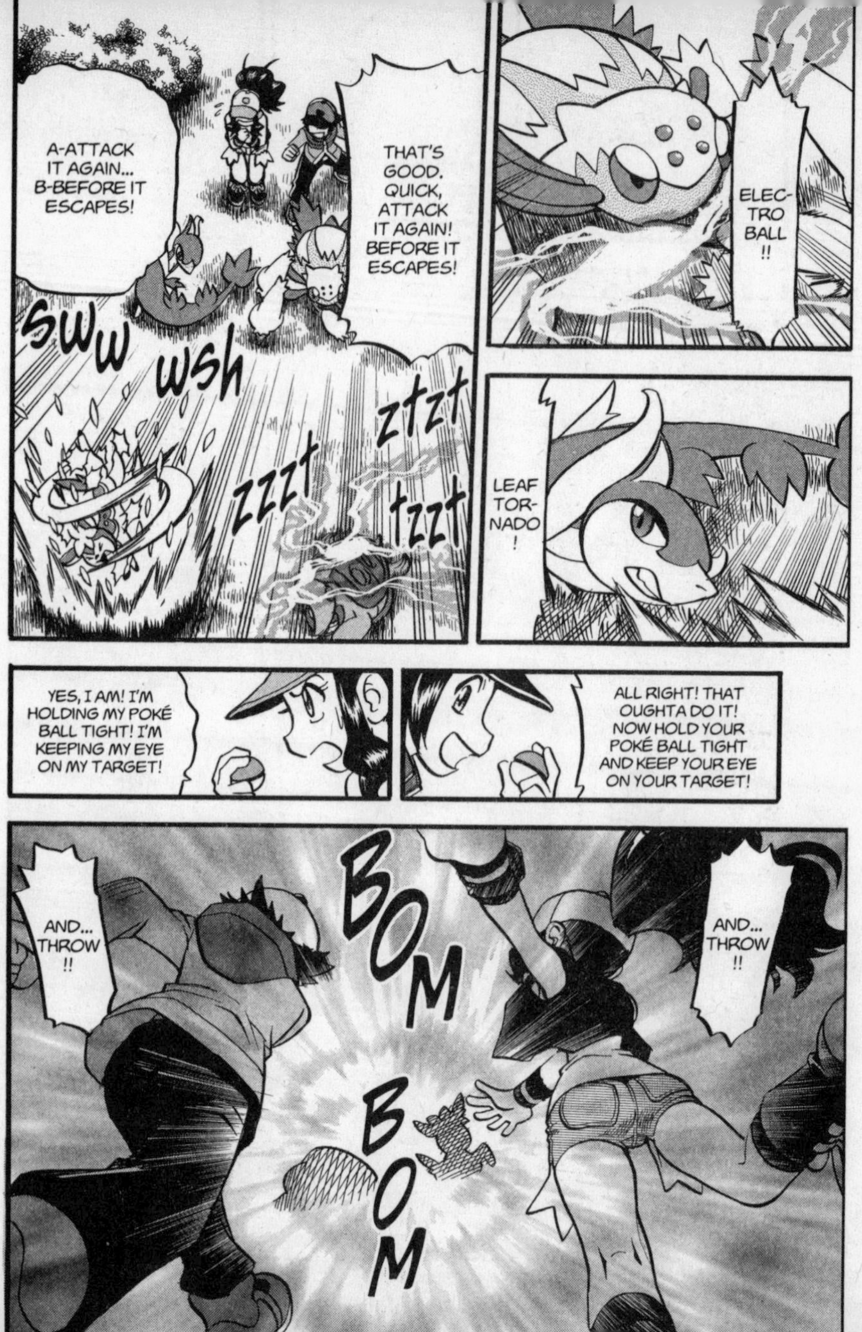
ELEC-
TRO
BALL
!!
LEAF
TOR-
NADO
!
THAT'S GOOD. QUICK, ATTACK IT AGAIN! BEFORE IT ESCAPES!
A-ATTACK IT AGAIN... B-BEFORE IT ESCAPES!
SWWWSH
ZTZT
TZZT
ZZZT
ALL RIGHT! THAT OUGHTA DO IT! NOW HOLD YOUR POKÉ BALL TIGHT AND KEEP YOUR EYE ON YOUR TARGET!
YES, I AM! I'M HOLDING MY POKÉ BALL TIGHT! I'M KEEPING MY EYE ON MY TARGET!
AND... THROW !!
BOM
BOM
AND... THROW !!

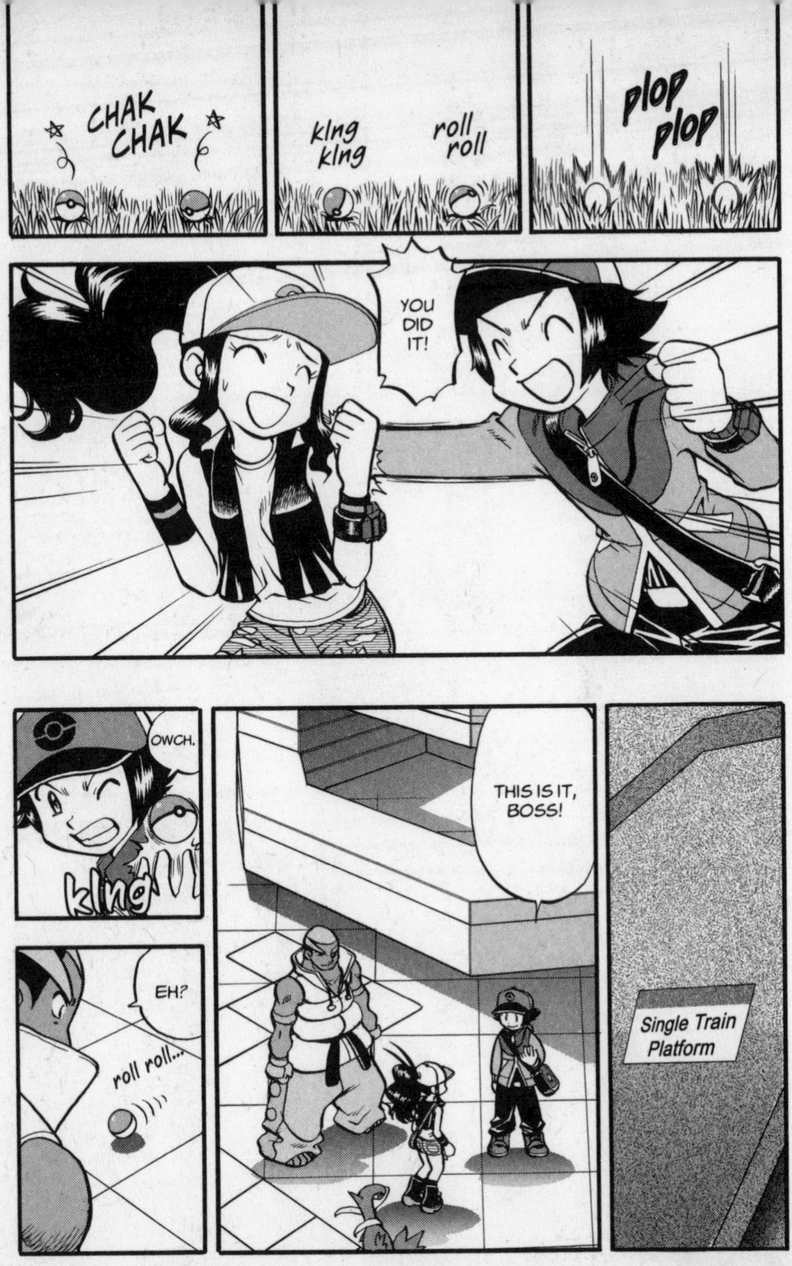
plop plop
roll roll
kling kling
CHAK CHAK
YOU DID IT!
Single Train Platform
THIS IS IT, BOSS!
OWCH.
kling
EH?
roll roll...

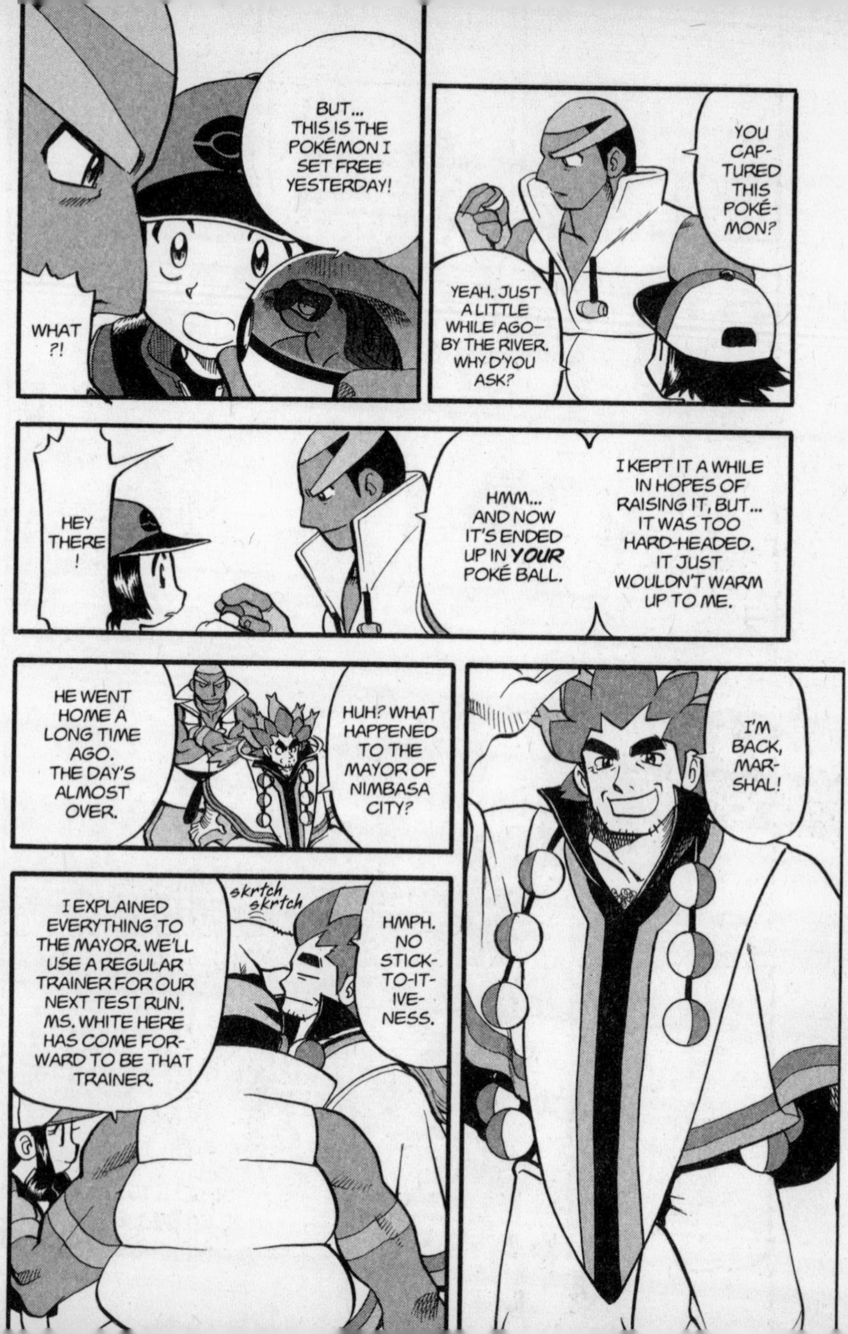
YOU CAPTURED THIS POKÉMON?
YEAH. JUST A LITTLE WHILE AGO—BY THE RIVER. WHY D'YOU ASK?
BUT... THIS IS THE POKÉMON I SET FREE YESTERDAY!
WHAT?!
I KEPT IT A WHILE IN HOPES OF RAISING IT, BUT... IT WAS TOO HARD-HEADED. IT JUST WOULDN'T WARM UP TO ME.
HMM... AND NOW IT'S ENDED UP IN *YOUR* POKÉ BALL.
HEY THERE!
I'M BACK, MARSHAL!
HUH? WHAT HAPPENED TO THE MAYOR OF NIMBASA CITY?
HE WENT HOME A LONG TIME AGO. THE DAY'S ALMOST OVER.
HMPH. NO STICK-TO-IT-IVENESS.
skrtch skrtch
I EXPLAINED EVERYTHING TO THE MAYOR. WE'LL USE A REGULAR TRAINER FOR OUR NEXT TEST RUN. MS. WHITE HERE HAS COME FORWARD TO BE THAT TRAINER.

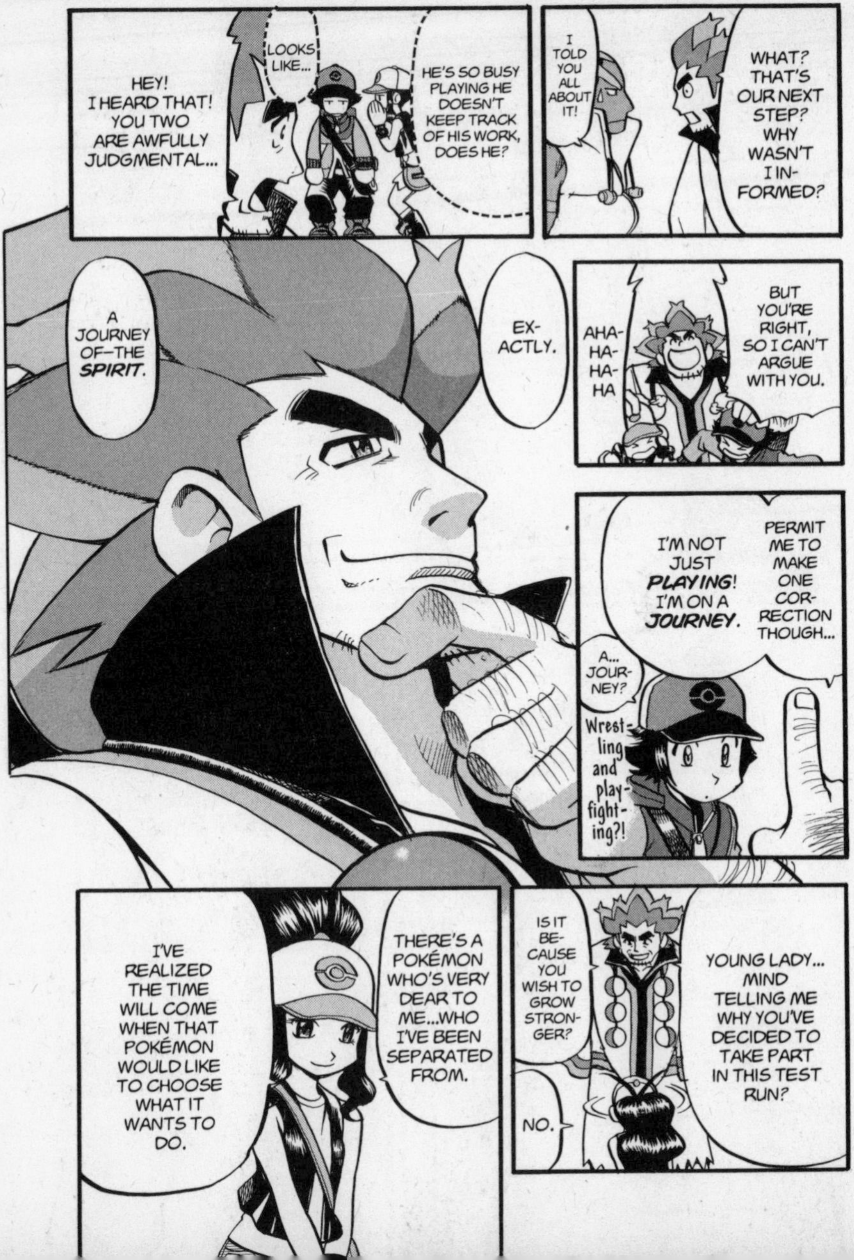
WHAT? THAT'S OUR NEXT STEP? WHY WASN'T I IN-FORMED?
I TOLD YOU ALL ABOUT IT!
LOOKS LIKE...
HE'S SO BUSY PLAYING HE DOESN'T KEEP TRACK OF HIS WORK, DOES HE?
HEY! I HEARD THAT! YOU TWO ARE AWFULLY JUDGMENTAL...
BUT YOU'RE RIGHT, SO I CAN'T ARGUE WITH YOU.
AHA-HA-HA-HA
PERMIT ME TO MAKE ONE COR-RECTION THOUGH...
I'M NOT JUST ***PLAYING***! I'M ON A ***JOURNEY***.
A... JOUR-NEY?
Wrest-ling and play-fight-ing?!
EX-ACTLY.
A JOURNEY OF—THE ***SPIRIT***.
YOUNG LADY... MIND TELLING ME WHY YOU'VE DECIDED TO TAKE PART IN THIS TEST RUN?
IS IT BE-CAUSE YOU WISH TO GROW STRON-GER?
NO.
THERE'S A POKÉMON WHO'S VERY DEAR TO ME...WHO I'VE BEEN SEPARATED FROM.
I'VE REALIZED THE TIME WILL COME WHEN THAT POKÉMON WOULD LIKE TO CHOOSE WHAT IT WANTS TO DO.

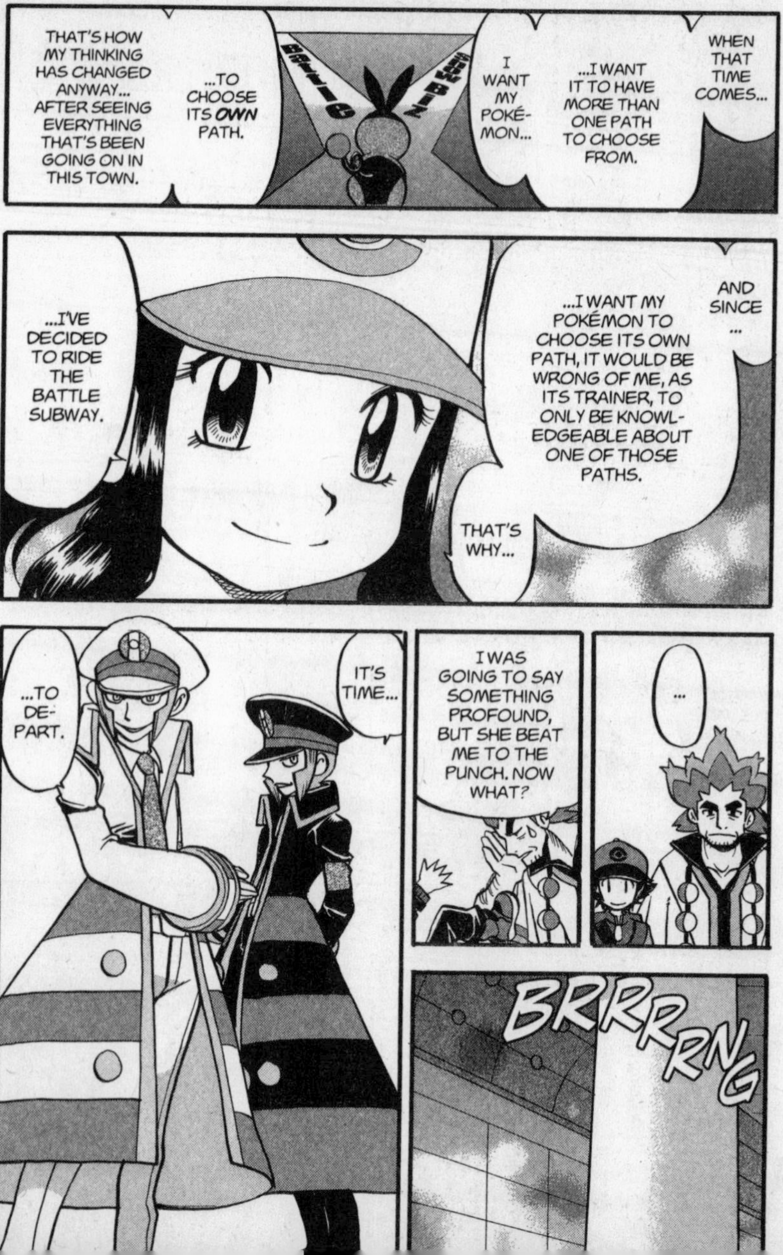

WHEN THAT TIME COMES...
...I WANT IT TO HAVE MORE THAN ONE PATH TO CHOOSE FROM.
I WANT MY POKÉ-MON...
...TO CHOOSE ITS *OWN* PATH.
THAT'S HOW MY THINKING HAS CHANGED ANYWAY... AFTER SEEING EVERYTHING THAT'S BEEN GOING ON IN THIS TOWN.
AND SINCE ...
...I WANT MY POKÉMON TO CHOOSE ITS OWN PATH, IT WOULD BE WRONG OF ME, AS ITS TRAINER, TO ONLY BE KNOWL-EDGEABLE ABOUT ONE OF THOSE PATHS.
THAT'S WHY...
...I'VE DECIDED TO RIDE THE BATTLE SUBWAY.
...
I WAS GOING TO SAY SOMETHING PROFOUND, BUT SHE BEAT ME TO THE PUNCH. NOW WHAT?
BRRRRNG
IT'S TIME...
...TO DE-PART.

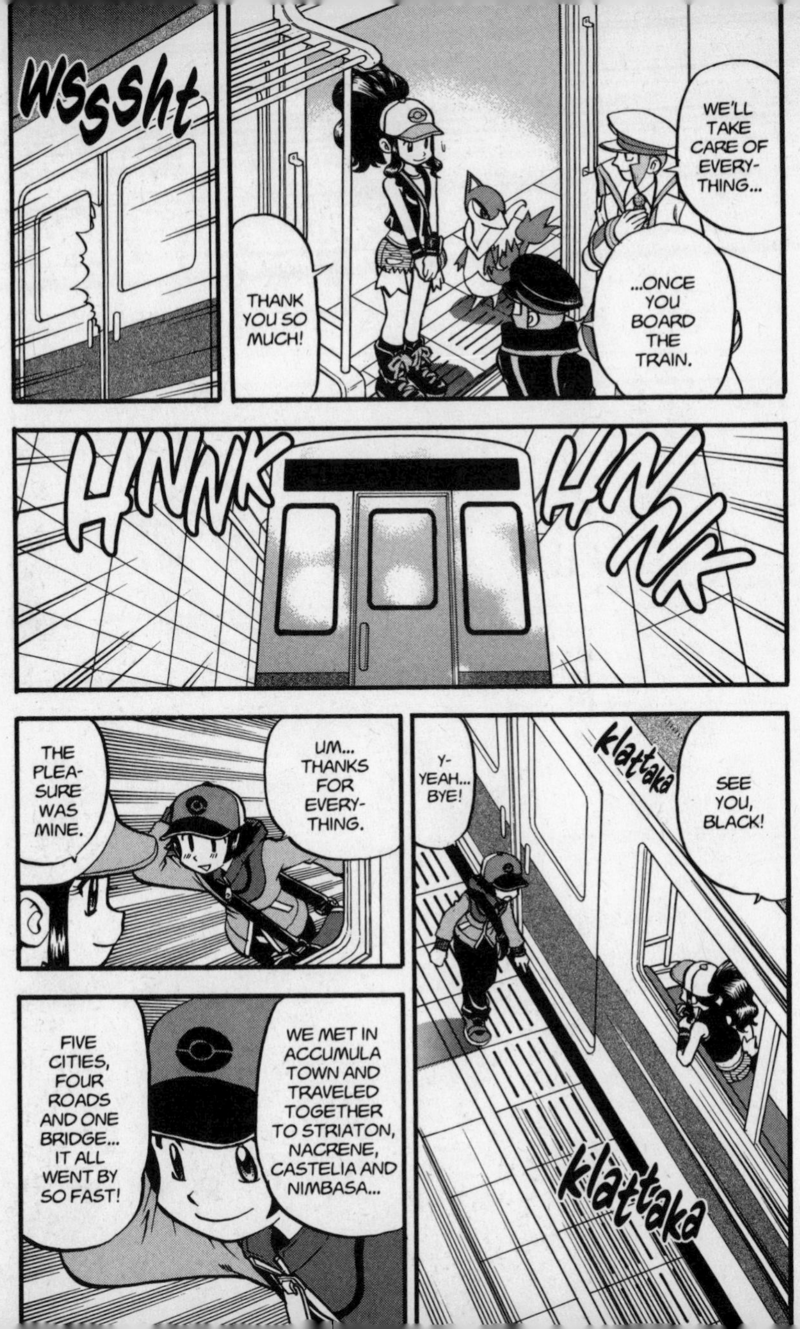
WE'LL TAKE CARE OF EVERY-THING...
...ONCE YOU BOARD THE TRAIN.
THANK YOU SO MUCH!
WSSSHT
HNNK
HNNK
klattaka
SEE YOU, BLACK!
Y-YEAH... BYE!
klattaka
UM... THANKS FOR EVERY-THING.
THE PLEA-SURE WAS MINE.
WE MET IN ACCUMULA TOWN AND TRAVELED TOGETHER TO STRIATON, NACRENE, CASTELIA AND NIMBASA...
FIVE CITIES, FOUR ROADS AND ONE BRIDGE... IT ALL WENT BY SO FAST!

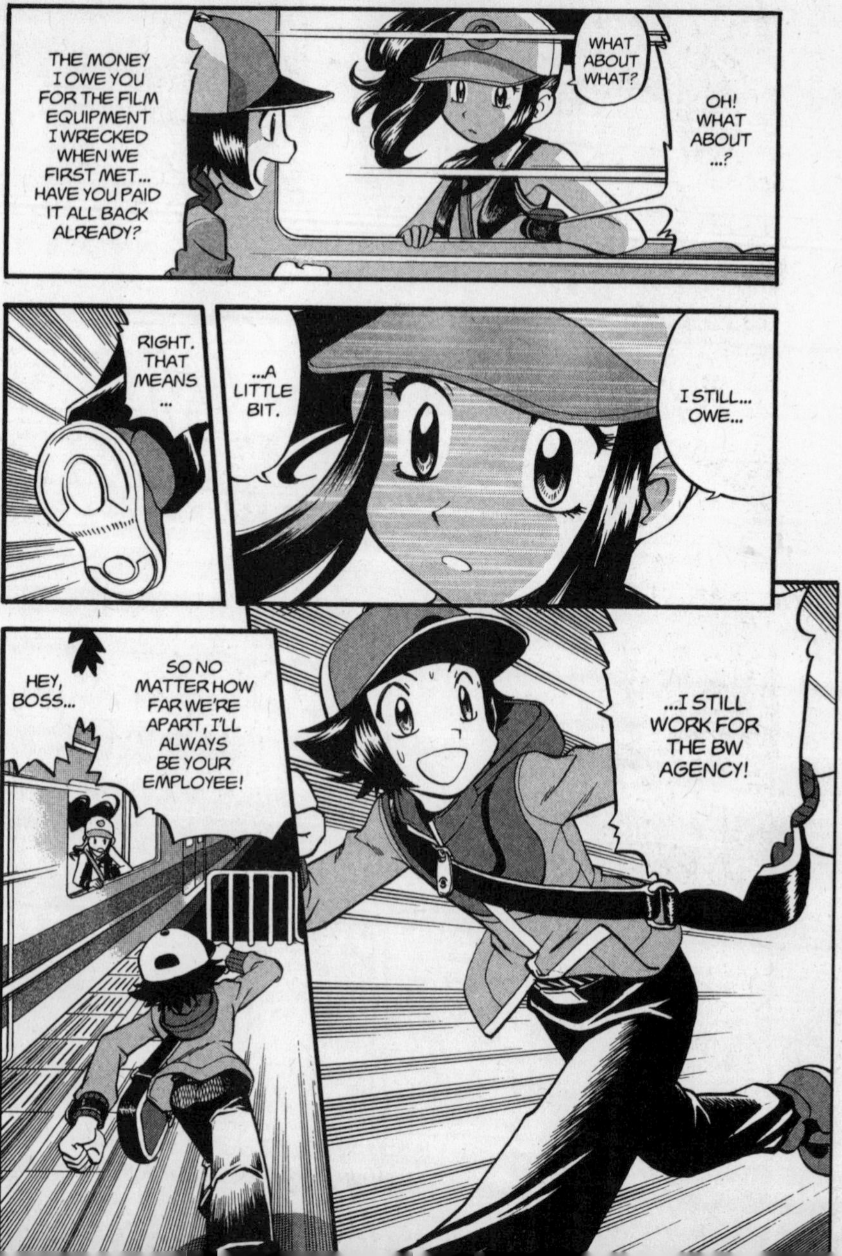
OH! WHAT ABOUT ...?
WHAT ABOUT WHAT?
THE MONEY I OWE YOU FOR THE FILM EQUIPMENT I WRECKED WHEN WE FIRST MET... HAVE YOU PAID IT ALL BACK ALREADY?
I STILL... OWE...
...A LITTLE BIT.
RIGHT. THAT MEANS ...
...I STILL WORK FOR THE BW AGENCY!
HEY, BOSS...
SO NO MATTER HOW FAR WE'RE APART, I'LL ALWAYS BE YOUR EMPLOYEE!

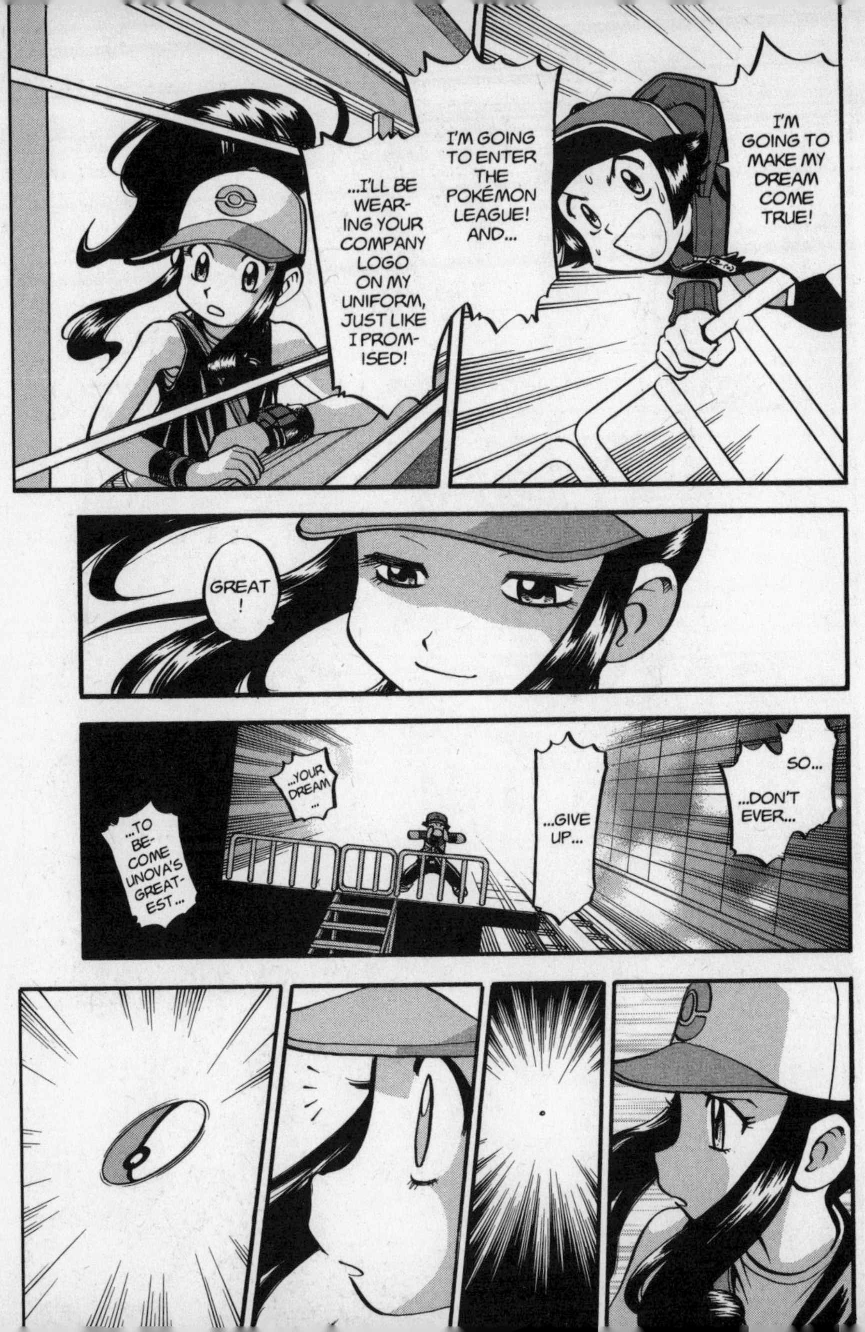
I'M GOING TO MAKE MY DREAM COME TRUE!
I'M GOING TO ENTER THE POKÉMON LEAGUE! AND...
...I'LL BE WEARING YOUR COMPANY LOGO ON MY UNIFORM, JUST LIKE I PROMISED!
GREAT!
SO...
...DON'T EVER...
...GIVE UP...
...YOUR DREAM...
...TO BECOME UNOVA'S GREATEST...

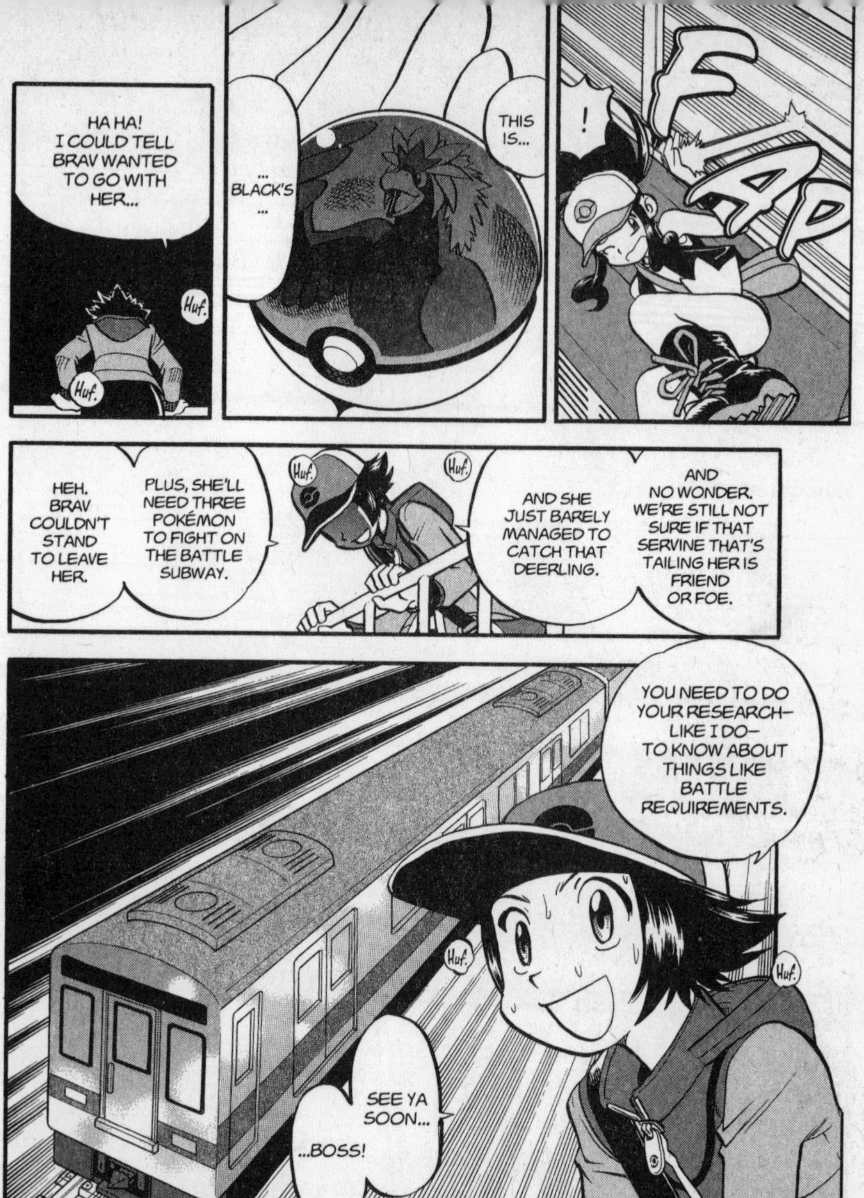
!
FAP
THIS IS...
...BLACK'S...
HA HA! I COULD TELL BRAV WANTED TO GO WITH HER...
Huf.
Huf.
AND NO WONDER. WE'RE STILL NOT SURE IF THAT SERVINE THAT'S TAILING HER IS FRIEND OR FOE.
AND SHE JUST BARELY MANAGED TO CATCH THAT DEERLING.
Huf.
Huf.
PLUS, SHE'LL NEED THREE POKÉMON TO FIGHT ON THE BATTLE SUBWAY.
HEH. BRAV COULDN'T STAND TO LEAVE HER.
YOU NEED TO DO YOUR RESEARCH—LIKE I DO—TO KNOW ABOUT THINGS LIKE BATTLE REQUIREMENTS.
Huf.
Huf.
SEE YA SOON...
...BOSS!
TO BE CONTINUED IN THE *POKÉMON ADVENTURES BLACK AND WHITE* GRAPHIC NOVEL SERIES—COMING SOON!

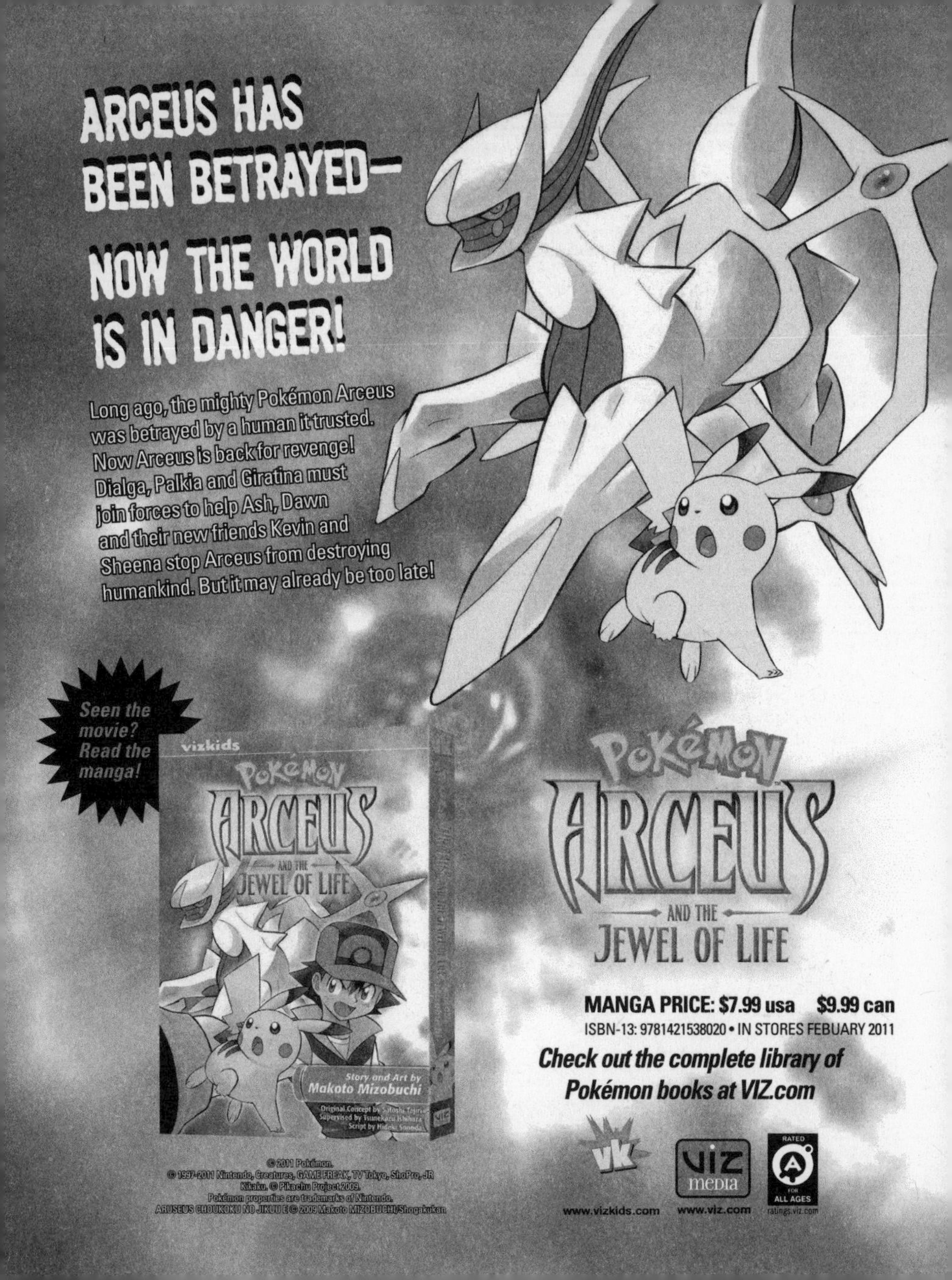
ARCEUS HAS BEEN BETRAYED—NOW THE WORLD IS IN DANGER!
Long ago, the mighty Pokémon Arceus was betrayed by a human it trusted. Now Arceus is back for revenge! Dialga, Palkia and Giratina must join forces to help Ash, Dawn and their new friends Kevin and Sheena stop Arceus from destroying humankind. But it may already be too late!
Seen the movie? Read the manga!
vizkids
Pokémon
ARCEUS AND THE JEWEL OF LIFE
Story and Art by
Makoto Mizobuchi
Original Concept by Satoshi Tajiri
Supervised by Tsunekazu Ishihara
Script by Hideki Sonoda
Pokémon
ARCEUS AND THE JEWEL OF LIFE
MANGA PRICE: $7.99 usa $9.99 can
ISBN-13: 9781421538020 • IN STORES FEBUARY 2011
Check out the complete library of Pokémon books at VIZ.com
© 2011 Pokémon.
© 1997-2011 Nintendo, Creatures, GAME FREAK, TV Tokyo, ShoPro, JR Kikaku. © Pikachu Project 2009.
Pokémon properties are trademarks of Nintendo.
ARUSEUS CHOUKOKU NO JIKUU E © 2009 Makoto MIZOBUCHI/Shogakukan
www.vizkids.com
www.viz.com
RATED FOR ALL AGES
ratings.viz.com

What's Better Than Catching Pokémon?
Becoming one!

Pokémon
Mystery Dungeon
GINJI'S RESCUE TEAM

Ginji is a normal boy until the day he turns into a Torchic and joins Mudkip's Rescue Team. Now he must help any and all Pokémon in need...but will Ginji be able to rescue his human self?

Become part of the adventure—and mystery—with *Pokémon Mystery Dungeon: Ginji's Rescue Team.* Buy yours today!

www.pokemon.com

Pokémon
Mystery Dungeon
GINJI'S RESCUE TEAM

Story and art by
Makoto Mizobuchi

www.viz.com   vizkids

© 2006 Pokémon. © 1995-2006 Nintendo/Creatures Inc./GAME FREAK inc.
© 1993-2006 CHUNSOFT. TM & ® are trademarks of Nintendo.
© 2006 Makoto MIZOBUCHI/Shogakukan Inc.
Cover art subject to change.

mameshiba
On the LOOSE!

stories by **james turner**
art by **jorge monlongo**
"Mameshiba Shorts" by **gemma correll**

PRICE: $6.99 USA $7.99 CAN
ISBN: 9781421538808
Available NOW!
in your local
bookstore or comic shop

It's a BEAN! It's a DOG! It's...*BOTH*?!

Meet **Mameshiba**, the cute little bean dogs with bite! Starring in their first-ever adventures, they rescue friends, explore outer space and offer interesting bits of trivia when you least expect it! Hold on tight–Mameshiba are on the **LOOSE**!

© DENTSU INC.

RATED A ALL AGES
ratings.viz.com

VIZ MEDIA
www.viz.com

vizkids
www.vizkids.com

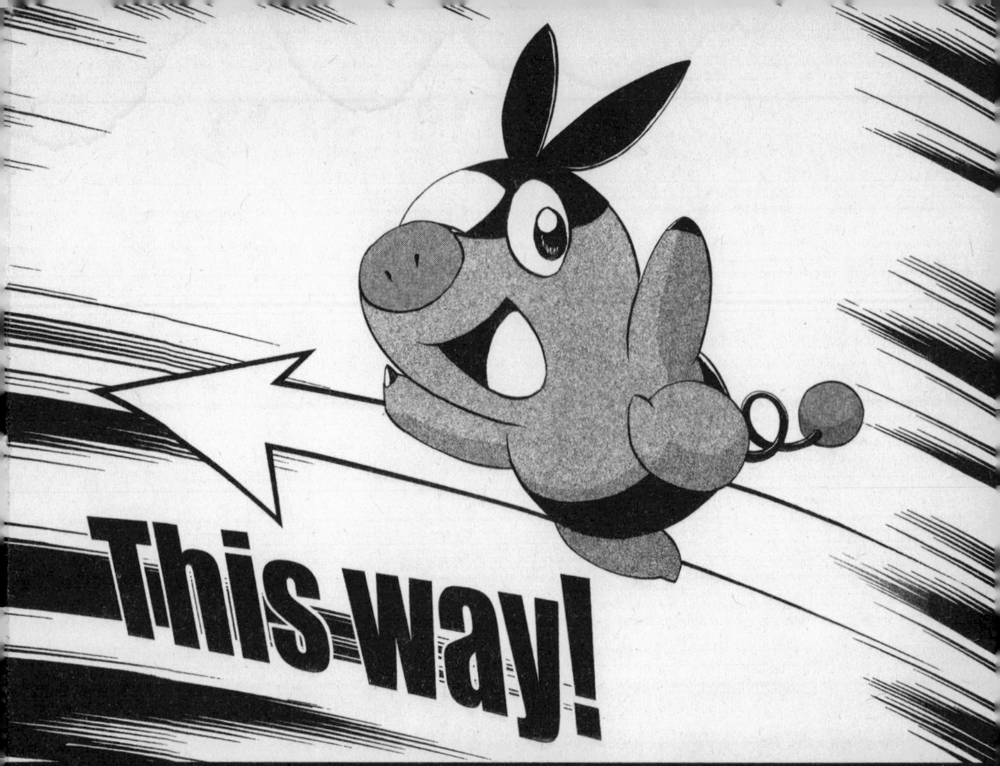
This way!

THIS IS THE END OF THIS GRAPHIC NOVEL!

To properly enjoy this VIZ Media graphic novel, please turn it around and begin reading from right to left.

This book has been printed in the original Japanese format in order to preserve the orientation of the original artwork. Have fun with it!

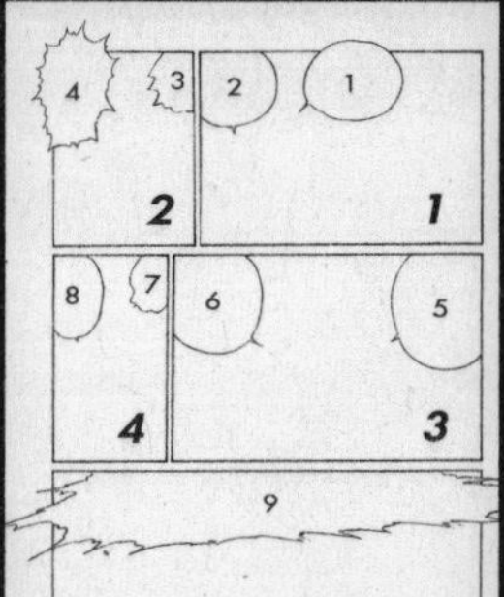

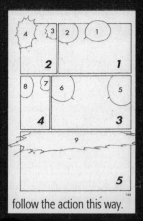

follow the action this way.